A Winter Harvest

Jane Beeson has been working as a writer since 1978. She has written poetry, short stories, plays for fringe theatre, radio plays and adaptations. Her first novel, *Apple of an Eye*, is also available in Pavanne. *A Winter Harvest* is her first television adaption.

Also by Jane Beeson in Pavanne

Apple of an Eye

Jane Beeson

A Winter Harvest

Pavanne

published by Pan Books

First published 1984 by Pan Books Ltd.
Cavaye Place, London SW10 9PG
© Jane Beeson 1984
ISBN 0 330 28321 9
Printed in Great Britain by
Cox & Wyman Ltd, Reading

All characters in this book are fictitious and any resemblance to actual persons, living or dead, is purely coincidental.

Acknowledgements

The lines from 'Leaflets' are reprinted from *Poems Selected and New, 1950–1974,* by Adrienne Rich by permission of W. W. Norton & Company © W. W. Norton & Company Inc 1975, 1973, 1971, 1969, 1966.

Permission to quote from *A Writer's Diary* by Virginia Woolf to the author's literary estate and The Hogarth Press Ltd.

'Shall I switch off?'

Probably Patrick hasn't heard. He is bent over the mower, freeing a massive tangle of grass from the blades. The tractor is running – the noise drowns all else. Caroline finds it agitating but Patrick from years of work with machinery is immune to engine noise – or so it seems.

She goes closer. 'Shall I switch off?' she shouts.

He frees the last blade, straightens up as though his back is hurting, and turns it off himself. In the silence all the sounds of summer come up – the rustle of uncut grass in the breeze, a lark singing above them, the determined buzz of bees.

'I'll have to go down to the house to sharpen this.' Patrick looks vindictively at the blade he has slid from its claw-like casing. The crop is heavy and has gone down in places making mowing an occupation to try anyone's temper.

Caroline and Patrick stand side by side staring at the troublesome grass that bends green and silver in front of them. Patrick starts to walk away down the field, a tall well-built man with powerful shoulders and narrow hips. Caroline, following behind, observes Patrick's back view with satisfaction. But it concerns her that after nearly two years of marriage she still feels oddly separate from him, in fact it sometimes seems that the only time they are really 'close' is when physically entwined. Patrick took for granted that they should communicate very little except by touch, but for Caroline the first year had been difficult. The intimacy and the distance. Now she began to accept it, stopped trying to force Patrick to respond to her sallies into verbal intercourse. Whether or not this was a good thing, or the beginning of the end she couldn't yet tell. It did mean there was much less friction . . .

'What we need is a new mower like everyone else round here,' Patrick calls back over his shoulder. 'Using a blade mower is a thing of the past.' Caroline's mouth forms a sulky set, why should Patrick spoil this perfect day by being in a bad temper? She resents him venting his anger on the mower, she feels it rebounds on herself. Aggravated by the injustice, she retorts, 'Why don't you get rid of all your old rusting machinery? Then you could afford a new one.'

The distance between them increases. Patrick shouts back, 'Who do you think's going to buy it? Most of it doesn't even fit behind a modern tractor.'

Caroline pulls a grass from the bank, chews the sweet bottom of its stalk, walks desultorily. She had come up to see him because the day was perfect and she was happy – everything had been in harmony – now, everything has changed. Patrick's bad humour spreads itself like a fungus over wood – her resentment ferments. Oh, she understands perfectly that he is worried about the hay, afraid the weather will break. For living up against the moor as they do means a cloud can touch the high ridge of Barrowdown and drop rain even when the weather over the rest of the country remains settled. But for all that she feels Patrick's temper unjustified.

The roofs of Greytor appear over the ridge in front of her, a tangle of old stone chimneys, modern stove pipes, and aerials all somehow sprouting joyously together. She feels happier at the sight of their confusion, it calms her, makes her feel more orderly herself and less open to criticism. She crosses the road, descends the steep drive, turning left into the cobbled yard, and arrives at the back door.

Inside the hall-come-scullery are three envelopes on the chest of drawers. She pushes two brown ones on one side and picks out a third – it is in Helen's large decisive hand. Black Biro on a white envelope. She goes into the kitchen and reads it intently twice before looking up to gaze absent-mindedly round the low-ceilinged room – the heart of the house. A dark heart though, even if a few red embers glow and smoke in the grate. She looks with affectionate distaste at the old prints of cart-horses set around the walls, all inherited with Greytor from Patrick's uncle. Likewise the dresser with a few old and faded rosettes pinned beneath one another down the side. She used to hate them, now she no longer sees them, but accepts them. Patrick had made such a fuss when she'd tried to remove them that they'd stayed, and would probably always stay. Her eyes shift to the wall beside the dresser where they rest with satisfaction on a large print of Cézanne's bathers pinned up by herself. The fact of its incongruity in the otherwise minimally changed room doesn't seem to worry her, for she looks at it for several moments with obvious pleasure before opening a drawer in the side of the hefty mahogany table and taking out a writing pad:

Greytor Farm
Meridan
5 August 1980

Dear Helen,
It was wonderful to get your letter saying you can come. Yes – it's a nuisance about Patrick and horrible for him. You wouldn't know there was anything wrong except he gets occasional very bad pains, the only outer sign is he's going yellow – his skin, I mean. Like jaundice. Anyway it's got to be done. I'll have Tom to help while he's in hospital so it should be OK – and with you coming I shall have something to look forward to. Also it will be good for me to cope with the farm on my own – *have* to be independent. There's still a terrible lot I don't know – people who grow up on a farm know by instinct most of the things I have to learn – like how an animal looks when it's off colour – not about to die, anyone can tell that. It's a question of catching them early . . .

Sorry, all this must be terribly boring for you, it's just that because I'm about to be left alone with it – the farm – I'm a bit obsessed by it. How are you? How's the work going? Have you done some brilliant articles? Have you heard any more about the job in Bristol, or has all that fallen through? And what about Alan? Are you still seeing him? There are so many questions, Hel, I just can't wait to have you here and squeeze everything out of you like a pressed orange. .... I want to hear about the flat and your latest replacement for me. I have to admit I'm rather glad none of your 'finds' have lasted too long, otherwise I should have grown jealous. I should hate it if you found someone to take my place – completely, I mean – not only in your flat but as your friend. That makes me possessive too, doesn't it? But how can I be otherwise when our relationship is so special? When I was younger I thought if a relationship bust up I could walk round the corner and find another the same. I've learnt better now – that it can only be replaced differently, and usually less well. So I'm not letting you go if I can possibly prevent it.

Caroline continues in this vein for another page, puts it in an envelope, seals it, writes Helen's address in her own characteristically delicate and spiky hand, and places it on the chest by the back door for the postman. Then, feeling childishly happy at the thought of her friend's visit and slightly guilty at the thought that Patrick's visit to hospital will allow them a week's uninterrupted intimacy, she goes down the central passage of the house – cobbled as the back yard – and out on to the small patch of lawn. The sky all at once is full of martins, diving, swirling, lifting up into the blue, their wings occasionally beating but mainly splayed and stationary, their movement that of miraculously guided darts taking part in some unimaginably intricate aeronautical display. The cause is a hatch of fly on the pond at the bottom of the field where they break the water surface, wings beating as they pick a delicacy from it, and soar up to dive down again and again to repeat the catch. For the most part they rise and fall in a silence only broken by the rush of air passing their small bodies. Suddenly noise is everywhere – Patrick has switched on the angle-grinder. It effectively jolts Caroline into the present; she lets herself through the small iron gate off the lawn and into the front yard. In the barn's murky interior Patrick stands bent over the blade in a vice. Caroline picks her way towards him looking distastefully down on the higgledy-piggledy oil cans, plastic bags, paper bags of dried-up spilling cement, all spread among numerous unrecognisable implements or parts of them. A work bench on her right is piled high with tools, on her left stands an ancient lathe seldom used. Patrick sees her and allows the motor to stop. He looks at her in silent impatience; she is holding him up – the hay still waits. Caroline for her part wonders how he can take so long to sharpen one blade . . .

'Helen's coming.'

'When?'

'The second week you'll be away.'

He nods and puts his finger back on the lever, successfully cutting off further intercourse. Caroline stands watching the sparks fly, then picks her way back into the sun of the yard. A hen makes a dust bath against the wall, another in the flower bed. Dust! She can hardly believe it – after so much rain. Summer at last, even if it has waited till August – she feels quite unaccountably happy.

'Aren't you pleased she's coming. I mean, pleased for me?'

'Yes' – Patrick keeps his voice carefully non-commital. Caroline knows what he thinks but resents it and is therefore determined to make him put it into words so that they will argue and she can convince him of his wrongness.

'You don't sound it.'

'I'm pleased for you. It'll be company. It won't affect me.'

'Why do you object to Helen?'

'I don't object to her.'

'You do.'

Patrick thoughtfully removes an inconvenient piece of ham from a back molar. He reaches for the butter. Caroline pushes it towards him.

'She always plays the same tune, doesn't she?'

'I don't know what you mean,' Caroline says indignantly, 'I should have thought just the opposite. She's . . . progressive.'

'Feminist.'

'Yes, feminist. But what's wrong with that?'

'Nothing in theory.'

9

Caroline knows exactly what he means but resents it on various counts, particularly that of criticising Helen.

'It'll be company for you while I'm away,' Patrick repeats, but she thinks she detects a patronising note in his voice. To her and to Helen.

'Actually I think I'd like to try it on my own for a bit,' she says, airily.

'You won't like it,' Patrick is definite.

'Why not? You were on your own here – for ten years.'

'I know.'

'Then why not me?'

Patrick stands up, putting his plate on the sink. Caroline looks at him in frustration – why will he never discuss anything? Clearly because he has the rest of the field to mow and another to carry. But that's not the real answer. He never will if he can avoid it – ever.

'Don't you think I should get some practice on the tractor before you go in?' Caroline chews her finger.

'If you like – but you probably won't need to drive it with Tom coming in.'

'I still think I ought,' she persists.

Patrick moves towards the door. 'You may have to help me get this cow and calf in too. If she's not letting it suck I'll need a hand.'

Caroline stands, pleased. She likes to be of use. Patrick, ten years older than Caroline both in years and experience of farming, will always do something on his own if he can. Caroline, who married him for various reasons, one of which was to be useful, spends much of her time feeling extraneous. Now she puts on her boots in spite of the dry season and walks across the fields beside him.

It is midday. The sun, powerful like a mountain sun, blazes agreeably on her bare arms and neck; her boots brush through the lush low-lying meadows. They arrive at the field gate and hang over it, surveying the grazing herd. Down in the rushes away from the rest, a cow grazes with her new-born calf. They watch it totter unsteadily round her, ineffectually poking at her with its nose. The cow remains unconcerned until the calf at last gets her teat in its mouth, then she abruptly walks forward with a half-kick. This slow, laborious process of the calf finding the teat and being rebuffed is repeated twice more before Patrick opens the gate.

'We'll have to get her in.'

Ten minutes later in a shed adjoining the barn, Patrick stalks the cow, endeavouring to get a loop of rope round its neck. Caroline peers anxiously over the top of the door. The calf stands unsteadily in the corner. The wild-eyed, long-horned cow rolls the whites of her eyes – she never comes in buildings and she doesn't like it. She is no friendly milking Jersey but a South Devon with a bit of Galloway blood. As she swings round Patrick skilfully casts the rope over her horns and draws it tight – the calf, knocked by its mother, collapses.

'Can you come in now?'

Caroline enters, fearfully. Patrick passes the rope through a ring, draws the cow up towards it.

'Right. Hold this and don't let go while I get the chain round her neck.'

He does so by slow degrees, dodging the thrashing horns. Caroline grips the rope tensely, murmuring prayers under her breath that Patrick shall not be irreparably gored, or herself and the calf trampled. There is nothing she hates so much as enclosed and thrashing animals. Her suburban upbringing, in spite of pony clubs, has not stood her in good stead for the minor rodeos that take place weekly on a farm.

'Alright – you can let go now.'

She lets out her breath in relief. The cow is chained, Patrick is loosing the rope that is sensibly throttling it, and the calf has staggered to its feet.

'What shall I do now?'

'Go up in the loft and throw down some hay – and fetch a bucket of water. I'll see if I can get the calf to suck.'

Caroline passes warily behind the cow and lets herself out of the stable door. Up in the loft above she drags a hay bale over, pulls off the string and pushes half of the hay down into the manger beneath. 'Enough?' She peers down. Patrick has the calf's nose pressed to the udder, with the calf sucking his fingers. As she speaks the cow kicks knocking the calf off his feet and Patrick backwards. Caroline asks no more questions but climbs down the ladder.

'Bloody cow,' says Patrick. But he persists with the calf – as a farmer he has no alternative. His calf is his income, the suckled calves sales in the autumn are the financial event of the year. Why should Patrick, an educated, intelligent man, have chosen to take on his uncle's isolated hill farm? God only knows.

Caroline hangs around in the yard. She sits on the wall, partly for the pleasantness of being in the sun and partly because she feels she may still be needed. After a few minutes she hears the lulling sound of sucking coming from the stable. She returns and looks over the top of the door. Patrick is squatting in the straw steadying the head of the calf; the cow jerks on its chain, eyes Caroline suspiciously, then turns its head and utters a low moo at the quivering, excited replica of itself.

Later that afternoon Tom's smart white Ford Escort van drives into the yard. He has come to help with the hay, in fact he has been coming to help Patrick on and off for the past 10 years for Tom is 25 and Patrick is nearly 40. Tom was only 15 when he first started coming out to work at Greytor – now he has a job in the Saw Mills at Meridan, as well as a wife and two babies – all acquired more by accident than intention. In this respect Tom is typical of the area rather than unique. He likes working for Patrick because Patrick lets him get on without interfering, because he's rather more capable than Patrick, and because the pay is generous. He also has as genuine a liking for the older man as Patrick has for him – a kind of remote, unexpressed understanding.

Patrick directs him up to turn hay.

Caroline, through the kitchen window, watches Tom. Tom is not tall, he wears a white shirt tucked into baggy black jeans, but his hair is thick and she likes his dark eyes . . . Patrick is speaking to her. 'Perhaps you could bring up some tea later?'

'You said I could do some turning,' Caroline challenges.

'You can. You can take over from Tom – let him go and put up the rest of the bales.'

Caroline walks up across the fields, swinging a basket. She doesn't walk as briskly as is expected of a busy farmer's wife but dilly-dallies, stopping to look at a huge bumble bee with an aggressive yellow stripe making its way into a speckled foxglove bell on the bank beside her. It slides back buzzing, then crawls up again in silent anticipation. A brilliant Red Admiral alights on a tiny blue scabious flower; Caroline stands spellbound, watching it spread its velvety wings to the full. But the weight of the basket reminds her of her duty, and she continues up the rough path. Cows and calves graze away to her left. She stops and shades her eyes to see them the better against the sun, now low in the sky, and before her sees a million silver filaments stretched between grasses. Each one dances and sparkles like a miniature tightrope. Her heart gives a thump, a sort of quickening – the sensuous perfection of what she observes seems to find a correspondence in her own feelings, her own nature. She feels in brief instants, and particularly on a day like this, a kind of rapture. She wonders if this is what mystics are on about, but no, it can't be, for mystics are always involved with religion and the spirit, whereas her experience is of the senses. Sensual. She hurries on, feeling almost guilty, as though she has imbibed more than advisable – taken a liberty.

The hay stands in a stack of bales. The elevator chugs and clatters rhythmically. A boy loads bales on to the bottom, while Patrick and a girl helper work high up under the curved roof of the barn. The mowing must have been finished or abandoned, Caroline decides – it certainly looks as though Patrick has been up there a long time for a bay of the barn is all but filled. At this moment he comes to the edge, peers down. The girl's face appears beside him. The boy goes forward and switches off the elevator motor. Caroline puts her basket down close to one of the posts and stands looking round. On the far side of the field Tom is rowing up.

Patrick climbs down the elevator followed by the girl

pulling hay from her hair. He wipes the sweat from his forehead with the back of his wrist, looks with satisfaction at the full bay, then turns to Caroline. 'You can take over from Tom if you like.'

'Do you want me to?'

'Of course – he can give me a hand with putting up the rest.' Patrick surveys a further heap of bales waiting beside him.

Caroline nods and walks across the field towards Tom who is rowing up with the 'spider wheel' – it rotates by the simple method of being dragged over the ground, the great crooked spikes looking more like a Van Gogh sunflower than a piece of farm machinery. Or so it seems to Caroline. She waits apprehensively for Tom's approach. She feels inadequate, incapable. The tractor in Tom's hands moves so easily, smoothly, with no apparent effort, but when she gets on it will go as awkwardly, as jerkily as a horse with a bad rider. Perhaps worse, for the tractor is even more reliant on the driver.

The breeze lifts the rows of hay, everything round her blows and dances, even the light. The tractor flashes and dissolves to a great lopsided star as she watches. In a matter of moments Tom draws up beside her, turns off the motor so he can hear her.

'Patrick wants me to take over from you so you can go and help him.'

Tom nods – gets down. She climbs up. He watches. She is wearing blue jeans and a T-shirt. He likes looking at Caroline. Down in the pub they tease him about her, not that he has ever said a word nor ever would, but everyone's thoughts as well as their actions are known on the moor – as though the granite receives them and radiates them out in thought waves like a psychic Goonhilly. As he watches her now he notices how her blonde straight hair slides over her bare shoulder and how tightly her small fingers grip the steering wheel – it's the grip that excites him. He takes a step forward.

'Go in six.'

She nods, pulls the lever, turns the starter. The tractor springs to shuddering life. She quivers inwardly, pushes it into gear, opens the throttle. It jerks forward, she lowers the hydraulic. Turning she sees the hay lift into rows behind her, but her wake is uneven; three rows instead of two have almost joined. Tom is gesticulating. She pushes over the wheel, corrects her course, but almost immediately the hedge looms in front of her. She circles wide and awkwardly, comes back into the next row. Perhaps the next time she will feel up to reversing and turning . . .

Half an hour later she sits on the bales, pouring tea from the thermos into mugs. The girl, the boy, yet another boy who has arrived, and Tom form one group; Caroline and Patrick another. Caroline would like to join in, sit with the younger group, but Patrick sits firmly beside her and the basket. She speaks to him but he hardly seems to notice, he has seen a bulge where the rick is not well built. He points it out to Caroline who studies it in silence. The other group seems to be sharing confidences, talking and laughing. Patrick goes over to them. She follows almost shyly, draws her finger along Patrick's brown arm as she comes up beside him. He frowns. 'Not here.'

'Can't I even touch?' Caroline is mortified. Could the others have heard Patrick's murmured rebuke? She feels instantly what she is – an outsider. She hates Patrick with the instantaneous blind hate that a clumsy remark can evoke in a sensitive person. And Caroline, having been an only child has all the precocious and highly developed sensibilities of that distinctive group. She withdraws her spirit from Patrick as a poked snail recoils into its shell, or a sea anemone shuts. She even shifts away physically and stands eating her cake with her back to him, looking down the long sweep of valley to where the sea sparkles through a distant gap in the hills. What is she doing here? Why does she stay with this man she detests and has nothing in common with? Black thoughts pound through her mind like nightmares – the beauty of the locality quite vanishes because she no longer sees it, only the oppressive and evil figure of Patrick talking to the others, shaming her in front of them . . .

Patrick, oblivious of the seething rage he has aroused in his wife, looks at the sinking sun, then moves towards the tractor. He hesitates, glances at Caroline. There's something about her back, her stance that conveys to him all is not well. He decides to ignore it. 'Will you drive?'

She pretends not to hear. He repeats, 'Caroline – would you like to drive while the rest of us load?'

'If you like.' She puts the cups, brought over by the others, into the basket and sets it back in position by the corner of the barn. She gets on the tractor, the helpers get on the trailer behind, Patrick and Tom walk. The tractor lurches slowly over the baked-hard ruts towards the field.

'Hold tight!' Caroline eases the tractor forward cautiously, the load sways unsteadily. Tom, on the other tractor, bales round the headlands. He finishes, drives over to them and gets off. Caroline stops her tractor by the final heap of bales. The two boys, helped by Tom and Patrick, throw up to the curly-headed girl on top, who cheerfully parries the sexist jokes of the men as she drags the heavy bales into position. Tom comes towards Caroline – he appears to her as some strange dark god in front of the low red sun. He says something to her but she doesn't hear it above the engine – she nods and smiles, imagining it to be a pleasantry. Tom, she notices, looks at her oddly, but backs away, arms folded. Patrick shouts, 'Right away, driver.'

She eases the top-heavy load across the field, negotiates the gate to the road, and proceeds along it to the steep drive and the open gate which gives access to the back of the barn. As she turns into the drive, although she is in first gear, the tractor's pace increases alarmingly. She puts her foot on the brakes hard, the tractor jerks forward, front wheels sideways and locked, unsteerable. By some instinct of self-preservation, she releases the brakes enough for the tractor to run sideways off the steep drive into the ramp of the gateway, but much too fast. She brakes again, the wheels lock and slide, coming to a juddering halt on the very brink of the ramp – one foot more and the tractor and load would have been over. The engine has stalled – there is complete silence.

Patrick comes forward – he and Tom have been walking and talking behind, hardly aware of the near tragedy enacted ahead of them. The position of the tractor shocks and frightens him, his defence is to joke. 'I thought you called yourself a tractor driver,' he says, looking up into Caroline's white face, accusing her to hide his own negligence.

'The brakes didn't hold.'

'Of course not. Why weren't you in low ratio?'

'You didn't tell me.'

She climbs off the tractor as Tom comes up.

'I told you back up in the field.' Tom searches her face. 'Didn't you hear?'

Caroline shakes her head, she can't speak, her knees are weak. She makes her way over to the drive wall and leans against it. Tom gets on the tractor. The helpers have climbed down from the load and stand in frightened silence, stealing pitying glances at Caroline who waits just long enough to see Tom skilfully manoeuvre the tractor and load to safety, then slips away in shame and humiliation. In the dark kitchen she sits motionless at the table, her entire body tensed and rigid. Then, with a sense of hopelessness, her neck and shoulders slump, and she buries her head in her arms. The only sound is a bluebottle's buzz and the tick of the clock on the mantel over the fire.

She is roused by the alien ring of the telephone and, with a feeling of dread, goes unwillingly through to the office and picks up the receiver. It is the hospital.

The light fades, the evening star appears, the white moon that has been in the sky since four o'clock shines palest yellow, but still the loads continue to be brought down from the fields. Finally Patrick, sweaty and exhausted, brings his haymaking team in. He looks round for Caroline, calls up the stairs but gets no answer. He gets the home-brewed cider and pours it into glasses for his helpers who sit themselves either side of the kitchen table. He drinks with them then slips out of the door and goes upstairs. He looks into their shared bedroom. Empty. He goes along the passage to the spare room that Caroline uses as her 'writing room' – looks inside. Caroline is on the bed, apparently writing a letter. To Helen, he imagines. Fuck Helen. He stands in the doorway in his grimy torn shirt, broad chested, lean faced. 'Aren't you coming down?'

'I've got a headache.'

'We're all having a drink.'

'I know – I can hear.' Caroline gets it out, 'The hospital rang. They want you to go in earlier.'

Patrick twists the door handle. 'Well I can't – it's out of the question.' He starts to back out, draw closed the door he has just flung open.

'They say if you don't take this bed there won't be another till next year – after Christmas.'

'I'll have to wait, then.'

'Patrick, you can't . . .' – but the door has closed and she hears his feet going down the stairs. Back in the safety of the kitchen Patrick fills his helpers' glasses with cider and his own secretly with whisky. He notices the top is not done up and wonders if Caroline has been at it earlier. To shut the impending operation out of his mind, he drinks his whisky like cider.

Caroline, propped on an elbow in the fading light, continues to write:

. . . so everything's a mess – because he'll have to go in. I don't know whether Tom will be able to come or not. I wouldn't say this to anyone but you, ever, but sometimes I think I can't stay here – that in spite of its beauty – Greytor's – in spite of caring for Patrick – I just can't live such a cut-off way of life. Oh not in the physical sense – as long as one has a car that's no problem except occasionally in the snow – it's just that I don't feel I'm part of the 'real' world, whatever that may be. I feel I'm out here but not contributing in any full sense. And though I know a lot of people in the area, I haven't really a friend. I miss you, Helen, I do. So unbelievably much.

Caroline lies chewing her Biro. She rolls away from the light and looks out of the window at the dark shadowy outline of the disused piggeries opposite. Through the floorboards floats up the odd discernible word and bursts of laughter. She would like to be down there joining in, but if she was she knows what would happen. The jokes would cease, the pauses would become long and awkward with herself struggling to make some sort of conversation, and shortly the hay-makers would carry their glasses to the sink and leave. No, it's better she stays away – let them get on with it. She switches out the light and lies staring through the old glass in the leaded window that distorts the stars making them elongate and flash.

Later she wakes to hear the party leaving. They have imbibed well, that's clear. Loud laughter comes up from the scullery, the back door bursts open and shrieks and laughter drift up interspersed with the lower tones of the men. One voice, Caroline notices, is breaking – high and peculiar, then suddenly deep. What must it be like to be a boy? She hopes she'll be reincarnated as one then her view of life will be whole – no wonder Tiresias and those who could, chose to be both or neither sex. She can't remember exactly . . . Suddenly she listens more attentively – Patrick and Tom are talking beneath her, the sound comes up through the hollow lathe and plaster partition. Is Patrick asking Tom to come sooner so that he can take up the hospital bed? She is almost sure he is. She leans over the side of the bed to hear them better, but all she hears is the back door close and Patrick's voice saying 'goodnight'. From the bed she can see Tom's white shirt in the darkness; his van lights go on; she watches him climb into a pool of light that goes off as the door closes. The engine starts – lights – she sees the red tail light as the van goes out of the yard. Downstairs Patrick shifts around. She imagines him switching off the lights, pulling apart the fire. His footsteps come up the stairs. She lies tense, aware she's not in their shared bed. Waits. The door of their shared room opens. Silence. Then Patrick comes along the passage to her door. It opens – the light goes on.

'Are you going to sleep here?'

For answer she gets off the bed and follows him meekly down the passage – she is, after all, still in her clothes. They undress in silence, each on either side of their double bed, once the possession of Patrick's uncle, brass headed but not very comfortable, tending to roll all occupants to the centre irrespective of their desires. Caroline slides under the quilt, Patrick slides in the other side. Tonight both balance firmly on their own sides of the bed, tense and separate. Caroline is the first to break the silence. 'You're late coming up.'

'They didn't go for some time, then I had some forms to fill in.' He becomes silent, then adds, 'She seems a good girl – strong too, she worked as hard as the boy.' He waits for Caroline to show some sign she's heard but when she doesn't he asks after her headache.

'Better,' says Caroline shortly.

'What's the matter?'

'Nothing.'

'Yes, there is.'

'I feel as though I'm not much use here.' Caroline's voice has a slight tremble in it that Patrick recognises with foreboding, it means she is near to tears – and that's one thing he hates. In fact he really rather hates an uncontrolled display of emotion of any sort, it disturbs him, makes him uncomfortable. He stretches out his fingers to touch her, hoping to avert the scene he feels to be imminent. 'Oh come on.'

But Caroline is not so easily soothed, she is in total turmoil – not only because her own near disaster on the tractor has produced a kind of shock effect; but also because Patrick must go in to hospital early and she is about to be left probably without even Tom. 'No – I mean it.' She continues to resist.

'Well you do live in your own world rather – you don't . . . join in.'

'I try to' – she is indignant.

Provoked beyond endurance she sits up sharply, dragging the bedclothes with her. Her voice shaking uncontrollably now with repressed hurt and anger she says, 'Yes, you know I do, but you shut me out. All of you shut me out.'

Patrick turns away from her, picks up a magazine from the table beside him, starts to read.

'Won't you ever talk?' She is almost shouting.

'I'm tired and you're being unreasonable. No one shuts you out.' He can hardly bear it, he comes in from a long hard day wanting nothing more than to sleep, yet his head is ringing with her voice, her demands. He swings his legs to the floor, sits with his back to her, head in hands. Caroline's tone changes instantly to anxiety. 'What's the matter?' He doesn't answer. 'Patrick, what is it?'

'Nothing.'

'Have you got the pain?'

He stands up, says with a tinge of the martyr, 'I'll be alright.' But as he walks towards the door she notices he doesn't look well and is immediately filled with guilt at her own selfish unreasonableness, or that is how she sees it although her feelings still rebel.

When he returns from the bathroom she says, 'You look a bit funny. Are you sure you're alright?'

'Yes – as far as I can be. It's no good fussing.'

'I wasn't fussing.' She sits watching him rather wistfully now as he gets back into bed. The sight of his thin naked legs beneath his T-shirt stirs her feeling for him, her compassion. She sits, chin on knees, watching him as he lies down.

'Patrick?'

'What?'

'We don't get much time to ourselves, do we?'

Still with his back to her he says, 'I should have said we were together all the time,' then: 'Maybe after my op we could get away for a week.'

'I wish we could . . . I'm not grumbling,' she adds hastily, 'just thinking about it. Being together and not together.'

'You think too much – about the wrong things.' He turns towards her. She allows herself to slide down a little towards the central dell. He reaches for her, draws her to him. She lays her head on his shoulder, she loves it when they lie like this not speaking, she sometimes thinks they would get on almost perfectly if they were mute. But before she can quiet her brain completely she has got to get it out. 'Why didn't you tell me to go in low ratio?'

'I understood Tom had.'

'I didn't hear.'

In the silence an owl hoots long and mournfully – an ides of March sound thinks Caroline nervously. 'You smell nice,' she murmurs.

'Of diesel you mean?'

'I like the smell of diesel.'

'You must have an unusual sense of smell.' Patrick's ironic response is an odd fending-off way of indicating he's pleased.

'You will take that bed, won't you?'

'Tom's going to see if he can fix it with the Mills to let him come earlier.'

'If not we'll have to get someone else.' Caroline feels an obstinate righteousness take her over. He can't go on as he is. They lie still and together, each following their own thoughts. Patrick puts out an arm, switches off the light. Out of the darkness Caroline says, 'The trouble is you make it so difficult for me by being so competent, so used to doing things on your own. I'm . . . superfluous,' but she says it lightly.

Patrick rises to the occasion, contradicts her, 'You're not. Why do you think I chose you in the first place?'

'Why did you?' The contentment and comfort generated by their two bodies lying tightly together is beginning to calm, soothe. The light of the moon, now much higher, slants on the old dark floor. The apparent stillness of night descends on the sleeping farm, only disturbed by the squawling toms who rattle the iron gate as they leap it and race up the yard. The leat's* trickle comes up clearly through the open window.

The day on which Patrick must leave Greytor for the hospital dawns thick with a chill mist. In the morning he prises himself from his bed, glances at his already packed case, and takes himself up to look at the fast ripening barley. It is definitely not ready, but one more week and it would be, given some sun to harden it off. The thought that the gold grain will be beheaded and put in the storage tower during his absence genuinely distresses him. He is

---

* *Leat:* a small waterway diverted from the main stream.

unable to imagine it can be as well done as if he were there. As the time approaches for him to climb in the car with Caroline beside him, drive himself over the winding moor road to Exeter his inward depression grows and his exterior expressions become more stoically cheerful.

Caroline has spent the morning gathering elderberries in the old piggeries, an activity she finds soothing – and sensuous. She snips off the shining heads dangling in clusters like massive earrings. Some of the tiny jet beads disappear into the periwinkle and nettle at her feet but who cares, there are more and more and more. Under her scissors the heads amass in her basket till suddenly she stops guiltily – a small wren ticks away in a bush to her left. She is no more than a thief marauding from the birds. When the ground will be hard with frost, the grass blades glacéd, then perhaps the birds' small bodies will stiffen for lack of elder's blood? At this intimidating thought, Caroline picks up her basket and goes back into the house. In the kitchen she finds Patrick writing out lists. He has been writing lists of this or that for the past two days – it started with a list of clothes he should take to hospital and has now got to lists of calving – who she shall expect to calve when. He beckons her over, shows her that Spotted Strawberry Cow and Sag Belly are the next two due. Caroline hopes fervently she will recognise them but says nothing to cause doubt.

'If you get into difficulties,' says Patrick, 'in any way at all, then ring Tom. I've arranged it, he's quite prepared.'

'Yes,' says Caroline, dubiously. She thinks of Tom's dark eyes, the hostility he emanates when crossed.

'What's the matter?'

'Nothing.'

'There is.'

'It's just Tom can be a bit moody.'

Patrick's expression makes it clear he thinks she's being tiresome. 'I've arranged it with him,' he repeats. 'It's not always possible to get him at the Saw Mills, but you can always ring Rita – leave a message with her.'

Caroline pulls out a chair and sits opposite Patrick. She takes a fork from the drawer in the side of the table and starts methodically pulling off the berries from the maroon-tinged stems with the prongs. They mount up in the white pudding basin in front of her, marks of their dark blood squashed brings back the image of the birds, then leaps uncontrollably to thoughts of Patrick's pending operation. To check her agitated thoughts she gets up and switches on the radio – a voice is in the midst of reading what she soon realises to be a poem:

If we needed fire to remind us
that all true images
were scooped out of mud
where our bodies curse and flounder
then perhaps that fire is coming
to sponge away the scribes and time-servers
and much that you would have loved will be lost as well
before you could handle it and know it
just as we almost miss each other
in the ill cloud of mistrust
who might have touched
hands quickly.

Caroline stands riveted. She experiences a kind of tingling feeling in the back of her neck and spine, so great is the impact of the words that she feels as though she is floating, could float up and bob ballon-like round the ceiling with joy, a joy and reverence that is almost divine. She has had this feeling before but seldom, oh yes seldom – once in the Tate Gallery before the paintings of Mark Rothko . . . She gives up the hopeless attempt to find words for feelings although it has just been proved it can be done by the poem, and goes back to her berries. Before she reaches them the radio wanders off station and the voice disintegrates into a shattering emission of distorted sound. Patrick looks up irritated.

'Can't you turn it off?'

Caroline does so, and her nervousness returns. She looks at the clock. In ten minutes they must leave.

She stands like Ruth amid the alien corn chewing grains

and spitting them out. Is it, or is it not ripe enough? She frowns with concentration, pushes a head of barley in her jeans pocket, and continues on her way to get the cattle in. Today is the test – for tuberculosis and brucellosis – the cattle must be got in, put through the crush, the syringe stuck in their necks by the vet for the TT bit, and blood drawn into phials from under their tails for the other. It is all a messy dungy procedure that she particularly dreads. The vet is loud-voiced and bossy and when he and the bull – who has similar characteristics – have dealings with each other, it is all apt to be extremely frightening. Caroline has decided during her time at Greytor that she is not at all brave, on the contrary, she judges herself to be rather cowardly with a strong sense of self-preservation. Well, you need to have the latter on a farm.

She opens the gate where the herd of cows and calves are currently grazing, and shouts. At first they turn a deaf ear, the grass is still quite lush and they curl their tongues round it, shifting with each mouthful to the next tuft. Happily one old cow spies the gate and, ever in hope of better pastures, starts to amble forwards, followed by her calf. Not to miss anything, another follows, and soon the whole herd are passing through while Caroline stands watching. They are a mixed and motley lot – Patrick believes in cross-bred vigour. Neither is he very good at dehorning and several are naked one side of their polls while projecting a classic horn of considerable length from the other. But Caroline looks at them with some pride – they are fat and glossy as they should be at the end of the summer, and only a couple look a trifle geriatric. They will be sold as barreners next year . . .

She closes the gate behind them, watching anxiously to see if they will take the right direction. The vet will be waiting – he has already rung earlier to tell her to have them ready.

'Shit. Shit. Oh shit' – involuntarily the short word spoils the clear air. Old grannies, first and second calvers, the bull, all with the impetuous delight that may be experienced by ourselves at the sight of a golden beach, take off and thunder down the field kicking their heels in silly fashion egged on by their circling, racing offspring – and in quite the wrong direction. Caroline, with an anxious glance at the yard gate, pounds down the field in pursuit. Digging their heels in and cutting up the valuable 'seeds', the matrons halt before the wrong gate as suddenly as they started. A shout comes from her left. It's the vet.

Instinctively she pushes her hair off her hot forehead and assumes the personality she has to wear in the vet's presence. John Robbins is suitably insensitive to the indelicacies he has to perform on the animals. He is equally insensitive with women, and delights in chatting them up in an overt and sexist manner. Caroline is in the unfortunate position of having to be civil to him, for he is the best vet in the area, and despite his other disadvantages, a good-natured man. So now she watches him advance out of the corner of her eye – as she circles to the left behind her unruly herd, the vet defends the field to the right. The yard gate being the only opening, the cows settle for it and plod towards it obediently enough.

Caroline and the vet come together at the gateway.

'On your own?' – the vet doesn't sound pleased. A woman in bed or the kitchen is one thing, a woman to help him with the bull, something else.

'Tom's coming, but he's late.'

The vet follows the last cow through giving it a prod in the rump to hasten it.

'Shut the gate, can you?'

Caroline bites her lip in anger. She would like to be reincarnated a mare able to lay back her ears, roll her eyes and snap – a gesture much more frightening and expressive than any given to a human.

In the yard John Robbins lays out his phial rack and box, his scissors and syringe, then takes off his jacket and rolls up his sleeves. He looks round impatiently. There is no sign of Tom.

'We'd better make a start. Got a rag, or something?'

Caroline hasn't. She fetches one from the boot of his car, puts it beside the paper where she is to write down the herd numbers. The sound of the gate catch makes them both look up. Tom comes through, he doesn't hurry but slouches across the yard. The way he carries his head, the set of his shoulders, his pace, make it apparent that Tom is coming as a favour unwillingly conferred. It has its effect, for the vet who has opened his mouth to tell him he's late, shuts it again. He doesn't want Tom to turn round and go away. Caroline is equally anxious. It is immediately clear to her that Tom, as much as the bull, will have to be humoured and handled carefully. To their encouraging greeting, he returns an unsmiling nod, and then casts his expert glance over the stock.

'We'll start with the bull – get him out of the way' – the vet's voice sings happily. Tom will do all the difficult work, edge the bull into the lane of the 'crush', force him up till his massive head and neck are caught and clamped by the vertical metal bars at the end. In the past, if the bull has chosen to cause trouble then the 'race' has been known to be smashed, his human tormentors scattered, and the unbendable metal distorted. So all now become united against the strongest force. Tenderly they coax him away from the rest till Tom and Brutus (for Brutus is his name) disappear into the dark shed that leads to the crush – for a few moments the only sound is Tom's voice, then Brutus comes plodding along towards the metal gate, stops, snorts, his eyes shining oddly maroon. Silence. No one speaks. Tom starts to prod and encourage from behind. Brutus tosses his head, takes a few more steps. The metal gate offers an inviting gap. He lowers his head, walks towards it – this after all, is how he smashes gates all over the farm, shifts himself from field to field if the other one's grass looks greener . . . The metal clamps close on his neck. He pulls back, forces forward. All hold their breath. Which will prove stronger? Fortunately the recently renewed crush doesn't give, and Brutus, whose temper is not yet at its worst is arrested. He is an old bull now and less temperamental than in his youth.

Tom vaults out from the race. The vet pushes his sleeves further up his pink hairy arms, and the business of the day commences. Caroline's duty is to hand the phials to the vet, receive them back filled with blood, wipe them free of dung, and settle them in the racks – and also list each ear-tag number. The rhythm mounts up. Soon it becomes automatic enough for her mind to wander. Patrick – is he alright? Is there something she doesn't know about? Something he's known all along but not said? He'd be under the anaesthetic now – perhaps it was all over and he was back in the ward – back in the white hospital landscape where beds undulate like fields of snow . . . or bodies laid out for anonymous burial. She'd dreamt last night of childbirth – on the delivery table – herself – pinned like a butterfly setting. Satin-white walls – splashes of red patterning them like carnations – white masks looking down from space. She felt common – a Cabbage White in a jar fluttering slower and slower. She smelt the ether as it came to meet her . . . Her mother had gone into hospital and never come out. She sees herself as a child in her best dress visiting – her mother tossing restlessly or lying apathetic, only her eyes following, herself an enquiring child, fiddling round the cubicle, examining everything . . .

A phial sees fit to join in Caroline's relived trauma, it slips through her fingers and breaks. In horror, past and present still confused, she gazes down on the scarlet pool of blood bounded by dried dung. She bends to pick up the fragments. Tom joins her, kneels beside her.

'I don't know how I let it go' – she feels embarrassed, humiliated. She is anxious they should think her capable.

Tom glances at her, but her face is hidden behind a curtain of hair that falls forward from her bent head. He says gently, half teasing, 'Where was you? Not here, that's certain?'

She looks up in surprise. Could he really have noticed? Before she can reply, the vet asks impatiently for another phial – he must re-do the cow owing to the woman's clumsiness. The sight of Caroline and Tom kneeling on the floor, both absorbed, gathering up the pieces, is peculiarly agitating to him and his response is bad temper. Everyone resumes their task.

Nearly two hours later the vet slams down the lid of his boot and calls to them that he's going over to the farm to wash. Tom and Caroline take a short cut back across the field. Caroline, oppressed by the silence, ventures a conversational gesture. 'I thought you weren't coming this morning.'

Tom takes it as a criticism, is immediately on the defensive and, in accordance with his nature, attacks. 'I've got another job to do. Patrick told me the end of the month – that's when I fixed. Now everything's altered. Rita was going down her mother's but she's cancelled that.'

Caroline, startled by Tom's vehemence, stumbles hastily along to keep up. Resentment has quickened Tom's pace.

'She mustn't do that. I don't understand, why does Patrick going in early prevent Rita . . . ?'

Tom interrupts. 'I have to have the van, see, if I'm to keep running out here.'

'But don't you have to have the van to go into the Saw Mills?'

Tom flattens a mole hill that has mistakenly risen in his path. 'I get a lift – but these last few days I've been taking the van in case I had to come out here sudden.'

Despair grips Caroline. She surveys Tom's sullen profile anxiously. 'I don't want you to come out here if you don't want to.'

Tom's pace is still increasing. She has to jog every few steps.

'It's easy enough to say that but then you go ringing up home all times and expecting me to be out here in five minutes.'

Indignation overcomes her anxiety. 'I don't – that's not true. This is the first time I've asked you to come out. The vet insisted I get someone.'

No sound but the thud of their feet and somewhere above a lark singing. Caroline makes an attempt to get things on a higher level. 'If you want to know, I nearly forgot it myself.'

They have reached the gate by the linhay.* It only remains for them to cross the road to reach the farm. Tom's van is parked by the entrance to the farm drive. Caroline

* *Linhay:* a small barn separate from other buildings.

decides to push her luck – if it is luck. 'Do you want me to get someone else then?'

Tom undoes the gate and crosses the road. Briefly they are separated by a passing car. She catches him up.

'Who could you get?'

Her patience is evaporating. 'Oh I'm sure there must be *someone*,' she says, airily.

They are now beside the van. Tom opens the door but remains standing, leaning in the opening. 'It upsets Rita if you keep ringing home.'

'Upsets her? I've only rung twice.'

'She doesn't like it' – Tom is dogged.

'I'll ring you at the Mills, then.'

'And lose me my job?'

An injured tone creeps into her voice. 'Well I'm sorry. What am I supposed to do?'

Tom gets in his van. Fortunately the window is open. Caroline leans down to speak through it. 'What about when the combine comes?'

Tom reaches for the starter key. 'When's that?'

'Tomorrow or the next day – I don't know for sure.'

Tom starts his engine. Radio 1 comes up at the same time. Caroline observes the interior carpeted in smoky blue – a rubber mat protects the nylon pile from the dung on his boots. As the van begins to shift forward he looks at her for the first time since the broken phial.

'I'll see what I can do,' he says – the flash of his dark eyes sear through her carefully built-up defences. He's got things on the right footing now – on his own terms. And Caroline where he wants her – begging. Power is all. He presses his foot on the accelerator – the banks on either side echo back his ill-suppressed exhaust. What Caroline sees distorts very slightly in the blue smoke.

Caroline and the vet sit opposite each other across the kitchen table. The vet is in the midst of one of his boring stories; she listens, chin in hand.

'. . . I said to my assistant don't help them, let them help themselves. It's all made too easy for them now – the less they do the more hand-outs they get. It doesn't make sense, does it?'

He looks across to Caroline for confirmation, but when she gives none, he goes on undeterred. Caroline is picturing her cats arrayed along the wall waiting for hand-outs. If she gives them none they become ill, so she has to take them to the vet who gives them a pill, tells her they are on the thin side. How, she wonders, does the vet reconcile this to his theory of not giving hand-outs, for after all there are enough rats and mice in the barns, not to mention young rabbits, to feed an army of cats . . .

The vet is still talking. 'I was up at John Hemmings' place yesterday and I said to him . . .'

The telephone rings. Caroline springs up. The vet nods sagely.

'That could be what you've been waiting for.' But she is out of the room before he has finished speaking. So he empties his glass, goes through to the scullery and lays his forms on the dresser. From this strategic point he is better able to overhear the conversation on the telephone. By the time she returns his enquiries are purely a formality.

'All well?'

Caroline's face beams her relief. 'Yes. He's round from the anaesthetic. I can go in tomorrow.'

The vet feels the need to quell her joy – sadly a natural human response. 'I expect he'll be pretty shaky – it's no small op. My brother had it a year back – he was off his feet for three months.'

He indicates the forms on the dresser, hands Caroline a Biro. Points. 'There. If you could sign – and there.'

She does so, holding the Biro tightly to prevent any tendency for it to shake. The skinny mother cat slithers past furtively in search of milk – she detests the vet's smell and only the anxiety of feeding kittens induces her to take the risk of passing him. Caroline's well-meaning visits with her to see him, if she could only explain, are nine times out of ten necessitated by morning sickness from which she suffers more acutely with every fresh pregnancy. The imperative nature of cruel desire makes her resistance to toms low . . .

'There we are then' – the vet tucks away the form and moves towards the door. 'See you Friday to check for reactors.' He backs out. 'Let me know how things go with your husband. Cheer him up – give him something to want to get home for, that'll do him more good than all the pills they give him . . .' Caroline wonders how many placebos that means he gives. 'You don't believe me, do you, but . . .' – he pats Caroline over-familiarly on the shoulder – 'if I was in Patrick's place I wouldn't want to be away longer than needs must.' He looks at Caroline as he might a box of delectable chocolate. He shuts the door as she forms her face into a grimace indicative of a smile. Surely there must be other vets in the area? – she must ask Patrick.

Left on her own her shoulders sag. She moves back unsteadily into the dark kitchen, takes the whisky off the dresser and pours herself a glass. She sits at the table tipping the fiery liquid down in a gulp. Tears of relief come into her eyes. She wipes them away with her sleeve but more come. The strain she has been under since delivering Patrick to the hospital and driving home across the lonely moor has been considerable. She lays her head down on her arms. After a few moments the whisky begins to take effect, when she looks up the room seems to be rotating round her very slowly. She stands, steadying herself on the edge of the table, moves through into the hall and struggles into her jacket.

Out in the yard she makes her way through a motley collection of game-chickens, interspersed with an odd ex-battery hen, various cross-bred ducks and a goose and gander. She enters a door in the side of the big barn and bends over the metal bins to fill a bucket with barley and pellets. Almost lunchtime and the laying hens are still shut up! – she should have got up earlier, done them first thing. Oh well! Suddenly she looks up attentively. A raucous, abnormal – at least she thinks it's abnormal – cackling comes from the root-house* used for the chickens at the back of the barn. She hurries along the pitch-dark passage at the back of the cow stalls and through the chicken-house

* *Root-house:* building generally used for the storage of root crops.

door. Most of the chickens are perched up as high as they can get, squawking and cackling – the rooster claws at the wire of a window. Caroline stands amazed – what on earth . . .? Then she sees it – a mink dragging a chicken by its neck across the floor. She grabs a stick conveniently at hand, darts forward, hits, misses, hits again. The mink, surprised, stops dragging, sums up Caroline and comes for her – fast. Caroline equally fast, turns, dashes out of the door slamming it behind her, stumbles along the dark passage to the yard where she stands trembling with fear and anxiety. What can she do? She runs round the buildings searching for a spade, at last finds one and armed with it starts back along the dark passage. The cackling has ceased as quickly as it started. At the door she hesitates, summons up her courage and pushes it open inch by inch, then stops horrified. Before her is a scene of massacre – five white birds lie dead on the floor, each one with its throat torn and ripped. The scarlet blood against the white feathers makes the sight more shocking. Caroline stands as though turned to the granite of the walls, only her eyes move round, hesitant and fearful, scanning each hole and cranny for a movement to give the whereabouts of the mink. But nothing moves, only the remaining hens eye her suspiciously and seem peculiarly silent.

She hastily opens the wooden doors that allow the hens access to the run. Guiltily she realises that if they had been let out first thing they would have stood a far greater chance of escape. She gathers up the corpses still glancing round nervously, and makes her way back to the yard. The day is still and perfect, the sky a hard blue behind the tors that rise to north and south of the farm. There is no sound but the leat that trickles reliably across the small triangle of lawn to the pond at the bottom of the field. It is so still that even the huge conker that drops its lower boughs over the domed ash-house* doesn't stir or lift its spanned leaves. Against this setting the five brutally slaughtered birds in her hands seem all the more startling. Nature has indeed manifested itself as red in tooth and claw.

* *Ash-house:* small building in which ash was stored in the past, to be used for fertilizing the fields.

Inside the house she hangs them at the far end of the chill lean-to adjoining the scullery, shutting the door to protect them from offending bluebottles. She decides to say nothing to Patrick but to go down to the market on Wednesday and replace them. In spite of the perfect weather and her relief that Patrick's operation is over, she feels oppressed. The mink hangs over all like an evil presence. It will attack again, of that she's sure, but what? From now on until it is dead she will start uneasily at every cackle of a laying hen, every quack of a duck. No duckling can be allowed on the pond, no chick from its run. A mink in a farmyard is like a Ripper in a city. No one is at ease – every time she leaves the farm to go up over the fields she will return in dread of what fresh slaughter she may find.

Greytor Farm
Meridan
10 September 1980

. . . Mist. Nothing but thick, grey, cloying mist. It has been like this for three days now and when I drive over the moor to Patrick it is a slow and laborious business – and always the dread of hitting the moorland stock that gather on the roads for shelter in bad weather. Alone here I live on an island without the sound of waves. Silence and more silence. Not even the noise of a helicopter above the cloud.

Caroline sits up in bed in the early morning, a writing-pad on her knees, chewing her Biro. The view from her window is non-existent, the only thing that shows through the mist are the white squares of the small doors spaced along the front of the old piggery. Even the shapes of the buildings, no more than ten paces from her, are invisible. She sighs and continues writing:

Yesterday I moved the ewes and got the ram with them . . .

Then pushes her journal to one side and draws in front of her an unfinished letter to Helen.

34

. . . I find relating to Tom amazingly difficult, yet I have to as we work together. I know he thinks I'm different to him, different to Patrick even. That's what scholastic education does, it estranges you from those educated more directly into a truer world of feelings. That's how it is with Tom and me – he thinks me aloof and I feel awkward and inadequate when he's around. Yet we feel the same about a lot of things, I can tell.

The other day I heard Adrienne Rich's 'Leaflets' on radio – I switched on just by chance, I had no idea what it was, and missed the end but looked it up later . . .

She stops writing and stares again at the dismal grey square of window. Why, she wonders, does she bother to write? Much better to ring. Perhaps she will later, tell Helen Patrick's alright. Try and persuade her to come sooner. At this moment the telephone seems like a lifeline, her only connection with the outside world. The house is certainly oddly silent. Somewhere out of the mist comes a mournful cock's crow.

Five o'clock the same evening finds Caroline driving their old battered Mini steadily over the moor to Exeter. The mist has lifted and hangs a heavy grey above the dark hard line of hills on her left. On her right rise the severe blocks of spruce planted after World War II by the Forestry Commission and which, year after year, perpetuate the destruction of the landscape.

Altogether the aspect might be described as lowering, bleak, and intimidating but Caroline's romantic nature experiences a distinct lift. The car zigzags waywardly as she gazes at the shafts of light from the greenish sun which silhouettes the row of savage rock clusters commonly known as tors. Suddenly her attention is even more sharply arrested, for coming round a hill she is confronted by what at first appears like a monstrous dragonfly but at a second glance proves to be a figure lying on its belly beneath the transparent wings of a hang-glider. She pulls up, winds down the window and watches. It hovers stationary, only the legs spoil the tail by falling apart. It seems to Caroline that it waits for another to descend and mate, stick a new shape on the dove grey sheet of sky. It looks green so its mate should be blue, in the kaleidoscopic, watery, set of the sun. She'd seen dragonflies up at the Miners' Pool zigzagging casually above fierce tips of reed . . .

Her thoughts are interrupted by the hang-glider's sudden swoop and disappearance behind the tor. At the same moment she sees another small black figure on top of the rocks also leap down out of her vision. This other reassures her that the hang-glider pilot is assisted and she drives on. From now on she hardly sees the landscape, so busy is she pondering on what and what not to tell Patrick. She feels a sense of both anticipation and dread at the thought of seeing him in hospital, mixed with a desire to tell him all she has accomplished. Managed. She wants to reassure him that his absence has not brought everything to a standstill. (She puts the thought of the mink from her mind). But her perceptions let her down, for in his heart of hearts there is nothing that would please Patrick more than to hear his absence has caused chaos. He likes to be invaluable, important, and in this is in no way exceptional. So Caroline has determined the outcome of her visit before she even enters the hospital, her failure lying in her lack of ability to put herself in Patrick's position. She slows down to cross a narrow bridge not wide enough for two cars abreast and at the same time makes a mental note to return by the main road along the valley; their car has a history of break-downs and although she has a passion for the moor land-scape she does not fancy being stranded on it at night.

Twenty minutes later she pulls up outside the hospital building. It is a large modern block, all windows the same, lights blazing from each in the darkness. She cannot help but connect it with the ominous moor prison she has passed which spreads its glow like a fire that burns all night long.

At the entrance to the ward she hesitates. Before leaving she has changed her habitual jeans for a skirt which she now adjusts at the waist nervously. It is an all male ward. She is well aware of the forty eyes that will follow her as she makes her way to Patrick's bed, for she has never quite outgrown her adolescent fear of being looked at. She pushes open the heavy double doors, goes in. Her eyes search the room anxiously, and finally focus on Patrick, almost unrecognisable for tubes and pillows. She makes her way over to his bed. He opens his eyes as she leans over him.

'I brought you a few grapes,' she says, helplessly, 'but I don't suppose you're allowed them.'

She puts them down on his table. Clearly with a tube up his nose speech is extremely difficult. A nurse sees the problem and sweeps down on them, deftly removing the tube which she says he no longer needs. Patrick begins to look more human. Caroline sits on a chair thoughtfully provided.

'Are you in a lot of pain?' – she has never been more conscious of the inadequacy of words.

'No, no,' Patrick grunts, tries to shift. His expression indicates the opposite. Caroline springs up with almost too much haste, tries to shift his pillow, make him more comfortable.

'If you could just call the nurse' – he successfully crushes her effort to offer loving care. She looks round for the required female symbol, opens her mouth to summon a matronly one passing.

'No – not that one – that one.' He indicates one of a younger and more conventionally appealing variety. Caroline is instantly affronted. Illogically it annoys her that he should be subject to the appeal of the feminine exterior, at the same time she is equally distressed if he never comments on her own. Meanwhile the nurse has vanished into the sea of beds and visitors that stretch beyond and down the ward.

'Never mind.' Patrick's voice is resigned.

Unexpectedly a further nurse arrives.

'I'm afraid I'll have to disturb you in a minute or two – for a wee drop of blood.'

She smiles benignly at Patrick who responds suitably.

'Blood?' Caroline looks at him.

'Of course – they have to test repeatedly.'

'Oh.' A picture of the blood-soaked feathers comes before her eyes. 'Why?'

'They always do. I must say these nurses are marvellous. They work incredibly hard and are amazingly efficient.'

Caroline folds her hands, thinks of her own efforts. Patrick's face suddenly screws up, conveying a momentary spasm of pain. She stands, regarding him with consternation.

'What is it?'

'Could you . . . could you possibly get me a drink?'

She looks round helplessly. 'Where from?'

'No. Here. There.' He nods his head to indicate a jug, covered by a cloth, on the table beside him. Caroline hurries round and pours it into a glass, holds it out. He makes an attempt to take it, then shakes his head.

'You'll have to hold it for me.'

She does so. He takes a sip which he declares enough. She puts the glass down and returns to her chair.

'How's the farm?'

'Fine. We did the brucellosis and TT tests. It took nearly all morning. Tom came to help. You know that cow with the white-spotted face and the ridgey back, well Tom said . . .'

Patrick interrupts. 'Do you think you could take home my pyjamas and wash them. And bring them back tomorrow?'

'Where are they?'

Patrick points to his cupboard. She opens it on a bedpan.

'The *lower* one.'

She opens the other, pulls out a pair of pyjamas, stares at them. 'Have you *worn* them?'

'No, but they're not very clean. I don't think the water in the washing-machine could have been hot enough. They smell funny.'

Caroline buries her nose in them furtively, conscious that others are looking in their direction.

'They don't.'

'They do.'

'I can't smell anything. You smell.' She holds them out to him. Patrick shuts his eyes, always his defence against what he considers to be Caroline's unreasonableness. He says in a tired voice, 'I know what they smell like.'

Caroline notices the pallor of his face and immediately feels guilty. How could she have argued? She pushes them into her bag, aware a nurse is once again passing. She sits in agitation, her hands folded to stop them fidgeting. She had come full of hope and good intention but in a matter of minutes all had been lost. Antagonism reigns.

She looks over the ward in silence. All around other visitors seem to be talking non-stop, in fact there is a perpetual hum like that of bees in the heather . . .

'You're not very talkative.'

'I'm sorry – I was telling you about the test. It's done. And the combine's coming as soon as he can . . .'

But Patrick can't let her talk. 'Is it ripe?'

'Yes.'

'Try to get Bob at once.'

'I got his wife – he was out on the combine.'

'Ring late night or early morning – explain to him I'm in hospital.'

'Yes' – Caroline's voice is flat. Patrick's irritating bossiness is hard to take. She is doing, has done, her best. He knows that combine-harvesters never come just like that. She feels limp, everything seems pointless. She and Patrick are poles apart – the cliché presents her with a satisfactory image. Slowly she stands.

'Probably I ought to go. I don't want to tire you – they said I shouldn't stay too long this time . . .' She fiddles with the shoulder strap of her bag. 'If I can't get in tomorrow because of the combine will your pyjamas do the day after?'

'Leave them – it doesn't matter.'

Caroline hesitates, then pulls them out of her bag and pushes them back into his cupboard. The nurse arrives to take Patrick's blood. Caroline who has an aversion to needles being stuck in herself, looks away, and only turns back when his arm is being dabbed with cotton wool. As the nurse moves to the next bed, Patrick lowers his voice.

'He's had his leg amputated – trod on a mine – outside Belfast.'

Caroline winces, and looks across. At least the occupant appears to have a talkative and entertaining visitor, not one reduced to muteness like herself. Guiltily she leans over to kiss Patrick. Of course she loves him, he's the only person she's ever really loved.

'It was horrible waiting for them to ring,' she murmurs.

'It took a lot longer than they expected – I was in the operating theatre from nine till twelve,' Patrick rejoices proudly.

'Oh Patrick, how awful.' Caroline's concern is heartfelt.

Patrick smiles bravely. She has a sense of *déjà-vu*. On the way out of the ward it comes to her that it must have been on television.

Patrick lies uncomfortably in his half-propped-up position watching Caroline's back view receding. Her shoulder-length straw-coloured hair, her slightly diffident way of holding her head, her infinitely quiet way of moving, all strike a chord in him of something like passion, which he carefully contains. Besides Caroline, the young nurse he rather fancies becomes meaningless, and he feels guiltily ashamed. On the other hand she is sexy, consoling and relaxing, and allows a side of him to emerge that he would be unwilling to show Caroline – an erotic repressed self which is nevertheless very much there. If he could only accept it, it would become less insistent and nagging, but this he cannot do so must keep the lid shut down tightly so his Jack may not escape the Box.

As Caroline vanishes through the ward doors, Patrick shifts himself and looks disconsolately round him. How will he face another fortnight in such surroundings? The farm is very much with him and he has not adapted to his new environment. He imagines Caroline going down the stairs, getting into their car, and setting off home across the moor. He allows himself to indulge in reminiscing, to relive in memory the first time he ever met her, temping in the NFU office while waiting for a job in the library. He had gone there full of righteous anger about the sheep scab notification, he seemed to remember, only to be faced with Caroline. He'd wanted to ask what someone like her was doing there, obstructing him from giving proper vent to his feelings, but of course had not. Instead his feelings had been quelled, she'd directed him to another department, and they might happily have not seen each other again had not fate seen fit to make them wait for the same lift. They had walked out of the building together and then found themselves walking along the street side by side so he had been almost forced into asking her for a drink. Oh no, it hadn't been his choice but fate's. So Patrick conveniently got through life – finding reasons for all his actions outside himself. That way he was never really responsible but passively fulfilled his destiny. If anyone was an Aeolian harp for others to play upon, it was Patrick – that is not to say he was weak but rather that it was how he preferred to be. He had been thrilled when the much younger Caroline had chosen him, for that was an approximation of what had happened. Caroline had simply decided on him . . .

The pain in his side is agony. He looks up and with relief sees the nurse of his choice approaching in a rustle of pale-blue and white starch. In no time at all she has beaten up his pillows, shifted him, taken his temperature and held his pulse. His pain is mitigated if not banished.

Caroline dresses, viewing her small but resilient body in the oval glass and frowning at it. Another year and she'll be thirty but she doesn't look any older than she did at twenty-four. At twenty she'd thought she'd be old at thirty, but youth has an agreeable habit of stretching – each ten years a new reprieve is allowed and age put off for yet another decade. Probably it was all an illusion like babies looking pretty in the eyes of the mother, but she didn't care. If you looked alright to yourself you could make other people believe you looked alright too, or so she hoped – and anyway there was no choice. Remembering that today she would be plucking, she ties her hair back from her face so that only her fringe falls forward over her eyes.

Downstairs she turns the radio on to give herself the feeling she is part of the real world instead of a woman on her own in a remote farmhouse. She makes herself tea and eats a bit of toast, not because she is hungry but because a routine, however flimsy, gives her a tether. Through the window the mist lingers and only with difficulty can she make out the pond at the bottom of the field. She is let off milking, for the house cow is heavily in calf, so once the animals have been gone round and the fowl fed and let out, she can find no further reason to put off the plucking. Accordingly she takes the five birds and seats herself on an upturned bucket in the feed-house with a cardboard box beside her for the feathers. Two hours later she is still at it, with a plaster on her thumb and forefinger. The birds are not young, the feathers are tough. Semi-plucked yellowy pink carcasses with bits of feather clinging to them surround her. She pushes her fringe from her eyes with the back of her wrist, looks in despair at the remaining unplucked bird at her feet. The wing feathers are unbeliev-ably hard to get out and boiling water hasn't helped – perhaps she should just cut the wings off, they are scrawny things at the best of times. But the thought of Patrick's, or worse, his mother's, face at the sight of a wingless roast fowl quells her, and she continues to wrestle with the stubborn feathers till a reprieve comes – the sound of a powerful engine approaching along the road. Caroline springs up, puts her head out of the door, listens. Yes, it's the combine. She hastily gathers up the plucked birds and puts them on the yard wall, then starts up the drive. The roar of the engine grows louder. Across the gateway at the top of the steep exit appears the yellow machine – immense, domi-nant, intimidating. The driver, high above, peers down on her, then switches off and himself climbs down. He is a short, thickset, pleasant-looking man in his thirties, dressed in a T-shirt and baggy trousers bound round the ankles with baler-cord. He takes a shrewd look at Caroline, gets a tin out of his pocket and starts to roll himself a cigarette.

'Do you think it's going to clear?' Caroline looks at him anxiously. He represents local knowledge, authority – what-ever he says she will be inclined to believe.

Bob Haines looks up, squinting at a glimpse of bluer mist above the general grey.

'It's clearing now' – he states it as a fact. She waits while he licks and sticks the paper of his cigarette, then looks up at her with shrewd blue eyes – 'Which field do you want me to make a start on?'

'The Big Field – the one up against the moor beyond the grain-tower field.'

Bob Haines nods, takes a shiny gold lighter from his pocket and lights his fag with deliberation.

'Have you got anyone on the trailer?'

'Tom Pritchard promised he'd come . . .' – she hesitates fractionally, 'but if not I can drive it.'

He surveys Caroline doubtfully. Indeed there is not a great deal of her in her denim jeans and V-necked shirt. His eyes wander over her bare, downy arms with the odd brown freckle and silver bangle. She guesses he is looking at the bracelet and flushes. She has forgotten to take it off since she last went in to the hospital . . . In fact Bob Haines is interested in other things than the bracelet and being an honest man his expression makes it quite clear. His eyes meet Caroline's.

'Perhaps I oughter go on to Downses – I can't hang around.'

'Oh no. *Please*. Tom'll be here by the time the mist lifts – and if not I can do it till he does come.' Caroline's grey eyes meet Bob's blue. He notices the delicate curve of her face to her chin. The thought of her on a tractor with a heavy load of grain brings out the protective side of his nature, at the same time he doesn't want to disappoint her – on top of that there's his own time to consider. And time's money, there's no getting away from that.

'Us'll give it a try if you think you can manage,' he says, still doubtful. 'I'll put the combine up in the field and go and have my dinner, make a start after.'

'Will it be dry enough?' – it is Caroline's turn to doubt.

'Soon dry off with this breeze.'

And sure enough the sycamore leaves beside them sway and rustle, waving their autumnal spotted black leaves. Bob Haines climbs back on his machine. Caroline stands downhill of it while he starts it and reverses back along the road to turn in an open gateway. But once out of sight of Bob, she frowns in concern. *Will* she manage it, or will the load run away with her? The Big Field is quite steep. Why isn't Tom here? Inside the house she goes straight to the telephone. Dials. A woman's voice answers. Caroline knows it is Rita.

'Is Tom there, please?'

'No – he's doing extra for the Forestry today.'

Caroline feels affronted. 'But he said he'd be out here. The combine's come.'

Rita's voice is sharp, but polite. 'I'm afraid I don't know his plans more'n he told me. Maybe he's intending to come out Mr Ashurst's place this afternoon.'

Caroline swallows the insult. She knows all too well that amongst the local people she is simply a 'bit of fluff' Patrick Ashurst's brought home. She controls herself – Tom is her lifeline and she must remember it. Casual labour is nearly impossible to get, besides Patrick trusts Tom absolutely . . .

'If he does come back home please tell him the combine's here,' she says, but feels no certainty that Rita will do so.

She stays by the telephone. Should she ring the Saw Mills, the Forestry Commission? What's the point? Her chances of contacting Tom are negligible. No, she'll have to manage. If she goes in low ratio it should be alright. Then suddenly an alarming thought occurs to her. No one has opened the top of the thirty-foot grain-tower, set the cyclone into the hatch.

> Greytor Farm
> Meridan
> 12 September 1980

My dearest Helen,

How are things with you? How's the paper? Have any really good stories come your way? I am counting the days until you'll be here. It's sad you couldn't have come while Patrick was in hospital but I do understand the impossibility for you of changing dates. If all goes well he should be home two weeks from today . . .

As for me, well, I am managing but it isn't easy sometimes, as you can guess. There's so much I've never done before and suddenly find myself having to do. Patrick has always been, and still is, so self-sufficient that he has seldom seen the point in wasting his time showing me how to do things. Now I am suffering from exactly this – a terrible lack of knowledge – practical knowledge. You can pick up a lot from watching, I know, but there is still more you can't. On top of that it would be a great help if I was six inches taller and twice as broad with decent-sized biceps. I cannot, literally cannot, shift half the heavier machinery and am not much of a hand at undoing rusted bolts – and somehow much of Patrick's machinery *is* rusted, I suppose it's because there are simply not enough buildings to put it all away in – or is it more that hill farmers have an aversion to putting anything away! No – that's not fair, it's more that a lot of the machinery won't go in through the narrow door openings of old buildings like ours. I say ours, but do you know, most of the locals round here won't even accept me as a farm partner – someone who shares the farm with Patrick. They make me feel like some town woman who's shacked up with Patrick for a weekend, not been sharing his livelihood for *two* years – almost.

Tom is proving a problem (I told you about him, if you remember) – he only comes when he feels like it. But I mustn't be critical because he's marvellous when he's here, and makes me feel safe and unloaded of responsibility. Oh I know you will scoff at me for saying this, but you try it, it's not so easy. No wonder Bathsheba Everdene married Gabriel Oak. It is very much like taking over a business you know almost nothing about. Up until now I have consistently *helped* Patrick, but he has made all the decisions and I have been happy for him to do so – it has left me free to write. I've got quite a few poems I want to show you – get you to read and tell me what you think. I started on a long one but that has had to be put on one side since Patrick went in.

The sky is a splendid blue and the breeze obligingly drying. As predicted by Bob Haines, the mist has cleared, and Caroline stands at the bottom of the grain-tower, shading her eyes, looking up. A wide metal pipe with a ladder beside it reaches from top to base. She steps forward and grips the lowest rung of the ladder, as she climbs on to it the satchel on her back swings out away from her. In the satchel is a stone with which she will batter the clamps that hold the hatch. Last year she watched Patrick. This year Tom has set the blower up, but the hatch must be left closed until the last moment, so as he has still not arrived, this task falls to Caroline.

Half-way up she stops to look down, clinging tightly to the ladder. The ground beneath her starts to revolve slowly. She shuts her eyes and swallows. When she opens them again it is to look up at the sky where small white clouds swirl across the hard blue like bits of drifting cottongrass. She mounts rung by rung, gripping so tightly with her hands that her knuckles show white through their thin covering of flesh. At the very top is a handrail which she must grasp to climb over the brink and stand upright. Her satchel sways, unbalancing her precariously as she grabs the rail, pulls herself up, then steadies herself and stands leaning against it, looking down at the reeling ground beneath. A strong gust of wind buffets her as she kneels, takes off the satchel and extracts the stone then batters at the clamps which hold the hatch. That done she opens it, looking down into the cavernous empty belly of the tower. Fall down inside it and in a few moments you're dead from lack of oxygen. She swallows and with difficulty pulls round the blower pipe and lowers the cyclone into the hatch. When she stands again she feels frighteningly dizzy – for some moments she does nothing but lean against the rail, trying to recover her equilibrium. The wind snatches at her, it seems to be getting up. She notices the stone lying by her foot and kicks it over the edge, listening for the thud as it hits the ground. Then she edges her way backwards to the brink of the tower, feeling with her foot for the top rung. Supposing the handrail is not secured properly, supposing the fixings are worn through? It *is* twenty years old. Shutting such thoughts from her mind she allows her body to slide over the edge, taking her weight on her hands.

Tom sits on the settee in the living room of his and Rita's shared council house, eating his dinner. He unfolds it from a piece of foil in which it has been carefully wrapped by

Rita earlier that morning. Indeed at seven a.m. Rita is industrious, quick on the uptake and efficient. Her great mistake in life has been falling for Tom – or so she thinks. Oh it's not that she doesn't love him, because she does, it's just that she let him have his way with her which has resulted in two babies with Rita herself only twenty-three. She feels older, years older sometimes. When she's pregnant and got pressure on the sciatic nerve she feels like an old woman. But looking in the mirror tells another story for Rita is a black-haired, blue-eyed beauty in a sharp, bird-like fashion. Just at present she is being sharp with Tom.

'You tell her not to go bothering me. Tell her I got better things to do than answer the phone all day. Who does she think she is?'

Tom scrapes up the last lump of fruit cake made by Rita and tips the crumbs from the foil into his mouth.

'Does she think I got nothing to do, or what?'

Rita is in full flood. Tom listens. Tom has learnt from his mother that when a woman gets going, listening is best. Or to be more accurate shutting off his hearing and concentrating on something else. Tom is adept at this, he settles now to think of how he will transfer an old Ford engine picked up from the local scrap merchant into the shell of his carefully fortified rally car. Tom has not yet rallied except in the dead of night over the Forestry roads against his friends, but it is his ambition. And Tom is ambitious. His downfall has also been Rita. Two babies is a considerable handicap to rallying. So Rita and Tom are tied by a local council house and an interdependent situation of need and resentment. Neither the one nor the other functions as well on their own; Rita is determined Tom shall be responsible for *his* children, and Tom likes a home from which to function. His mother's would have been better but as soon as she heard from Rita's mother that Rita was pregnant, she kicked him out.

Nothing annoys Rita more than Tom's silence. It frustrates her almost beyond endurance and Jenny grizzling and grasping her skirts doesn't help. She slaps Jenny who runs into Tom's arms. Tom is roused.

'What did you want to slap the poor maid for?'

'Are you going to answer me or not?'

'What do you want me to say?'

'Are you going to tell *her* to stop ringing me?'

'Yes – if that'll quiet you.' Tom gets up, disentangling himself from Jenny's clutches. 'I must get on.'

'Up there, I suppose?'

For answer Tom bangs the door. Marriage is awful, he can't abide it – but he hates it worse when Rita goes off to Sharon's and he comes home to no stove lighted, no evening meal, a bare house. He can always go out with some of his mates looking around for women, that's true, but somehow he doesn't fancy it. So instead, he's learnt to keep silent, go out in his shed that serves for a garage and lie under his car.

Now he climbs into his van and slams the door. A slight lift of his feelings comes as he mounts out of the village on to the stretch of road from where he can see Greytor chimneys at the end of the valley. He wonders whether the combine will have started and if Patrick Ashurst's woman is out there, making a fool of herself and everyone else.

Rita watches Tom's van depart through the window. Her mouth is set in a sullen line – resentment still burns. She has no evidence of any sort to suggest Tom is receiving 'favours' from Mrs Ashurst, but the other night it was more than hinted at during the darts tournament, and what annoyed Rita even more was the implication that Tom had struck luck, done well for himself. Typical of a man, Rita thinks, to land her in for two kids and then make the most of his own time. In a sense it had been her fault, she's bound to admit, for she wanted the first to make sure of Tom. But the second was Tom's fault entirely, she'd told him he'd got to come out and he hadn't. Or he had, but too late. Now she is on the pill but she's done for anyhow with two, any more and she'd be in a looney's place or whatever . . .

Jenny is sobbing quietly behind her high chair. Rita sweeps her up in her arms and kisses her. The tears vanish miraculously at the promise of a visit to the village shop for a packet of Smarties. The baby, already sleeping in the pram, is wheeled out of the door and jolted down the steps which seems to make him sleep all the better. Jenny trails along beside the pram, her toes turned in, clutching the handle.

In the shop Rita is greeted by Christine who runs it.

'Hullo, Rita. I just seen Tom.'

'He hasn't been in, has he?' Rita is puzzled.

'Yes. He came in after stamps.'

'Stamps?' Rita is frankly amazed, Tom never writes a letter. She's not sure that he even can, he certainly didn't make the most of his years at Taverston Comprehensive. She opens her mouth to make this comment but then thinks better of it. Another thought has occurred to her. She buys the Smarties and a few groceries and leaves the shop. Christine prices bananas and watches Rita cross the road with Jenny and the pram. Christine knows as well as Rita who Tom has been buying stamps for, but it's not for her to say. Let her guess. Christine has a soft spot for Tom and she's noticed Rita looking at Jimmy Weber where she'd got no right to at the darts match, being a married woman . . . Christine squeezes a banana till it's black as she sticks on the tag. She really likes Jimmy.

Rita meanwhile has pacified Jenny with Smarties and is absorbing the information that Tom is running errands for the 'Ashurst woman' – for that is how they refer to Caroline in the village. Few of them, other than Christine, have actually spoken to her, in fact at first no one knew he had a woman – a wife – up there until the postman brought the news. But early this spring she had made her debut in the village so to speak – she had attended the jumble sale. It had been generally noticed that she was young in appearance (her exact age was an endless topic of conjecture), blonde with that strangely perfect skin that few people possess and all desire, and had grey eyes with black lashes. That her face was not astoundingly pretty but was astonishingly arresting; and that though she dressed in the most normal clothes imaginable she had an indefinable air about her that made her stand out from the crowd so that people felt it necessary to either know her intimately or hate her.

Caroline had not stayed long, she had bought some faded velvet curtains and a rickety milking stool, and then left as unexpectedly as she had arrived. But her image had imprinted itself indelibly on the village, and it was this image that danced before Rita's eyes. For she has not seen Caroline since, only spoken to her on the telephone.

She now begins to see the wisdom in saying nothing to Tom about the stamps, but knows her own nature well enough to deem it unlikely she will restrain herself. With difficulty she drags the pram back up the steps and into the front hall. She eats a Smartie wishing it might have the same calming effect on her as it does on Jenny.

Caroline stands at the bottom of the tower looking up at the ladder she has just descended. She takes little pride in her achievement, merely a profound hope she will not have to undergo such an ordeal again. Her terror of heights seems to be increasing with age, she remarks regretfully. She fumbles in her jeans for a piece of paper with a diagram drawn on it which she examines in relation to the blower engine at her feet. She turns it round, finds the indicated lever, closes the air vent and turns on the blower. A loud whine starts up with the motor and a look of profound relief crosses her face. After a few seconds she returns to the first lever and opens the air vent. She watches it with some satisfaction, then gets on the tractor beside her and drives the trailer up to where the combine waits. Perhaps due to nerves she fails to swing wide enough to manoeuvre tractor and trailer through the gateway and, in spite of the help of Bob Haines who has got down to signal her through, she scrapes the trailer against the granite gatepost. She jams on the brakes, reverses. There is a further scraping. Caroline embarrassed and anxious drives hopefully on. The scraping becomes a rip, but she is through. Bob Haines advances on her, grinning.

'Most of it's still there.'

Caroline gets off full of foreboding and joins him to examine the damage. She touches the tear in the wood with her fingertips as though her touch will heal, but the offending rip remains.

'It does show, doesn't it?' – she bites her lip in frustration at herself.

Bob Haines runs his expert eye over it. 'Touch'n up with a bit o' varnish. Nothin's busted.' He turns back to his combine. As he climbs up he mutters under his breath 'Not yet it isn't.' He settles himself in his seat, leans forward and talks down to Caroline who is waiting beneath for instruction.

'You wait here until you see me wave, then bring up the trailer alongside of me. You'll have to hold it steady, mind, or us'll have the grain sowed nine months early.' He smiles cheerfully. Caroline nods. She wanders along the edge of the barley beside the hedge, leans against it chewing at the grain and spitting out the husks while she watches the combine move away from her up the field. She listens to the roar and rattle of the great machine consuming the grain while the straw slides out behind leaving a gold wake. The sky is cloudless above the pale corn, while two buzzards circle over the moor beyond. Caroline shades her eyes and watches them. The beauty of her surroundings makes her forget her fear of driving on the steep field. She stretches herself on her stomach and gives herself up to the sensuous pleasure of the present . . .

Bob Haines is bending over her, shaking her shoulder. She starts up in embarrassment. Bob grins at her flushed face.

'What are you then? A sleeping princess?' He chuckles broadly. Caroline's discomfiture seems to amuse him all the more.

'I was waving and waving, then I guessed what it was. She've falled asleep, I tells myself, that's what she's gone an' done.'

'I'm terribly sorry' – Caroline presses her hands to her flaming cheeks. 'Shall I get the trailer?'

'Yes – you bring it up alongside of me and us'll see how us gets on.'

Caroline does as she is bid. To her immense relief it is easier than she had thought. She drives the tractor at an even pace along beside the still-moving combine, and listens to the hiss of the grain rattling through the shoot as it is spewed across. As soon as it ceases she drives away down the hill and reverses back to the hopper. Arms folded, she stands watching the hydraulic slowly tip the trailer to allow the grain to slip through a hatch at the back into the hopper. All sound around her is drowned by the whine of the blower, the rattle of grain ascending the pipe. Suddenly alarm is written all over her face. She darts forward, pushes back the hydraulic lever but too late; the barley instead of trickling steadily through the hatch, floods over the back – a big heap spreads on the ground. Helpless to counteract the flow, Caroline covers her face with her hands, then looks again. The blower, jammed, cuts out.

'Shit. Shit. Oh shit.'

By degrees the trailer lowers and the grain ceases to pour over. She looks despondently on the heap of waste, then up at the now silent tower. She glances anxiously at the field where the combine continues its methodical course, unaware of her predicament. But in ten minutes it will want to discharge its grain again and the trailer will be in no state to receive it – neither will the blower. She would like to sit down and weep – everything had been going so well! She feels overwhelmed by her own stupidity, for all she knows the blower is broken. She does the only thing she knows how to do – gets a shovel and starts shovelling the grain on the ground into a heap beside the hopper. Soon her forehead is covered in beads of sweat, her hair clinging to the sides of her face. She pushes her hot fringe out of her eyes, straightens her aching back, only to see Bob Haines within a few yards of her. A slow grin spreads over his pleasant face. He stops, surveys the situation.

'Some spilled.'

'So it did.' Bob nods, arms akimbo, enjoying Caroline's sweaty proximity. She has beautiful hair, he would like to touch it. He would like to touch her altogether, all over, but the chances seem slight. He looks at his watch.

'Combine's ready to empty,' he says.

Caroline turns distressed eyes at him. Desire mounts in him – his trousers feel unduly restrictive. As a release, a safety valve, he becomes angry.

'Well what do you want me to do,' he says, looking at Caroline, hotly belligerent.

'The trailer's almost empty,' Caroline says terrified he may drive off never to return. 'I'll come up and get the next load, then you can go on.'

'Then what?' – his desire is still mounting and he is even more surly in consequence.

Caroline really has no answer. She simply does not know how to dismantle and repair the blower, doesn't know where to begin. But fate chooses to be kind – an engine sounds from the rough lane. Through the gate Caroline glimpses white. Tom? Minutes later Tom approaches them. Caroline could not have been more pleased to see Jesus walking towards her over the waves.

Bob grunts. 'Looks like your problems are solved . . . temporarily.' He nods at Tom and walks off up the field. His brief acquaintance with Caroline has only confirmed his opinion that women should be kept in the kitchen.

Tom takes in the situation. Takes in Caroline. Notices the shovel in her hand.

'What's that for?'

'I was shovelling it up. I tipped it too steep.'

Tom makes no comment. He looks up at the tower.

'Who opened it up?'

'I did.'

He nods. A warmth seems to steal over his body, he feels no particular desire to move, do anything but go on standing beside this hot, distracted woman. He feels her dependency on him, that she is hanging on his words, his action. It is immensely comforting after Rita's fierce independence.

'The combine's full – it's waiting for the trailer' – Caroline looks at Tom anxiously. 'Shall I go?'

With an immense effort Tom pulls himself together.

'Can you manage it?'

'I did the last' – but her confidence since the blower episode has been sadly undermined.

'You take the trailer on up while I sort out this muddle.'

'Is it broken?' Caroline's voice expresses tragedy of a far greater order than the event.

'No. Jammed – but I'll have to dismantle the lower section of the pipe to get at it.'

They regard the silent engine and jammed hopper. Then Caroline turns to the tractor, climbs on. As she passes Tom he allows her the indulgence of a smile.

3 Rails Road
Taunton
15 September 1980

Dearest Caroline,
I don't pretend to understand you – 'a challenge', you say – is that what you call giving up your independence? Oh I know you were between jobs and hated temping, but to have chosen what you have as a way out, chosen to bury yourself in a crumbling hill farm that gives you no alternative but to forsake your own talent for a dull monotony of daily duties. Caroline, I'm sorry, but your last letter made my blood boil – you seemed so cowed somehow. (Forgive the pun!) Why don't you make up your mind to get out of it before you have children, while you still can?

Greytor Farm
Meridan
18 September 1980

My dear Helen,
You're quite right – you don't understand. It's no good my repeating what I've said before – that I care about this place built up over the last ten years by Patrick from nothing. I hesitate to add that I care about him.

Caroline is in the spare room which she has always used as her writing room and which has become her bedroom during Patrick's absence. She prefers it because her books are around her, because it faces east, because it has a low sill so that she is able to lie in bed and watch the scarlet, pink, and orange dawns spread across the sky from behind the conical peak of Scarhill. In the distance she can even see the sun glint on the clock face of the church tower. To be honest she doesn't terribly like their shared bedroom, certainly not on her own. She finds the big old walnut bed that belonged to Patrick's family oppressive, with one side empty. Also it still has the wallpaper on the wall from Patrick's uncle's time and when she'd said she would paint it Patrick had demurred. Generally he was reasonable enough, but in this case he had insisted that the wallpaper was perfectly good, an immense amount of work was needed to strip it down, and it was inadvisable to paint over it. Truth was on his side and Caroline was discouraged. So the vertical gold stripes and wreathes of roses had remained to remind Caroline of the past. A past she would have preferred to forget, for Patrick's family seemed to her to have too great a hold on him, make him singularly disinclined to change. Caroline looks round the agreeable white walls of her present room and derives satisfaction from them – she had painted them herself last summer soon after she'd finished the living-room.

But even the white walls and comfort of her books can't entirely allay the turmoil she feels as a result of Helen's blunt letter. She feels Helen is over-stepping the boundaries of even the most intimate of friends. She frowns and curls a piece of hair round and round her finger. Or is it not perhaps the *duty* of a true friend to be blunt – a sign of how much they care for you? Caroline, unable to make up her mind, thinks of herself and Patrick, of the peculiar loneliness of their shared life. She pulls her journal out from under a pile of papers, flips the pages back, reads:

10 June 1979.
Why are you lying away from me, Patrick, why aren't you closer? Am I what you wanted, expected? Am I more particular, special than those . . . others you never admit to? Are you cold to me now? Do you, like all men, take me for granted because you have had me? Deny it of course, but you do, don't you? I know you do. Why am I not tranquil, happy, so close to you – the two of us forming the grass like hares. Or that's how we were till you rolled away, withdrew even your fingers – left me alone – not cold because the sun caresses the little bits of me that are naked

55

– but cold for fear you are satiated by me, that the helping I put on your plate was too rich, indigestible. Why is your face turned away?

She sighs, closes her journal. She had written that after a day they had been walking together along the cliffs soon after they were married. It was one of the few days they'd spent away from the farm . . .

A loud knocking sounds on the back door. Caroline starts out of her reverie and looks cautiously out of the window. Jim Thurley from the next farm down the valley is standing there as though he doesn't mean to go away. Caroline hastily puts on some shoes and goes down stairs. She opens the door. Jim Thurley raises his pork-pie hat.

'Good afternoon, Mrs Ashurst. I just dropped by to ask after Mr Ashurst.'

Caroline regards her neighbour warily. She wonders the real reason for his visit, but says politely, 'That's very good of you.'

Jim Thurley shifts his weight, crosses one leg over the other and rests his elbow against the wall, his hand on the back of his red, creased neck.

'An' I thought I ought let you know I seen some of your sheep going up the hedge next my barley. Now I don't want to cause trouble knowing your husband is away, like, but I figured if you was to get Tom Pritchard to go up along the hedge looking for holes . . .'

Caroline, who deems it meet to stay on the right side of her ambivalent neighbour, asks him in to tea. Jim Thurley removes his hat and follows her into the dark kitchen. He pulls a chair out and seats all of his thirteen stone before the table. Caroline puts the kettle on the hot plate and gets out cups and saucers instead of the usual mugs. He pursues his inquiry about Patrick and she answers to the best of her knowledge. She assures him she will give Patrick both his and his wife's regards when she goes in tomorrow. Jim looks satisfied but still slightly sly. She gives him his tea. He stirs it while she waits for the conversation to return to her sheep and his barley, which it does.

'You got a beautiful crop you was getting in today. I

seen the combine – Haines, wasn't it? – up in your top field. My own's coming on. Needs a few days yet, and as I was saying if you could get Tom Pritchard to put up a stake or two along your hedge . . .'

'You see Tom only gets out here when he's got time, otherwise he's down at the Mills. But I'll put some stakes up there myself tomorrow.'

Jim Thurley looks at Caroline with a calculating light in his eye. He doesn't see her as much of a hand with a crowbar, let alone a mallet.

'I wouldn't want to go putting you to any trouble, that wouldn't be a neighbourly thing to do with Mr Ashurst in hospital – but if you could let me have the stakes – and tell Mr Ashurst I'd be glad if he could let me have some of his straw, not too pricey like – then I could put up a bit of fence along that hedge for you. There's wire there, but it's growed in under where it doesn't do no good to anyone.'

Caroline replenishes his cup assuring him she will ask Patrick about the straw, but will do the hedge herself in spite of his kindness in offering. Jim Thurley accepts partial failure and stirs his tea while taking in the Ashurst kitchen.

'Changed it a bit, then?' He looks at Caroline's print of Cézanne's bathers stuck on the wall. 'Is that what they call modern h'art?'

Caroline at once feels embarrassed and defensive, why shouldn't she put things she likes on the wall, why should paintings of Patrick's uncle's carthorses be the only acceptable decoration. This is not quite fair of her and she knows it, for anything realistically copied will suffice, but the print she has chosen is particularly likely to cause comment. Not only is it of naked women – and the Thurleys are Methodists – but the women are distorted into strangely cubic forms. Jim Thurley feels affronted by them, women to him should widen and narrow, curve in a pleasantly voluptuous fashion. His eyes stray to Caroline without gaining satisfaction – there's not enough of her to make a smart maid . . . His gaze suddenly intensifies. Caroline who is sitting facing the sink with her back to the door turns to see what he is looking at. Tom faces her, holding up a half-plucked, mauled chicken. He walks into the room and lays it on the table. No one speaks. Caroline turns it over. The breast is badly chewed.

'Where did you find it?'

'Up on the road as I come along . . .'

Caroline doesn't wait for him to finish. The door slams as she goes out in search of the rest. Jim Thurley and Tom eye the dead bird before them.

'Looks like a dog,' says Tom.

'Last week there was a dog up on the Common worrying sheep' – Jim's expression is openly innocent to the point of being devout.

'It's chewed the half of it.'

Jim bends to examine it the better. 'A dog, you say? I don't know that that looks like a dog tooth.'

'Must've come right down in the yard.'

'What dog would come right down in the yard, then?' Out of his eye Jim catches sight of his own pass across the window. He moves a little to block it from Tom's view. The clock ticks. Silence. Caroline returns with the remaining chickens, puts them with the other on the table.

'Another's been bitten – dragged down off the wall. All that work!'

Jim shifts towards the door shiftily. 'I can see I'm in the way. Remember me to Mr Ashurst, and if you get time to ask him about the barley straw I'd be very grateful. I thought I'd come to him first, like – before trying anyone else.' Holding his hat before his chest like a shield, Jim Thurley backs out.

Tom resettles himself against the stove, one leg crossed over the other, arms folded. Caroline sits by the table. After a few moments Tom announces, 'He knows whose dog it was.'

Caroline looks at Tom, adjusts herself to his implication.

'Not his?'

Tom shrugs.

'Surely his dog wouldn't touch a chicken?' Caroline is disbelieving and shocked.

'He doesn't feed it proper, does he?'

'Couldn't it be the mink come back?' she almost feels she

must support her neighbour, now suddenly seen in this more wicked light.

'I never known a mink touch anything cold' – Tom's mind is made up, his aspect grimly threatening.

'Whatever it was I'd like to shoot it!'

Tom looks at Caroline as if to say something then changes his mind. Instead he says he must return to the combine, adding that he only came over because the tractor was out of diesel. He doesn't want her to get ideas, think he's hanging about the house for nothing . . .

Caroline follows him to the door. 'Could you teach me to shoot – I mean shoot better? Patrick has showed me but I don't feel very confident yet.'

Tom edges his way out of the door. 'You might shoot the neighbour instead of his dog' – he grins to soften his sarcasm.

Caroline ignores his remark. 'It wouldn't take long. When you've time.'

But Tom can't bear to be cornered, manipulated. He'd rather Rita's shouting than that. And Caroline's big eyes staring at him increase his exasperation rather than soften it, his own weakness makes him doubly resentful.

'Too long. I'm too busy for anything like that.' He begins to close the door.

Caroline says quickly, 'I've got to get the sheep off the moor at the end of the week, so that'll mean dipping. And the vet comes Friday, will you be able to come?'

'I'll have to think about it.' He closes the door, walks up the cobbled back yard. Everything about his walk, his carriage, expresses his defiance and inward rage. He will be asked but not ordered and the sooner the Ashurst woman learns that, the better for her. He completely ignores the fact that Caroline *has* asked him, rather than ordered him. But the implication is that she expects him to come and that is the one thing he won't stand for. One way and another she gets his goat. He can't see what Patrick had to go choosing a town woman for, far better to have got himself someone from the area. Rita was from the area, well almost – down off the moor a bit, it was true.

But then when they'd started going round together they hadn't had any plans for settling down. If it hadn't been for the baby . . .

Tom, like most men however moral, feels that the baby was little to do with him. And during Rita's worst bouts with him – for any row or scene is always her fault, her carrying on – he sometimes wonders whether it is his at all. Given another year and he'd have known better than to get caught out like that. They'd got the two now. For one on its own, Rita'd said, was more trouble than two. Tom wasn't so sure about that but, all in all, he liked his children. They didn't affect him too much one way or the other. Rita reared them and he worked. That's the way it had to be if they were to pay the interest on the van, the telly, the three-piece leather suite Rita'd insisted on, and the rent to the Council. Tom perspired at the thought as he climbed on the tractor. The diesel that he had left filling the tank while he took the chicken down had over-filled and flowed down the drive in a long stain. Tom swore. Still, what did it matter, the Ashursts had money, didn't they? It wouldn't hurt them over much. And starting the engine Tom jolts off over the cobbled yard.

Caroline, watching him from the bathroom window, bites her lip. Why does he have to be so moody, so difficult? Patrick had never entertained the idea of her having anyone other than Tom, but she is beginning to think it would be better to have someone easier, someone she could rely on. Perhaps she might suggest it to Patrick at the right moment, if he was well enough.

Greytor Farm
Meridan

Dearest Helen,
Thank you for your letter, which as always I seized upon and ravished. I feel like a dog that is only fed once a week on real meat, I am so hungry for it that it goes down in one gulp. But then I have plenty of time to digest it later. And that is what I have been doing with your last, digesting it. But I shan't write all the ideas it has given me, questions

it has raised – on the contrary, I shall wait until we are together which is so soon now I can hardly believe it. I keep feeling afraid something will happen to stop your coming. But no, why should it? Why shouldn't we be together? Is it a feeling of guilt I have for coming out here that makes me think I have something to atone for? Actually, I am atoning daily for any rash or wilful step, but I am prepared to. For surely there comes a stage in everyone's life when one must put reason out of mind and step down boldly to where there is a possibility of a ledge. Otherwise no motion, *real* motion I mean, would be possible. One could neither move up nor down but must forever stay trapped in circumstance.

No, I shan't write any more. In spite of the temptation I shall wait with my fingers crossed till you are here. I have to confess to loneliness, Helen, though I despise myself for my weakness and am really used to being on the farm alone. The nights by myself no longer worry me – except for that last moment of darkness when I switch the lights off and go up. Tom comes when it's essential . . . Patrick had expected to be back for the dipping – it is now almost a month since he went in. They say his operation was a complete success but they seem powerless to deal with the infection. I shall try to corner the Ward Sister this evening when I go in.

The blackface sheep form a pale winding stream as they move slowly forward over the moor between brown bracken and gorse. The sky is grey with clouds racing hastily on their way pushed by a strong wind. Caroline stands on an outcrop of rock, her eyes shaded, watching them. As they move past she steps down from the rock and walks along parallel but at some distance, guarding their flank. They move on steadily, warily, halting every now and then to take in the positions of the three figures that are driving them, four with the dog who follows behind, mouth open panting, relieved to walk after the energy expended in the gathering. Tom and Johnny, the twelve-year-old brought along to help, are on the other flank. The entire pageant now comes out of the bracken and moves across a patch of grass towards a group of rocks on the brow of the hill prior to plunging down to the farm some hundred feet beneath. This next is the tricky part, the part that takes care, patience, and a knowledge of animal psychology, for to get the sheep off the Common they must pass through a narrow hunting-gate, down an ill-fenced lane and across a ford into the buildings. The hunting-gate is the main problem for the blackface rightly sense captivity ahead – a thing their nature is bred to combat – and break back up the hill at the slightest sign of a gap.

Accordingly the sheep bunch up on the top. They are as fine looking as any animal with their elegant curled-back horns, long silky fleeces and fine legs. In many ways closer to goat than sheep, feeding off little and preferring to go over a wall than through a gate. The owners of blackface lose friends due to the sheep's breaking capacity.

Caroline and Tom take a count, agree on numbers. All have been found which is of vital importance, for to leave a sheep on the moor during a sheep scab clearance is illegal and may result in the loss of sheep. Now slowly they edge them down over the steep ground – Caroline takes her eyes off them a moment to look anxiously at her watch, only to hear a shout from Tom and see him pointing from above. Two sheep are breaking away to the left below her. She leaps down over the steep ground, unable to see the rocks beneath the bracken. The dog joins her and between them they push the breakers back to the main flock who hesitate before the gate. Two others break away the far side, are pursued and brought back. No one dares push them, everyone waits. Then one takes it into its head to risk the gate, another follows and the whole flock pour through the bottleneck spreading out as the lane broadens the other side. Caroline runs, leaps up a wall and gets in the field on the lane's left; Tom is on the other side, miraculously ahead and in the right place, Johnny and the dog, behind.

Once in the lower lane the sheep keep moving until they sight the ford, then try to break to right and left. Quickness is all, and Caroline *is* quick, there's no denying that, Tom thinks, watching her. In fact she's pretty neat with this sort of thing altogether. Never scares the animals, senses where they're going and gets there first. Could Caroline have read Tom's thoughts she would have felt more than gratified, as it is she looks again at her watch – another fifteen minutes and she *must* go for Helen who is arriving off the bus in Meridan. She feels bad about not having fetched her from the main line station, but what could she do? Fortunately the sheep cross the water without too much fuss and are coaxed into the buildings by the dip. All heave a sigh of relief, wipe their hot faces. Tom looks round for a drink of water which Caroline fetches from the house. She offers him cider but he declines. What does she want him to do – fall in the dip?

She places the tray with two glasses and a jug of water on the wall, announces guiltily her need to fetch Helen and, to assuage her conscience, pours Tom a glassful and takes it over. He thanks her, takes it. Drinks. Hands her back the glass. Their eyes meet briefly but what they say no one would care to hazard. All Caroline knows is that she needs Tom's respect and feels an odd little thrill of pleasure on receiving it.

'I'll leave the jug on the wall in case you want more,' she says. And goes. She is conscious of Tom's eyes following her as she walks away and walks awkwardly, stiffly. Tom in fact is more concerned with mixing the dip. Perhaps because of a sense of achievement, perhaps because of her recent exertions, Caroline's face is flushed and her eyes very bright. She seems lit up, her sense of guilt overlaid.

Inside the house she looks round in despair at the disorder, seizes a bunch of yellow daisies out of the sink and puts them into a Matisse-like jug she carries up to Helen's room. She wipes some dust off the sill with her palm. Then, smoothing her hair quickly in front of the mirror, picks up her handbag and goes out by the back door to the car. Twenty minutes later she is parked opposite the chemist in Meridan, waiting for Helen's bus.

Patrick lies on his back in the men's ward staring at the ceiling. After almost a month he vacillates between moods of resentment and extreme passivity. The hospital habit to a certain kind of nature is oddly subversive, having much the same effect as a tranquilliser. The habit and routine of the days follow each other for the patient neither ill nor entirely well with a monotony that drives some to any lengths to escape, while others it lulls, making it increasingly difficult for them to muster the will to shake off the infections their body is fighting. So it is with Patrick. A streptococcus has invaded his blood stream and decided to stay, his response to antibiotics while good at first, later seems to flag. Repeated changes of pills are to no avail, and recently one of the more enterprising doctors has concluded Patrick's resistance to antibiotics might well be due to his repeated absorption of them while treating animals. Be that as it may, Patrick is not responding as he should – his temperature goes up and down, and no one will discharge him.

He whiles away the hours by reading, watching television, writing a letter or two, listening to Open University programmes through earphones, and walking about the corridors. As is normal, he has become increasingly infatuated by a young nurse of his choice who is quieter and shyer than the rest, goes by the name of Vanessa, and is equally infatuated with Patrick. Their silent unvoiced love affair gives a tang-like frost to the air each day. On her days off, time seems to pass twice as slowly, and Patrick lies on his back as today, staring, or appearing to stare, at the ceiling.

He has also got friendly in a distant kind of way with one or two others in his ward – a naval captain and a travelling salesman. With the former he has a love of the sea in common, the latter he only listens to perforce, but enjoys the continuous succession of anecdotes in spite of their inevitable crudity. But most of the time he lies in apathy fantasising about Vanessa or thinking about Caroline.

Vanessa was everything that Caroline was not. She was agreeably subservient and made clear by her every gesture that she would like God to be made in Patrick's image. Caroline was immensely complicated, blew hot and cold in a flash, and often gave the impression she thought less highly of him than he would have liked her to. She certainly was not relaxing. Her own standards were high and she expected equally high standards of others, which was not easy, for under Patrick's authoritative manner he was more lackadaisical than he liked it to be known. But he cared deeply for Caroline and was as fascinated by her as when they had first met, so he spent much of his time wondering if he had, or could, make his wife of two years' duration happy. That she was nine years his junior also worried him, he sensed a kind of generation gap between them that oddly enough did not seem to matter when it came to the even younger Vanessa. Vanessa was so much more outgoing, more . . . he looked for the word and lighted on 'continental'. Patrick was one of those people who imagine continental women to be an entirely different species to that of his own cold island. Caroline, it seemed to him, had withdrawn since their marriage. He wondered sometimes whether he should have insisted they marry for she had said plainly she would have rather they lived together. But it would have made so much awkwardness with his mother, not that he saw her often, and the village. And really he himself believed in marriage. If they were going to live together, share their lives, then why not? And Caroline had given way surprisingly meekly. If truth be known he didn't think she cared one way or the other, it was that other woman she shared the flat with that caused the trouble. He detested her. She had a strong hold over Caroline he'd never been able to break. She was a feminist with a capital F, of the militant breed. Caroline professed to be one too, but she was no separatist. He suspected the other woman of being lesbian . . .

So Patrick's thoughts revolve round his head in a confusion of building aggression, and it is only his sleeping pill at night and Vanessa in the day that allay his inner turmoil, allow him to become calm and filled with the holiness of happiness.

Then of course there were Caroline's visits, when she sat by his bed watched by all the other men in the ward and he felt jealous and possessive. As a result they sparred silently while remaining polite and civil to each other on the surface. He longed to draw her between the hospital corners of his sheets. She remained aloof beside him, her hands folded, her hair smelling of Jojoba shampoo. She always brought him something, fruit or flowers or a book, and kissed him when she arrived and departed. All she left him with was a pain of desire that lasted many hours after she had gone. In the main she talked about the farm and he bullied her because he almost resented that she should have grown so interested in it during his absence, whereas in the two years they had been there together she had shown little interest and even less aptitude.

Patrick turns on his side and pulls the pillow over his head. Probably she will come this evening.

The bus that conveys Helen ever closer to Caroline, winds and stops and starts along innumerable lanes. It has no hesitation in taking one and a quarter hours over a journey that would take thirty minutes in a car. It is a long-standing institution, giving trustworthy service to many country inhabitants without cars or unable to drive. It also regularly transports school children on five days out of seven, and it is from this worthy service that Helen has suffered most. She has had her feet trodden on and her head knocked – two boys have fought for the seat opposite and her trousers have narrowly escaped a bottle of Coca-Cola. To increase her discomfort two girls have sat behind her, giggling and squirming, the sharp knees of one frequently jabbing her through the soft back of her seat. So when the driver calls back to tell her Meridan is the next stop, she stands with alacrity and takes her suitcase and polythene bag from the rack above. Moments later she is in the road hugging Caroline, who clasps her like an affectionate daughter might a long-lost mother.

To Caroline, Helen seems to have grown taller. Perhaps it is her high-heeled boots beneath her smart baggy trousers that give this impression. The women take each other in in a minute, as women do. Caroline notices along with the tallness that Helen has shortened her hair since she last saw her and that it fires off red tinted lights. She wishes she wouldn't wear lipstick. Helen observes Caroline to be a bit thin in the face but otherwise as beautiful as ever. To herself, of course, for Caroline's face is not exceptional but rather grows on people the longer they know her. What is special about her, Helen has decided long since, is the aura that is a part of her, a way of dressing and choosing colours that sets her apart in a crowd. Helen almost wishes Caroline's disastrous choice of life might show more in her appearance, but on the contrary, her face, though thin, has a glow to it that is enviable.

Caroline takes Helen's bag and together they cross to the car, open the boot, talking all the while. That they are happy in each other's company is unmistakable.

Tom is well into the dipping. He catches each sheep and drags it forward, heaves it over the edge of the dip to drop with the splash and thump of a body entering a swimming-pool. Dip sprays out fierce red drops. Johnny, standing at the side dunks each one twice with a wood mallet slightly resembling those used for croquet. The terrified sheep blink the stinging dip from their eyes, swim to the far end, heave themselves out, shake themselves, and stand shivering in the pen. Another is put through, and another. Tom's rhythm of catching, dragging, dipping, builds up. On occasion he shouts at Johnny, gives him an order, otherwise they work in silence – until the sound of a car in the front gate makes them look up. Caroline and Helen have returned. Johnny stares up the drive at the car coming down; Tom makes a point of ignoring it. When Caroline gets out and leads Helen forward to watch, he doesn't even appear to see them. Caroline asks Johnny if the bus has come and gone without him, but he shakes his head, and sure enough five minutes later the bus appears and he runs off, stinking with dip to plague both bus and school.

Tom rests. Leans against the side and smokes. Caroline knows he is waiting for her to take Johnny's place and hurries Helen in the house to make herself at home while she covers herself in protective clothing and goes to help. She treads warily along the side of the dip – a slippery enough place at the best of time without the fear of being knocked by a sheep. Tom pushes the first sheep in and stands back to watch what she will make of it. Caroline, eager to do well, ducks the sheep down vigorously.

'Not too long or you'll drown it' – he looks at her earnest face beneath her sou'wester in amusement. What a get-up! But his heart lifts at her proximity. The arduous labour of the work at once becomes more tolerable. He notices her flush at his correction. Caroline wishes she had goggles to protect her eyes. The crombing* of the sheeps' heads, the guiding of them along the bath becomes a part of her lot. Tom sends them at her in quick succession, then seeing her tire, slows down his pace. The hollow slop of the body entering the water, the motion of swimming, the pumping action of pushing the sheep under, all combine into a glut of sensation excluding words. And all the time the churning red water, shaken from the fleeces, runs back into the bath in a continuous trickle. Caroline's arms and the back of her neck and shoulders ache until she becomes numb to everything but the pain and the need to endure. Only Helen's arrival finally brings Tom to a halt. She has found some old waterproof clothing and decked herself out like Caroline who smiles and can hardly refrain from laughing, her transformation is so complete. She climbs along the dip on the opposite side as Tom hands her a dipping stick. Caroline's attempt to tell her to watch out for the slipperiness is drowned in the splash of a sheep entering the bath. They work at first in silence. From time to time Caroline glances anxiously across at her friend to see how she's taking it, but Helen, who has a strong body and iron will, takes it in her stride. Her help certainly relieves Caroline whose work is now halved.

'Even I . . .' Helen gets spray in her mouth as she speaks and spits, 'didn't anticipate this.'

Caroline laughs – Tom too smiles.

'I'm sorry Helen, I really am. Are you alright?'

'What does it look like?'

'Six more to go' – Tom is enjoying himself. Helen's presence eases the tension that is always present when he is alone with Patrick Ashurst's woman, although he would

---

* *Crombing:* Catching with a shepherd's crook.

68

deny it if asked. He is able to work with both of them as easily and naturally as he does with Patrick. Helen amuses him, he admires the way she has rolled up her sleeves, joined in. He glances at Caroline's face and a sensation steals over him he can't control. In anger and relief he throws the last sheep in the dip, straightens up.

'That's it.' The sheep climbs out the far end and shakes itself. Tom stands, his hands hanging limply, palms slightly turned out, almost like a figure of sculpture. He has suddenly the exhausted stance of someone who has worked himself beyond his limit. Caroline is quick to notice and makes her way round the dip to him.

'Shall we go and have something to eat before we move them?' Her voice registers her concern for him.

'I got to drench them yet.'

'After lunch?'

'You didn't think I'd go right on and do it now, did you?' He looks at her with contempt and resentment.

Caroline looks down, trying to contain her hurt. Why does he have to take everything she says the wrong way?

'Of course not. I thought you'd come and have cheese and pickle with us.'

'I've brought my dinner with me.'

'Don't you want tea?'

'If you're making some.' Tom starts to unroll his sleeves, button up his shirt. Caroline, about to say something, thinks better of it and instead climbs over the rails along the side of the dip to join Helen who has been looking round her while not appearing to listen to the interchange. The two women shed their protective garments in the porch and go upstairs to wash themselves. Tom enters the house after them, washes himself in the sink thoroughly and methodically, including his face and neck. He dries himself on the roller towel, goes through into the kitchen and takes up his characteristic stance in front of the stove. Above him he hears running water and laughter, then Caroline appears in the doorway in white shirt and clean jeans. Her hair, which she generally wears tied back, is damp and falls loosely round her face. The same sensation he has felt out at the dip repeats itself, he shifts his weight, uncrosses one leg and crosses it over the other. Poor Tom, what else can he do? Unfair forces are at work beyond his control which he cannot account for and has no wish to accept.

Caroline busies herself with making tea and putting plates, knives and a hunk of Cheddar cheese, a bottle of Branston pickle, and a round silver-papered garlic cream cheese (for Helen) on the table. She pours tea into a mug for Tom and hands it him. Tom accepts it, spooning sugar from the bowl she holds. She adds milk as he holds the mug towards her. The whole is an odd kind of ritual of communication that works better than words. Indeed, it could not work worse.

'Milk out of a bottle?'

She looks at him. 'Daisy's dried up. Her calf's due next month.'

Tom accepts the information without comment. They drink their tea in silence. Caroline, due to her upbringing, feels a need to break the silence. She has been taught to feel that silence, unless with your children, husband, or some other with whom you live daily, is undesirable. To be in the room in silence with friend or stranger is completely alien to her, producing an uncomfortable tension. Tom, on the contrary, being less 'educated' and entirely natural, sees no need at all to speak unless he has information of interest to impart. Silence to him is as good as speech; being in the same room as someone is company enough for him. So it is Caroline who speaks first.

'I'm going in to see Patrick tonight.'

Tom looks at her but says nothing. Caroline struggles on. 'Perhaps they'll say when he's able to come home?'

Tom drinks his tea and makes a face. He puts his mug down. 'What kind of tea is this?'

'The usual.'

'Not like you make most times, it isn't.'

'It's all I've got.' Her expression verges on the tragic – even at this level she has failed. 'Perhaps it's too weak,' she says hopefully. In fact she knows it's because she's put a teaspoon of china in it because of Helen.

He places his mug down expressively on the edge of the stove, alters his legs again and looks out of the window.

'Would you rather have some coffee?' she removes the instant Nescafé from the shelf, waves it, her hand on the lid.

Tom picks up his mug. 'This'll do.'

A silence follows in which Tom sips his tea and Caroline feels depressed. It sometimes seems to her she could communicate better with someone who spoke a different language.

Tom tips the mug up drinking the dregs and spitting a tea leaf in the sink. It is clear she should have used a strainer as Tom's mother or Rita would have done. He places his mug on the drainer and makes for the door.

'I'll get back out and have my dinner while you have your "lunch"' – he makes it pointed.

Caroline absorbs and ignores it, asks him why he doesn't bring his food in and eat with them. But at this moment Helen enters, meeting Tom in the doorway. He stands back to let her pass.

'You got company – besides I've got to get on or I shan't get through.' His tone is unbenign, sullen.

Caroline's colour rises with her anger. Their eyes meet. His mocking, hers flashing. Curbing her rage against what she considers his sheer ill manners, she says with spirit, 'If you want help with the drenching you'd better come and tell me.' Let him play the beggar for once!

For answer the door closes. She looks after him with resentment and regret. Regret that he has pushed her into showing her temper. She knows, or thinks she knows, it will only increase his contempt for her. In fact the fierce intensity, the brilliance of her eyes when angry, has had exactly the opposite effect.

Helen has sat at the table and is helping herself while observing Caroline.

'What's up?'

'Nothing' – Caroline's pink face and agitated manner belies what she says. Realising this and wanting sympathy, she adds, 'It's just Tom. I don't known why he's like he is.'

Helen disparages the Boursin and helps herself to a slab of Cheddar and pickle.

'How *is* he?'

'Like a spoilt child – when he's with me, that is. As if he hates me.'

Helen makes no comment. She glances at her friend shrewdly and gets up to make some toast. 'I'm starving.'

Caroline immediately feels guilty at her own self-concern. 'Oh I'm sorry, Helen. You sit still – I'll do it. There are masses of eggs. Would you like one?'

'No – this is a delicious Cheddar.' She munches happily. 'Have I done my work for the day or is there another little job lurking outside for me this afternoon?'

Caroline relaxes and laughs. 'You were wonderful. Dipping's horrible, isn't it?'

'Let's say I *have* done things I've preferred.'

'If Tom doesn't want me this afternoon I'll show you the rest of the farm. The nicest parts.'

Helen catches a bit of dripping pickle with her tongue. 'I get the feeling he almost certainly *will* want you this afternoon.'

'Why do you say that?'

'He's got you round his little finger – anyone could see that. You're like a mother with her first-born son.'

Caroline is both startled and mortified by Helen's comment. And also oddly pleased.

'Thanks,' she says in mock offence, 'he's not *that* much younger.'

Helen licks her fingers carefully, one by one. Age, she replies, was not her point, though it might well have been. She reaches for an apple. Caroline pushes the bowl towards her. Nothing further is said about Tom, but Helen's words continue to recur in Caroline's mind. She prefers to take it as a joke rather than show herself disturbed by the appositeness of the remark.

Shortly after this, Caroline goes back to help Tom catch sheep for drenching. She has not kept her threat that he must come a-begging. She knows he never will. So she enters the space in which the sheep are penned and 'catches' for him. Helen hangs over the gates, watching. The sheep are large and powerful and it is quite a rough house – in catching one Caroline is nearly knocked off her feet. Helen would like to interfere, tell Tom he should do the catching and let Caroline hold the drench, but thinks better of it and goes back into the house. She searches for matches to light a fire – a thousand feet up at Greytor means the drop in temperature is considerable and the air a lot colder than she is used to.

Caroline continues to do the catching until Tom takes pity on her and suggests a rest. For no particular reason that she is aware of, his manner towards her has entirely changed and he speaks in a straightforward fashion with no edge to it. Thankfully she nods, pushes her hair out of her eyes and finds a corner with an old log stump to sit on. Tom sits on an upturned bucket opposite and smokes. Their silence is a silence of exhaustion where she feels no more need of speech than he does, in fact apparently less, for it is Tom who looks across and says, 'She doesn't come from a farm, then?'

'No – she's a journalist from Taunton.'

'Out for the day?'

'She's staying for a week.'

Tom is looking at the rest of the sheep, taking in how many more there are to do. He looks back to her. 'Can you keep on?'

'Yes.'

But she's rather pale he notices, and his better nature comes to the surface despite himself. He suggests that if they put a hurdle across the corner and pen the remainder up tighter, he can manage them on his own. They do so, confining the sheep and making them easier to catch.

'You go on in the house. I don't reckon your friend will be happy without someone to talk to.'

Caroline marvels at his unprecedented pleasantness, but sets her chin and helps him finish. Her reward is a momentary look of approbation she gets from Tom over a struggling sheep, but it is enough to make her happy for the rest of the day. That, and Helen's arrival.

It is early evening. The October light is fading rapidly through the whorls of ancient glass that constitute the window panes. Caroline lies on her bed and Helen sits at its foot.

'You can't. You mustn't.'

'But I told him I'd be coming.'

'Ring the hospital. Leave a message to say you'll be in tomorrow.'

Caroline looks up with worried eyes. 'I can't do that. Imagine if it was you.'

'But you've been at it all day and you look like a ghost. It's nearly an hour's drive.'

'Forty-five minutes,' Caroline corrects her, 'well, say fifty.'

'I still don't think you should.'

'I'm feeling better, Hel. Honestly. All I needed was a rest. What's happened to Tom?'

'He's gone.'

'He must have been absolutely worn out.'

Helen laughs in a rather humourless tone. 'He's used to it, don't you see. You're not.'

'Well that's my fault, isn't it?'

'Oh rubbish – of course it's not "your fault". You haven't been raised as a strapping farm worker.'

'So I've got to learn to be one now.'

Helen sighs – she picks a tooth. She finds Caroline obstinate to the point of unreasonableness. It seems ridiculous to her that Caroline who is quite gifted enough to make her own way in the world should be acting the role of a supportive skivvy. However, she curbs her normal bluntness and refrains from saying so – after all the poor thing has got enough on her plate just now. She's got to keep the place going while that patriarchal man she has chosen to live with lolls in hospital. Helen brings herself up short, sees that uncurbed emotion is taking over from reason, and mentally chastises herself. Nevertheless, it does distress her to see Caroline exhausting herself – surely Patrick could have afforded to pay another man to work with Tom. Tom? She looks thoughtfully at Caroline, voices her opinion.

'I have to admit Tom's got something about him . . .' – she sees Caroline's eyes are directed intently at her – 'something not very pleasant,' she finishes. She returns Caroline's gaze. Caroline drops her eyes.

'Why? What are you thinking?'

'Where does he come from?'

Caroline describes Tom's home and family, explains he has been working on and off for Patrick since he was fifteen. Helen listens. She fervidly hopes Caroline's not going to make a fool of herself over someone of that sort, but decides it wiser not to say so. She doesn't much like the slightly reverential tone that Caroline uses when she speaks about Tom.

'You see, he can do absolutely everything. He knows the place and Patrick's ways – he's quite invaluable.' Caroline looks to Helen for support.

'Yes,' says Helen, automatically. But she knows and Caroline knows that's not what she thinks.

Caroline suddenly sits up. 'What time does your watch say?'

'Ten past five.'

She gets off the bed hastily, takes a skirt off a peg and puts it on, zips on a pair of boots and brushes her hair. Helen sits watching her.

'I'm truly sorry to leave you on your first evening, but I'll have to go. I won't be long – I'll come tearing back.'

It's your guilty conscience driving you, Helen thinks, but says, 'Please don't. I want you alive to talk to.'

She then suggests she go with her and wait outside the hospital in the car. But Caroline demurs, says it will be better if she comes with her on the next occasion when Patrick will be strong enough to argue with her. She makes a joke of it, but it doesn't conceal from Helen that she is worried at the thought of them meeting. Caroline, perhaps sensing the track of Helen's thought, puts her arms impulsively round her. Helen returns the embrace and for a moment the two women cling together, yet their minds are steering separate courses, but not so separate that the one can't comprehend the other.

Caroline frees herself as Helen says gently. 'Tell him there's too much to do for one person, Caroline – tell him he must let you get someone for the days Tom can't come. He must be insured.'

Caroline picks up her handbag. 'No,' she says, briefly, 'he's not – only his life.'

Helen stares. 'He must be mad.'

'No, not mad. Just a typical hill farmer. Insurance to most of them's like paying tax. They consider it a form of insidious robbery. Anyway,' she goes on, 'I can't start worrying him at this stage, there's no point. We couldn't afford anyone else – the overdraft's phenomenal – we never have any spending money because any profits go on paying interest to the bank.'

As she talks she makes her way along the passage to the stairs. Helen follows her. Caroline runs down ahead, turning at the bottom to look back at Helen, a dark figure at the top of the stairs.

'I might have a bath – if it's possible.' To climb back into a warm watery womb might be a relief, Helen feels.

'The water *may* be hot enough – you could try. If not' – Caroline is on her way to the back door – 'put some more wood in the stove, and leave the bottom door open until it draws up . . .'

The door bangs. Helen is on her own. She descends the stairs slowly, dragging her fingers across a patch of discoloured wall. She looks at them, surprised to see they are wet and smeared with a greenish mildew. Down in the kitchen she tackles the stove, prods the hot ashes and fills it with logs, obediently following Caroline's instructions. She feels the hot pipes. Tepid. Helen swears. She pulls the door at the bottom wide, then opening her briefcase on the window-sill sits at the table to write up a report – 'Should country buses go?' After a few moments of thought she adds 'straight'.

Tom flings open the front door by putting his shoulder against it. How he hates this door – always jammed. It's because the whole place is badly built. Put up after World War II – cheap – thin partitions, poor foundations. As fast as they decorate it is spoilt by new cracks. It's one thing he and Rita are totally in accord over, the inadequacy of their house. But it's all they can afford and they were lucky to get it – if the Rogers hadn't decided to move right out of the area, their name would never have come top of the list. So they grumble to each other and everyone else, but in a sense they're sitting pretty and know it. For otherwise how should they have got a home? They would have had to live with Tom's mother and that's a thing Rita would never have borne because Tom can do no wrong in her eyes at all. Darling son, spoilt child. It enrages Rita to even think of how his mother treats him. She's not going to be like that with Ernest. Ernest, at the present, is yelling. When Tom opens the door he meets it full volume. He looks grimly at Rita.

'Ain't he been fed?'

'Course he's been fed. What do you think I do all day – write letters?' A cat whose tail he's trodden on could not be more fierce.

Tom slumps in the chair by the stove, unlaces his boots. Ernest's volume increases. Rita reaches from where she's sitting and rocks the pram where, apart from the breast, Ernest's life has so far been spent. She rocks it with the force and vigour she would like to direct at Tom. It is effective, the yelling subsides into snuffles then into silence. Peace if not order descends over the small square room which would have no character were it not for Rita who adores bright colours, so that the room dazzles. Even the nappies stretched on two strings over the stove are pink – admittedly this was by accident as they happened to go in the washing-machine along with Tom's red 'Canadian' shirt. The washing-machine, bought on credit, is her most precious possession as well as giving her status. It is a sign that Tom is 'getting on' and prevents her having to sit in the inadequate village launderette which comprises a single ancient Frigidaire washer that doubtfully improves the 'whites' but is alright for 'coloureds'. Sometimes she drops in there to talk to her friends who use it, other young women in the same predicament as herself. Having experienced the 'launderette', Rita feels sorry for them, but not quite sorry enough to invite them to use hers. She knows what that means, her paying the water and electricity, not to mention the repair bills, and all of them messing up her sitting-room while they wait. Oh she's offered it to Sharon on occasion, but then Sharon's her best friend and her best source of information other than Christine in the shop . . .

She looks across at Tom more kindly. He does look worn out. She opens the oven door and pulls out his tea – a large warmed-up pastie made by herself because Tom won't stand for bought stuff, and baked potatoes in their jackets. She puts all in front of him and sits Jenny up to the table on a cushion to make her high enough. She herself sits opposite – casts an expert eye over the table. The ketchup is missing. She gets up, takes it off the shelf and pushes it towards Tom.

'Isn't he home yet, then?'

Tom stares. If he does understand, which he almost certainly does, he pretends not to.

'Mr Ashurst? Isn't he home?'

Tom tips a dollop of ketchup on the side of his plate, replaces the top.

'I ain't seen him.' Tom speaks a broad dialect at home that, out at Greytor, he drops completely, so that only his use of syntax and soft emphasis of 'r's remain to give a flavour to his speech. He's got a keen ear, and had life disposed him in more favourable circumstances, might well have been a linguist. As it is, life has imposed a hard lot on Tom, and the shift from an adoring mother to a fierce young wife has been no easy matter. Once when he and Rita were getting adjusted to each other he brought his fist down so hard on the wooden draining board it split in two.

But Tom has much to redeem him and Rita knows it. Not only is he the most attractive and desirable man in the village, making Rita the secret envy of all, but he is hardworking and ambitious, as well as being intelligent. He also has other qualities of sensibility that Rita's never plumbed. Perhaps in an obscure way she feels them; perhaps if she knew there was no part of Tom she could not contact at will she would feel secure and not afraid another person might be able to offer him more than she can. Her reasoning is quite irrational for at the merest hint Tom might share interests elsewhere, she immediately withdraws all she generally gives, instead of allowing him her usual offering and more.

Tom himself vacillates between rage at Rita's unjust accusations and a strong feeling of guilt he hotly denies but nevertheless feels. The more she accuses him of being 'wrapped up' in the Ashurst woman, the more righteously he denies it; and the more he comes to think about it and find it true. If Rita had never accused then doubtless the whole thing would have simmered on for months without ever coming to a head, but with Rita lighting him up with her stabbing comments, his imagination is set on fire.

Rita has been quiet for all of three minutes and she can't stay quiet any longer. She is dieting and so doesn't eat except for an apple – she chews her fingers and nudges Jenny to eat up.

'Say something, then?' she says sharply. Tom looks startled. 'Well, what have you been doing up there today?'

Tom jabs his knife into his baked potato, splits it open, then fills the centre with butter. He stares belligerently at Rita. 'Can't you smell?'

'Dipping?'

Tom doesn't answer, he takes more butter, puts the potato back together and bites it with disastrous result. The butter trickles down his sweater. Rita watches him bitterly.

'I only done that one yesterday. Done it by hand. I can't put it in the machine unless you want it to come out the size for Jenny.'

Tom dabs at his front.

'So who done the catching?'

'She done it.'

'Her!' Rita's laughter is as humourless as a green woodpecker's – 'I'd like to see her.'

'Then you should've come out.'

Rita's sarcasm is biting. 'Oh yes. See me walking two and a half miles with the pram an' two babies. Since when have you left me the van so as I can go anywhere? I can't even get down the shops except Wednesday on the bus, and that's a lively business with the two of them.'

Tom is having further problems with the potato so he

keeps silent, but in his mind he goes back over the dipping, the two women on either side of the dip, Caroline's hair slithering out beneath her sou'wester like . . . like . . . like a TV ad. Well, it was the same colour . . .

Jenny knocks her mug over and Rita deals a sharp slap. Jenny screams. Ernest wakes. All is pandemonium. Tom looks at his watch. Later tonight he's meeting Martin Weller and they hope to do a bit of poaching, go down in the Forestry woods, see if there's an unwary deer. The Forestry don't mind as long as you don't say nothing, they're pleased to get rid of them, they do so much harm to the young trees. Meanwhile he shifts from the table and settles himself on the low chair by the stove, his socked feet resting up on its edge, and ruminates. Rita stares bitterly at his handsome face; that he looks tired fills her with hate, love and satisfaction – the emotions he inspires in her are much too complex and involved to unravel.

Patrick lies on his side watching Vanessa. She has been 'on' all afternoon and it has passed in a flash. Any moment now she goes 'off' but Caroline should be in shortly, that is to say she said last time she would be in this evening. Caroline, having been brought up by parents who were continually ringing each other if they were to be five minutes late, tended to be reliable. She has learnt the consequences are too dire if she's not, so that he has really no need to worry. But he does. He lies glimpsing Vanessa shifting from bed to bed at the far end of the ward, working himself into a fever of anxiety as to whether or not Caroline will come. Vanessa eventually makes her way back to his bed where she pauses for a little longer than is medically necessary.

'Goodnight, Mr Ashurst. See you again Thursday.'

Thursday? She'll be gone until Thursday. Patrick is immediately swamped by a wave of self-pity and depression. He's fed up with this bloody place, he has to get out of it. He'll tell Caroline tonight to fetch him the next day. They can't detain him any longer against his will, he can discharge himself. He smiles at Vanessa.

'Have a good day off!' He means, I hope you miss me

and long for Thursday; tomorrow will be a long and wasted day. 'Get some more of that scent you wear. I like it – it makes me better' – he smiles to show it's a joke, which it isn't.

'I'm not made of money,' says Vanessa briskly. 'One bottle has to last me six months. My brother brought it back off the Roscoff Ferry – duty free.'

She sees the man who has replaced the previous patient on Patrick's right is listening, so she makes a pretence of shaking up his pillows, letting her soft arm brush against his cheek and her apron-restricted bosom loom in front of his nose. Patrick gives himself up to this momentary bliss, he hasn't exactly had much of it lately. Under the round arm he catches sight of Caroline in the doorway, at the same time Vanessa moves on to the next bed.

Caroline approaches slowly in that rather shy tentative fashion she has, her face solemn, nursing a bunch of yellow daisies. She reaches his bedside and sits.

'How are you feeling? I brought you these. They're all that's left in the garden now.'

'What about the wall garden – how's that?'

Caroline has stood up again, is looking around in her slightly helpless manner for a vase for the daisies.

'There's one over there – under the sink.' He points and she goes obediently and returns with the daisies spread out in a white jar.

'I rather like them,' she says, looking at them proudly. Then, 'The frost's got the beans – the frost's got everything it can get.'

'Didn't you pick them?'

'Of course I did, they were over anyway, so it didn't really matter. It's just the garden looks awfully dead and tatty.'

'I should pull them up – get rid of them. You could keep the sticks, they're good ones. They'll come in for next year.'

She looks at him solemnly, making no response.

'How are the cabbages and sprouts?'

'Some of the sprouts snapped off in the gale – and quite a lot have got clubroot.'

Patrick frowns, murmurs 'Shit.'

They share the full impact of this unhappy news.

'You gathered the crab apples, didn't you?' He looks enquiringly at her.

'We're going to – tomorrow.'

'We?'

'I told you – Helen is staying. I met her this morning before we dipped.'

'That'll hold things up, won't it?'

'No – it's a help to have someone else around' – Caroline is increasingly defensive. Patrick shifts himself. He is dressed, has been up and about now for over two weeks, and is on the bed rather than in it. Caroline watches him, her expression tells very little of her thoughts, for his attitude to Helen prevents her concern for him showing.

'Last time she came out she tried to turn in the field and got stuck.'

'Well this time she's come by bus.'

There is a long and not too happy silence.

'She's going next Sunday.'

Why does she have to say this like an excuse, she wonders? Why does Patrick's intolerance of Helen make her feel almost guilty for liking her. It irritates her that it does so, and yet it does. Patrick's opinion of people definitely affects hers, however much she may defend them and despise herself for being affected.

'With any luck I shall be home.'

'I'll ask the Ward Sister again as I go out. The trouble is they'll never say anything definite, but now you're up all the time it can't be more than a matter of days . . .' her voice trails away. On two previous occasions they have been prepared for Patrick to go home but both times at the last moment they have been disappointed. The doctors are not happy with the way his wound has healed, in fact it hasn't healed properly, there seems to be some kind of infection there as well and he is continuing to prove almost immune to treatment by antibiotics. His temperature is inclined to go up suddenly, why they seem uncertain.

'They're all terribly overworked,' Patrick says tactlessly, implying to the over sensitive Caroline that she is not – 'I'm still amazed at the long hours the nurses do.'

'I thought all that had been changed' – she tries to hide that she has been hurt.

'It certainly hasn't' – Patrick's prolonged convalescence, his feeling of total frustration at his own inadequacy, makes him aggressive. Caroline glances round this buzzing ward of busy efficient nurses – it blurs and dissolves in front of her eyes into her own disorderly house. As if reading her thoughts, Patrick asks her to search through his letters on his desk to see if she can find the form for the hill cow subsidies, it must go off by the end of the month. She listens to his explanation of where it should be, but silently dreads the thought of searching through his papers. He is not an orderly man, that's why he admires it in others; the disorder of his desk is only understood by himself. Their untidiness, thinks Caroline, is one thing they unmistakably have in common.

Patrick looks at her unenthusiastic expression. 'What's the matter?'

'Nothing – it's just there's quite a lot to do.'

'Tom's coming in, isn't he?'

'When he can – yes.'

Patrick looks at her anxiously, feeling genuine concern that it is all too much for her. He also feels guilty that he has made no reasonable provision for the prolonging of his stay in hospital. He knows that he is asking a lot of Caroline, at the same time he has no real way out of doing so. Without an insurance the cost of a relief worker is prohibitive for people with their means.

'You're not managing' – his voice is worried.

'Yes I am.'

Caroline's head spins. She looks round at the hospital landscape of beds, visitors, nurses, whiteness. Quite suddenly she feels she must get out. She leans forward, about to explain to him, make a move, then checks herself, overwhelmed at her own selfishness. There is still twenty more minutes of visiting time. How terrible it must be for Patrick who is detained day after day, how weak she is to have almost fled in panic. She reaches for his hand and they sit in silence which works better for them than speech.

*

Helen, having given up the idea of a bath, sits beside the fire which she has piled up with logs. It blazes enthusiastically up the huge chimney which is no surprise to her, for the force of the draught behind her back she believes would turn a mill. She drags one of the home-cured sheepskins round her shoulders and curls her feet up on the sofa for warmth. In the corner stands an old television set. She gets up and fiddles with the switches. Nothing. She might have known that was too much to hope for. The rest of the room consists of plain white walls and a low ceiling supported by massive beams. It is a rather beautiful room, Helen decides, but lonely. For company she goes and retrieves the transistor from the kitchen, switches it on. With a human voice emitting from the speaker she feels more normal, as though she is not as many miles from civilization as she feels. Her admiration for Caroline increases. How can she stand it here on her own? – *she* certainly couldn't. It would drive her mad. She picks up her book – *The White Hotel* – and immerses herself in its Freudian case histories. She doesn't like it, how could any woman *like* a man attempting to pretend the sexual fantasy of a woman? It's a kind of horrific male trip and fairly repulsive. But it's compelling reading and Helen wants to be able to hold her own if it should come up in discussion, so she persists. She also learns from it, for however much she dislikes what it says, there is a kind of brilliance in the writing.

Nearly three hours later Caroline returns and flops down on the other end of the sofa. Helen studies her sombre face.

'No better?'

Caroline sighs. 'You can't get a word of sense out of them. No – they don't think he *is* better, that's the answer.' She tells her at some length the details of Patrick's detention, the reasons they give for it. Helen listens sympathetically, but her anxiety is for Caroline rather than Patrick. How much longer must she continue struggling along on her own in this bleak place with no help but from the Heathcliffean Tom? She stares into the fire.

'I've made myself cosy but I didn't have much luck with your television.'

'It's broken – the tube's gone. I don't really miss it as

long as I've got a radio, though now I'm on my own I'd probably watch it more.'

'You could hire one.'

Caroline assents but Helen knows she won't get one and doesn't press it. Instead she shows the cover of her book. 'Have you read it?'

'I tried.'

'What do you think?'

Caroline screws up her face. In a matter of moments she and Helen are outside time and place – they are involved in a discussion of the book and its relation to their own attitudes and thoughts that takes them swiftly into an intimacy that is the very soul of their relationship. When finally the conversation lulls, Helen asks Caroline if she has had anything to eat, and on learning that she hasn't goes to fetch the remains of her own supper she's kept hot on the stove. When she returns Caroline is in the passage putting on her boots.

'I haven't looked at that heifer – the one I said this morning looked about to calve. I forgot her – that's terrible of me. I'll have to go now with a torch.'

Helen puts down the plate. 'You'd better eat this first.'

'I can't.'

'You must.'

Caroline sits with the plate on her lap and eats hastily.

They walk through the darkness side by side, mainly in silence except for the brush of their boots through the sodden grass. In the beam of the torch a misty rain falls continuously, limiting visibility. Several rabbits shuffle into the hedge in front of Helen, and quite suddenly they come on a fox, head up, brush outstretched on a knoll of ground the far side of a gate. His eyes shine in the torch light like rubies. He stands poised for a full twenty seconds before leaping up a hedge and vanishing.

Helen is jubilant. 'Now I only have to see a badger. A fox and a badger – my two ambitions for this week.'

Caroline laughs. 'As long as you don't wish up a mink I don't mind.'

Silence closes round them again. They have one more

field to cross before they come to where the cows are grazing. Caroline's mind drifts back to her childhood amongst dark rhododendrons and tall pines, with only an occasional lamp to illuminate the darkness, make it even more frightening by casting deep shadows, with herself beneath it and visible to all. Footsteps following, breathing – she dared not look round – she would tell herself it was nothing, force herself not to panic and run – run like she had as a younger child coming home from the bus stop – running, running for her life, bursting through the front door in terror, slamming it. Into her mother's arms. No one was there – no one was ever there . . .

She grips Helen's arm, not with fear now, but affection. Nevertheless there were still times she was afraid of the dark – oh not so much out here in the open fields, but in among trees, in narrow lanes . . .

'I can't have been eating enough carrots – I can't see a thing,' says Helen reassuringly, stumbling yet again. Caroline laughs, as much in relief for Helen's comforting concrete presence as for her discomfort. She hands her the torch.

'Take it – I know the ground by heart.'

'You amaze me.'

'What have I done now?'

'Become a kind of nature woman, a Eustacia Vye finding her way along the moorland paths by her bare feet.'

'Did she really?'

'Something like that – yes. It made a deep impression on me at fifteen. How we change! I'm so unromantic now.'

Caroline remains silent. She suspects that she is not.

'I hope we're not heading for a mill pond' – Helen pursues the same train of thought, 'I'd certainly fall straight in.'

But a bank looms squarely ahead of them with stones projecting from the wall to form a rudimentary style. Caroline climbs up and flashes her torch round the field beyond. Helen looks up at her dark figure, partially silhouetted against the beam. Fine drops of drifting mist fall through the light giving a halo effect, faintly coloured. She climbs up to join her.

'Is that it?' A cow's hulk shows in the distance.

'No, but this is the field. She was over against the far hedge at lunchtime, but she could be anywhere now.'

They drop down the far side and walk along the hedge. Every now and then dark forms of cattle loom up at them out of the darkness, but mostly the cows are lying down, often with their calves close beside them. Some heave themselves up as they flash the torch over them, others don't bother to shift. Suddenly Caroline halts. They have come upon a single heifer alone in a patch of rushes. She's unmistakably in the process of calving; her back arches and she contracts as they watch. Slime trails from her.

'What now?'

Caroline doesn't answer. What now indeed? Her fingers tighten nervously on the calving ropes she has in her pocket. She edges round to get a better view of the back of the heifer, directs the torch on her rump. Her heart gives a thump of anxiety as she sees the two protruding hooves. How long has she been in this state? The heifer contracts again.

'I think we'd better try and get a rope round the hooves – help pull.' She hands Helen the torch and extracts the rope from her pocket. At the same time the heifer collapses in the rushes, turns agonised eyes on them. Caroline advances on her stealthily. The heifer heaves herself up, but goes down again almost immediately. Caroline is able to get the loop of rope round the two protruding hooves and draw it tight just as the animal once again drags herself on her feet.

'Quick Helen, help.' The heifer contracts. The head starts to emerge. The two of them put their weight on the rope, dig their heels into the slippery ground, heave. The contraction ceases.

'Won't we hurt her?'

'No – if we don't get it through her pin bones it'll die. Now – *pull*.'

The heifer contracts again, and then again. With each contraction they brace themselves on the rope, but the calf does not come.

'Is it dead?' Helen's voice utters Caroline's dread. She

goes in close, tries to release and ease the head with her hands. A further contraction and desperation gives them strength. Suddenly with a rush the head slithers out, one more heave of heifer and helpers and the dark wet body is precipitated into the rushes in a caul of slime. Caroline hurries forward, Helen retrieves the dropped torch.

'Is it alright?'

'I think so.' She goes to lift the head but it lifts it itself, utters a low undiscernible sound. The mother, who stands shuddering a few feet off, responds with a low crooning moo. She advances, Caroline backs away. The heifer noses at the wet shivering body, laboriously, methodically, licking away the slime; the afterbirth that has come with it lies in a pool of blood-tinged jelly.

The women watch spellbound. Now their eyes are accustomed to the darkness they can see moderately well without the torch. They listen to the sound of the rhythmic licking.

'Do we leave it here?' Helen's voice is not quite steady. The impact, the overwhelming emotional happening of birth, has affected both profoundly. Caroline wipes tears from her cheeks, glad that Helen can't see in the darkness. Oddly the shared experience has pushed them apart, rather than together. They feel stiff and almost awkward in each other's company. It is as though it has touched on depths too unfamiliar, too disturbing for them to be able to share.

'Yes' – Caroline answers Helen's question.

'But we ought to wait and make sure it's up and sucking.'

So they find a nearby rock and sit patiently waiting until at last the damp body of the calf lurches to its feet, staggers, falls, gets up again and noses its way along the mother's side to the udder. She utters her croon moo, turns her head, tries to lick its tail as it pushes further beneath her, gives up and stands placidly until the sound of sucking, the quiver of pleasure of the calf's body, indicates to them that all should now be well.

The drama over, they notice they are tired, stiff and soaking wet – and that the torch battery has dwindled to a dim circle of light that is of less use than their eyes. In complete silence they plod back across the field. Only when the chimneys of Greytor emerge as dark towers in the mist does Caroline lay her hand on Helen's arm and say, 'I couldn't have managed without you.'

'Yes you could. You'd have got Tom.'

'Would I?' says Caroline, doubtfully.

Caroline wouldn't have got Tom for he is sitting in his van in the middle of a Forestry road in total darkness waiting for Martin Weller who has disappeared down into the trees a good half-hour ago after a deer whose tracks he claimed to detect. Tom thinks they're old tracks and waits with the van, his temper worsening with every minute. Bugger Martin – where's he got to? He'd told him he was on a false trail hadn't he? He starts the engine, the screen wipers whine wearily back and forth. He turns it off again. Footsteps sound from nowhere, a knock comes on his window, a helmeted head silhouettes itself indelibly in Tom's vision. Now it's all up. There's no escape – he'll have got the number. Tom winds down the window, turns off the engine.

'I'd like to ask what you're doing here?' The constable's voice is neither friendly nor affable.

'Waiting—' Tom is about to add for a friend but stops.

'Waiting? Are you on your own?'

'Yes.'

The constable's head is well in the window, he withdraws it, opens the door so light floods the interior, glances round the inside, sees Tom's incriminating shot-gun.

'Poaching, eh?'

'I haven't fired a shot.'

'But you intended to.'

'Only after rabbits – they told me they'd be glad if I could shoot some.'

'You understand you're trespassing. All this land is Forestry Commission property.'

Silence. Tom understands all too well. It's his unlucky night, a chance in a million a copper will be wandering about the woods at this hour. Someone must have put him up to it. Through the opened door, faint in the distance, Tom hears a twig crack. So does the constable.

'If you aren't waiting for someone what are you sitting here for?'

'Hoping to see a rabbit in the lights.'

The constable withdraws; truth, he has learnt from years of experience, is seldom got except by barter. He writes down the number and other details, looks at Tom's licence, then tells him to go home, that he will be hearing from them in due course. Tom doesn't argue, he's tried that before and it doesn't get you any further, not unless you've got a woman with you. He drives off fast, flinging mud at the muttering constable who is fairly convinced Tom is poaching deer. At the gate of the Forestry ground, Tom has to stop. As he pulls up a figure emerges from the trees, and attempts to get in beside him.

'Oh no you don't, you find your own way back. I been picked up by the police because you was so long in there.'

Martin Weller pulls himself up to his full height which is several inches more than Tom and for a moment it looks as though there must be a fight. But Tom's fighting reputation runs before him and Martin makes his own way home on foot, uncertain as to whether or not Tom has given his name along with his own.

When half an hour later Tom slides into bed beside Rita he rolls on top of her to show that if he can't tame the law at least he can his woman. For he considers Rita his property, if a doubtful acquisition. Rita fights and bites, swears he will wake Jenny and Ernest in the adjoining room, but finally submits in agonised joy. Sex for her is only enjoyable if it is a sort of rape. She is the possessor of what feminists feel to be backward and primitive instincts. It is this blend of sado-masochism that uncomfortably cements Tom and Rita's relationship. With Ernest and Jenny to raise, perhaps it pays off.

Caroline and Helen huddle round the stove, the fire has long since gone out. They have made themselves hot milk and whisky, which is the only alcohol in the house – other than home-made brews and a bottle of wine bought by Helen – and sit over their mugs, burning their tongues and talking. The warmth, the intimacy of the dim lighting in the old room, are both conducive to confessions and this is precisely what they are about. Caroline's fair hair falls forward concealing her face; Helen's dark wavy mop leaves her fine-looking face displayed to any who might wish to see it. She removes the skin from her milk with a carefully manicured 'natural' nail.

'My career? It's been "progressing", as they say' – her tone is mocking, derogatory.

'And that's enough, it makes you happy?' Caroline takes too big a gulp of hot liquid, feels it burn its way down her throat.

'I don't know about happy. I enjoy it – yes.' She doesn't continue so Caroline prods. 'Go on.'

'Nothing.' She places her mug down on the corner of the stove. 'I suppose there was that person I wrote you about a few months back, but it's come to nothing.'

'Tell me.' Caroline pulls her socked feet up for warmth, curls them beneath her.

'It's hardly worth telling – it's the story of my life. You know it already. A friend introduced us at a party – he rang the next day, took me out to lunch. We saw a lot of each other for a few months, in fact we lived together – only thank God I wasn't silly enough to let my flat go, then . . .' she takes her mug off the stove, drinks, puts it back, 'he started being busy when I rang, having "appointments" he couldn't miss. I met him by accident at a film – *The French Lieutenant's Woman* – it's awful, don't go and see it – I was on my own and he was with a girl who looked sixteen, a student I should think.'

She stops. Caroline makes a sympathetic murmur. She can see this story is taking more out of Helen than her casual tone betrays. 'I rang him up the next day,' Helen goes on, almost aggressively flippant, 'when I felt calm enough – asked him why he couldn't have told me there was someone whose company he preferred. He said he didn't prefer her company, he preferred mine, but he got satisfaction out of being able to teach her – for teach read "manipulate" – whereas I knew it all already. He said he found me assertive, even aggressive, at times. So I said

91

what did he mean, and he said "All those peace marches you go on."'

Caroline laughs. 'I don't believe it.'

Helen rubs her head, bear-like, as though by doing so she will erase the bitterness of the memory.

'It's true. I took it as a marvellous example of male logic.' She stares at the floor for some moments, hands clasped between her knees. 'So that's all over. I really think I'm better off without men – without allowing my emotions to get involved anyway. Do you know, Caroline, I don't think I've ever met a man who genuinely likes me for my mind or my conversation – that's only a lead in to what comes next. It makes me feel more than insulted, sort of mentally damaged.' She sits back, stretches out her legs. 'I don't know why I care, but I do.'

She looks penetratingly across at Caroline. 'You . . . manage?'

'Yes.' Caroline hesitates. 'I have to.'

'*Have* to?'

'I've settled for it, haven't I?' Caroline braces herself, she rather dreads Helen's ruthless probing because it also implies judgement and she feels she does not fulfil Helen's expectation. Helen is always somehow trying to get her to be stronger, more anti-men than she really feels. Oh it's not that she isn't a feminist because she is – she's always saying so. It's just that frequently she feels as anti-women as men and is not able to think of them as 'sisters' as Helen does. That it is a sign of Helen's sincerity and greater strength of purpose, she has no doubt – like Adrienne Rich. But in spite of sleeping with successive volumes of Adrienne Rich, Kate Miller and Dale Spender under her pillow it still does not give her the requisite amount of strength never to have relapses. She relieves her anxiety by curling her legs on the other side, she has got pins and needles in one foot.

Helen frowns. 'Does one settle for things?'

'I do.' Caroline feels as though she is hanging from a ledge on a cliff face by one hand.

'You think one can?' Helen turns clear honest eyes upon her friend.

'I don't know for other people.' Caroline has caught the ledge with the other hand and is edging along it.

'I get the feeling you've closed off – almost – a side of yourself.' Helen's eyes are still resting on her, expecting an answer of deeply considered truth.

Caroline prevaricates, plays for time. 'Why do you say that?'

'I just feel it.' If only Helen would not feel, not in that particularly investigating kind of fashion. It forces Caroline to look at facets of her life she would rather not.

'Does it work – you and Patrick?'

This is the moment surely to let go and drop. Instead she remains clinging, waving her feet around for a foothold. 'Sometimes it does, it works so well I can't imagine how it ever couldn't – but then other times I don't know what we're doing together at all.' It has worked, her toe has felt something, even if only a tuft of sea pink.

'In a way you're very masochistic.'

Indignation gives Caroline strength. 'I'm not – I'm absolutely not. Whatever else I am I'm not that.'

There is an uncomfortable silence. Helen perceives she has overdone it, but she refuses to retreat.

'Why do you say that?' Caroline demands.

Perhaps it's the hot whisky, but Helen is in full tongue.

'You're forcing yourself into a way of life quite alien to you. All physical struggle – if it isn't the animals it's the elements. What about the writing – your poetry?'

Caroline frowns. 'I keep a journal – and read. I do write a poem now and again – try to.'

'Write a poem now and again? What sort of way is that to talk?' No, the sea pink will not hold, Caroline's fingers slip, let go. She feels herself falling and falling out into an immense void of pale blue sky. It is not as frightening as she had thought, but it will be, when the sea comes up to meet her out of the mist into which she is about to plunge.

'So you've settled for living second-hand – through Patrick?' Helen magnificently pushes on.

Caroline seizes at a tuft of vegetation in falling. 'I *want* to do what I do. I chose it. And in no sense is the quality of my life second-hand.'

Their eyes meet. Caroline drops hers first. Why should Helen have this capacity to make her feel guilty, unrealised? 'Obviously I'm doing much more at the moment.' She gets up to prevent herself hitting the sea – makes up the stove with logs. 'The woodstacks going down at an alarming speed.'

'That's it. It's all so difficult, so ... inconvenient. Couldn't Patrick have made sure there was enough wood before he went in?' Helen is aware immediately of the cruelty of her remark, wishes it unsaid, feels herself diminish.

Caroline rightly is defensive and antagonistic.

'He could have but he didn't. He wasn't, after all, feeling particularly well.'

'Of course not,' Helen agrees hastily. 'I didn't mean to be critical ...' – but she has been, oh yes she has. Of Patrick. And as he is not present to defend himself, it makes it seem a thousand times worse – 'but the thought of you sawing wood all day with a hand saw ...'

Caroline interrupts her. 'Don't you see, it's my fault – for not being able to use the chain saw.' She grips the stove rail against which she leans as though it alone will save her. Lets herself slide down on to the couch beside it.

Helen raises her finely shaped eyebrows, looks at Caroline in frank amazement. 'For god's sake – it's not your fault.'

In the pause that follows they both take stock, recover balance.

'Tom will probably saw some for me when he gets time.' Is Tom, then, the bush that will hold, her last chance to prevent herself shattering like a broken doll when she hits the savage black ripples of the dark blue surface?

Tom is a variable with which Helen is unable to deal. She had forgotten Tom. Instead she moves across, joins Caroline on the couch, puts her arm round her shoulders, draws her to her, kisses the long straw hair that divides them. 'I'm sorry. Sorry.'

But Caroline is rigid from latent emotions inside herself that have laid dormant for the past two years, and have now been revived. She would like to burst, scream, hit

Helen. Instead she disengages herself gently, and stands up.

'I'm absolutely worn out, so must you be,' she says. Normality is restored – reality firmly put away. Helen goes in search of her hot bottle.

There is something about the way Tom has made love to Rita, for that is what they both consider it to be, that has awakened her resentment. Or was it Christine telling her he'd been buying the Ashurst woman stamps? Whatever it is instead of Tom going whistling to shave and Rita lying with dilated pupils in the bed as is commonly supposed to be the normal follow up of 'good sex', Tom doesn't get up at all and Rita lacerates him with her tongue. It makes her feel a thousand times better. She starts quite low key, in seductive tempo. Indeed had Tom had the insight to give the right response, allay her fears, the morning after might have proved better. But Tom is haunted by the helmeted figure at the window and in no mood to think what he should be saying.

'Tom, it wasn't me you were thinking of last night, was it?' Tom doesn't answer, so she goes on, 'I could tell by the way you acted – different to usual.'

Tom pulls the bedclothes higher round his ears. No – if he'd been thinking of anyone at the time to which she refers it was almost certainly the copper. He doesn't really want to tell Rita about it, she'll probably rage at him anticipating a fine.

'Tom?' She pulls the bedclothes back from his head, shakes him. 'Tom – can't you answer?'

Apparently not. Rita roused even further, continues: 'No – and I know why not, because what I say is true, isn't it?'

What does she say? All Tom knows is that if he doesn't get up, get moving, he'll be late at the Saw Mills and get fired. With a monumental effort of will he pushes the bedclothes back.

'You don't love me, do you? It's her, isn't it? Oh I know you run her errands for her. You're a creep really, aren't you Tom?'

'What are you talking about?' Tom blunders through to

the bathroom, squeezes foam on his face and wrenches a new polythene razor from its cellophane case. Rita stands in the doorway behind him.

'Where were you last night? It must've been half past one before you came in, leaping on top of me like the dirty great animal you are.'

Tom shaves methodically. He is a methodical person. What has happened to the bloody children? Have they died in the night or something, that they can't wake and divert Rita's attention? Most mornings they are awake at six-thirty, kicking up and making themselves heard.

'What's happened to Jenny and Ernest?' He feels a guilty anxiety. He loves them doesn't he?

'They're still asleep. It's early yet.'

'Early?'

'Seven.'

'Seven? Eight.'

'Seven.'

'Shit.' Tom flings his razor down. 'Why didn't you tell me?'

'You didn't seem to be hearing anything I said.' Rita sits in front of her dressing table mirror in her see-through shortie nightdress and examines an eyelash that is sticking down into the corner of her eye instead of following the gradual curve up of the rest. Tom looks longingly at the bed he's just left, but getting back in will only involve him in a further effort of will to get out again shortly, so he finishes his shaving and dresses.

'Can't she buy her own stamps, then?' Rita's back is still towards him, she is watching him in the mirror.

'What?'

'The Ashurst woman' – it is out. Rita feels quite surprisingly relieved. She waits hopefully for Tom to deny it, though she won't believe him if he does. But somehow denying will make it seem that he still cares for her, but if he admits . . .

She is quite safe. Tom denies. He has grown up in a family, a clan, who have always preached denial. It is safer. And certainly in this case it proves true. Rita pads across the floor and slides her warm arms round him, he feels her

96

soft naked body up against his. There's time to spare, why not? He pushes her backwards on to the bed, buries his face in the comfort of her body to obliterate the helmeted silhouette. But to his surprise the Ashurst woman comes before his eyes – only briefly, for one moment, her fair hair on her brown skin. Thin, she is. Too thin. He draws Rita's more ample proportions to him to shut her out. After all it is Rita's own fault for talking about her, otherwise he'd never have thought of her, would he?

The early morning sun falls on the pages of Caroline's diary, laying the window bars across it in grey lines of partial shadow. The dazzling white of the page between almost makes her blink. She has been struggling with a poem she now crosses out savagely, and instead starts on a circular doodle which no sooner gets in motion before it too is checked. On the opposite page she writes:

4 October. *Pony round-up.* Helen and I are being lent ponies so we can ride. It will be quite like old times. Saw Patrick again last night – much better, but I couldn't get anything definite out of the Ward Sister. In the car on the way home, I thought of Helen's and my conversation. Why is it I can never explain to anyone, hardly myself, what I feel for Patrick? What made me come out here with him? I suppose because he attracted me more – much more – than other men. I couldn't separate him from his life and it was the way I thought life ought to be. He hadn't lost contact with nature, animals, the earth – or so I thought – he hadn't allowed himself to be reduced to a robot city dweller walking round a cash and carry buying pre-packaged food in cartons. He seemed to me unconcerned with the trivia with which most of us concern ourselves, and in some way to compliment me with, dare I say, his archetypal maleness? What I didn't appreciate was the stress, the loneliness, a marriage of opposites brings – for with that unconcern for trivia goes an unconcern for chatter and detail, for nuances of relationships and thought, the infinite possibilities of communication that occupy me deeply as a woman – all that and more is unapproachable territory to

Patrick. Only by our proximity, our physical touch, almost through a body language can we communicate on any deep level; and this for me is of prime importance but still I am left longing for the other . . . *Important*. White-faced heifer must go in with the bull. Ram is lame, must ask Tom to give me a hand with his feet. Vet coming back to recheck a possible reactor – thinks it's probably nothing. Cake for whist drive. Have I time? I think I'll have to be firm and say no. Such a force of wind yesterday doors didn't shut it out, nor walls – the fire was sucked from the hearth without a housewarming.

Helen enters clutching a long cardigan round her, her teeth chattering. 'My god, it's freezing. How do you live, Caroline? If it's as cold as this now what must it be like in midwinter?' She crawls beneath Caroline's quilt. Caroline regards her anxiously.

'Didn't you have enough bedclothes?'

'Oh yes – in bed. It's getting out. My nose must have been uncovered – it's frozen.'

Helen's sense of the ridiculous seldom fails, and Caroline never ceases to enjoy it. She doesn't find it as easy to laugh with a man as a woman, although she doesn't quite know why. So she laughs now joyously and tells Helen she doesn't have much time for feeling cold. Helen extracts herself from the quilt, crosses to the window and peers out, wiping the misted-up glass. 'There's no frost – not to be seen. But the poor old cherry's naked as a hairless man.' She looks over her shoulder at Caroline earnestly. 'The house – the boom of wind down in the kitchen chimney is really frightening – it must be rather like this in a lighthouse. You should have told me to bring thermal underwear . . .'

Caroline prises herself from the self-created warmth of her bed, starts to dress. 'We're sheltered down here, wait till you get up on the top.' She looks up to see Helen's eyes on the bed, her expression serious. 'What's the matter?'

'It seems funny to think Patrick usually sleeps there?'

'Why funny?'

'Forget it.'

'I shall' – but Caroline doesn't. She thinks about it on

and off throughout the day, particularly two hours later when they plod slowly up the long stony path to the moor on their two borrowed ponies. They are out of the wind and surprisingly sheltered. Overhead the clouds race fiercely, vying with each other, pushing and jostling to cover over patches of sky that are blue, or even white. On either side are clumps of gorse, some yellow with bloom in spite of the season, and beyond that, rolling hills of bracken and heather. The path dissolves into an area of closely cropped grass, with a few old wizened thorn. Wool around the trunks indicates it's a spot frequented by hill sheep. In the centre of this ancient and idyllic sward is a clear, glossy pool three parts covered with reddish-tinged leaves of weed.

'The Miner's Pool,' Caroline announces.

Helen takes it in in silence. She finds the motion of her pony strangely lulling and speech quite an effort. Caroline, on the contrary, seems to be in her element.

'Is it deep?' Helen finally asks as its surface suddenly blackens under a darker cloud.

'I don't think anyone knows because the bottom is all weed and mud, but you can swim in it. Someone drowned in it a few years back.'

Helen looks at it with distrust. 'I'm not sure I'd care to – it looks a sinister place.'

'It looks quite different in summer under a clear sky. Sometimes I've been up here on my own and there's nothing but water-boatmen scudding about the surface and emerald green and prussian blue dragonflies. It's like another world.'

'What a strange little private life you have! What was the pool for exactly?'

'For feeding the tin workings lower down. All over the moor there were tinners – in fact about 400 years ago the moor wasn't the empty and wild place one imagines, but seething with people . . .' She reins in her pony, shades her eyes. 'I thought I saw something – someone moving up there.'

They scan the landscape while their ponies nibble at the vegetation. Informally dressed, they merge easily into the

99

landscape, completely unlike the formal over-dressed crowd to be seen barging across the landscape after the hunt.

Suddenly another figure on horseback appears on the skyline above them; a moment later three wild ponies come cantering over the ridge below.

'It's them.' Helen glances at Caroline, struck by the excitement in her voice. Although they have ridden together before it has always been a sober sort of hacking, and this element of her friend is one she has not seen before. Caroline, in fact, seems almost to have forgotten her presence as she sets off up the track through the heather at a fast trot.

Before they reach the ridge, a sea of thundering ponies sweep over it just ahead of them, thirty or forty at a minimum, manes and tails flying, nostrils distended.

'On your left,' Caroline says suddenly. Two mares and a sucker have broken away from the rest and are veering off round the brow of the hill. Caroline and her mount vanish in pursuit with a scud of hooves and flying turf. Helen sets her jaw and murmurs a prayer as without encouragement her own pony follows over the rough ground littered with rocks. Whereas she is struggling to slow her pony, gain greater control, Caroline she notices is leaning forward, urging hers yet faster.

She's mad, Helen thinks, she'll kill herself. But Caroline is already wheeling round ahead of the breakaways, heading them back up to the ridge. Helen alters direction, and by a short cut reaches the top almost at the same time. As they near each other Caroline calls, 'Are you alright?'

'Yes thanks' – Helen is crisp. Actually her knees are sore from the stiff stirrup leathers and her hands beginning to feel blistered from managing her rather hard-mouthed mount. Caroline, oblivious to Helen's suffering, turns ecstatic face and shining eyes upon her.

'It's quite something, isn't it?'

'Oh yes, it is,' says Helen, 'quite something.' She wipes a speck of mud from her eyelash. A shout from their right indicates a further batch of ponies coming over the top towards them. Caroline wheels her lathered black charger and plunges forward over what appears to be an almost sheer incline. Helen takes a look and decides it's not for her; she directs her mount firmly along the flat ground on the top. Soon she joins a wide and gentle path that takes her in the direction she wishes to go. She has no sooner broken into a canter than she sees a scarlet headscarf in the heather – Caroline's. Dutifully she reins in and goes back, dismounts, pushes it in her pocket, and goes on. By this act she puts herself out of the drift, for by the time she comes out from behind the long hill the path traverses, there is no sign of ponies or riders. The whole landscape is curiously still and silent, so much so that she is uncertain in which direction to go. The sky is altogether more ominous and she notices with some anxiety that the mist on the hills ahead has descended and is drifting slowly but surely towards her.

Now what? Shall she go back, try to retrace her steps by following the tracks she has come by, or should she go on in hopes of catching sight of someone? Against her better judgement she decides to go on, into the face of the low line of cloud rolling forwards like an oncoming army. Already the tops of the hills with the tors differentiating them have disappeared. She descends a small valley and crosses a stream, encouraged by tracks showing others have passed the same way. She follows up the path which is small but quite well trodden, hoping to see someone over the top of the rise. The first wisps of chill, grey mist touch her face; the wind increases a little. She checks her pony, cups her hands to her mouth and shouts. Her voice seems as nothing in the emptiness that surrounds her, but miraculously an answer comes back. She shouts again. This time the answer is clearer. It's Caroline, she's sure of it. They continue to call and by this method Caroline quite quickly appears out of the mist beneath her, trotting up a sheep path that could hardly be called a track.

'Helen, I'm so relieved. I thought you might end up anywhere in this fog. I'm terribly sorry I lost you. Where did you get to?'

'I stopped for your scarf.' Helen is looking a little old-fashioned, Caroline observes.

'You found it. How did you manage?'

'That's what put me so far behind – I thought I'd better stop for it.'

'Thank you, Hel. You shouldn't have bothered.' Her pony, its coat curly from sweat, snatches at the reins and snorts, sidles impatiently. Helen can't help but feel envious of Caroline, she looks so much a part of it, completely natural.

'Will you be able to find the way?' She herself, ignorant of the territory, is quite lost.

But Caroline has every confidence.

'As long as we keep to the tracks we'll be alright, but I must admit it's come down quickly. Everyone else is down at Wallace Prior's place sorting ponies for tomorrow, but I think we might as well go home.'

So with the wind now behind them driving the mist against their backs instead of in their faces, they set off on the long ride back – Caroline leading, Helen following. They are too tired to talk and only when they pass a long line of granite stones standing up out of the mist and ending in a prehistoric barrow does Helen break their silence with, 'My god, this is an eerie place. I couldn't live here, Caroline, absolutely couldn't.' And then again much later when their ponies' hooves ring comfortingly on the tarmac road, she says curiously, 'How do *you* know your way around so well?'

Caroline answers vaguely, 'I don't really but I think I've got a fairly in-built sense of direction.'

Tom stands in the yard, leaning against the wall, hands in his trouser pockets. Caroline faces him holding a bucket of barley.

'If you'd've telephoned, I'd've come right out.' Tom's tone is particularly amenable. Is it because Rita's suspicions, fanned by public conjecture, have put ideas in his head, or is it because he hasn't turned up at Greytor for most of the week Helen's been staying and is feeling guilty? Whichever the reason, Caroline remains in ignorance. She is actually engaged in imagining the result of disturbing Rita during the night. So she says carefully, 'I didn't want to bring you out for nothing. I thought it might worry Rita – it was one a.m.'

Tom responds by looking darkly at the ground and stamping out his cigarette. Caroline puts down the barley bucket. Generally these sessions with Tom take a long time before he gets round to saying what he means. 'If you want me another time when I'm home, ring me up directly.' Caroline thinks of the previous telling-off she has had but presumes it to be because she had rung when he was out at work, so refrains from reminding him about it.

'Steer calf, is it?' Tom looks at her enquiringly.

She looks vague. 'I'm not perfectly sure. I forgot to look at the time, and since then I haven't been able to get close enough to see.'

Tom is triumphant. 'Didn't look? What are you going to tell the boss when he asks?'

'You'll have told me by then' – she smiles at Tom. It really is much easier to put about, let him regard her as ineffectual, than continue to tack into a rough sea. She steals a furtive glance at his Apollo-like profile. Perhaps she is deluding herself, and he is behaving in this way for totally other reasons? She puts such a disturbing thought from her mind quickly, picks up the bucket, and swings it. Tom glances at the house which not only lacks lustre, but life.

'Where's your friend this morning?'

'In there.'

He raises his eyes to the upstairs windows, looks his contempt for late risers. He turns, leans his hip against the wall, so that he is looking up to the road. 'Vet's late, isn't he? I'll go on over in case he comes from the other direction.'

'You'll want me, won't you?' Caroline is horrified to hear a pleading note in her tone. Tom, no doubt, has heard it too and says, 'Two of us is enough.' Then as an afterthought, 'You're going down the pony sales, aren't you?'

'I don't know.' Caroline, for no good reason that she can think of, feels let down. The pony sales don't appeal to her at all, she detests them. Swallowing her ill humour she goes in the house in search of Helen. Helen will want to go and see them, she knows that – she will want to write an anti-pony meat tract. Oh well, everyone's entitled to their opinion, but Caroline can't see why it's any worse for ponies than all the other poor wretched animals. It just seems particularly ironic in their case that it is the same pet lovers who want to save them that produce the trade in pony meat by having pets to feed. Of course if they didn't go for meat no farmer would keep them because there wouldn't be enough trade to make them worth the trouble. It was the same old farming story. Caroline scrapes her boots revengefully on the boot scraper and goes into the dark central passage of the house.

A sea of ponies undulates throughout the pens of Asherford market – each has a number stuck on its rump, each has become a commodity for purchase. Gaitered farmers wander round in their best suits. Transactions, it seems, cannot be conducted unless farmers and dealers alike profess an outward show of honesty by a 'respectable' appearance. Women are in a minority, their dress is much more diverse, so are the reasons for their being there at all. Some, in fact a majority, have come for the love of horseflesh live; a few, like the men, are as keen on the same flesh dead. Others are into pony trekking and hope to pick up a quiet pony to break and use the following summer; and still more, like Helen and Caroline, have just come to watch. Cattle trucks parked round the perimeter enclose the market, their drivers, almost without exception, have resorted to the Golden Lion. One or two small children are about mounted on the shoulders of their parents, but in general the market is empty of them because they are in school.

Caroline and Helen appear standing in the big market gateway. Caroline says something to Helen and they start to make their way through the crowd towards the ring. As they pass, faces turn and look after them, some indeed look at Caroline as though they would be as happy to bid for her as a horse. Helen, following behind, observes their expressions and tugs at Caroline's sleeve indignantly.

'Talk about men being like animals,' she murmurs.

'Given the choice I'd prefer to be like the animals here than the men.'

Caroline smiles, but can't help agreeing. As they near the ring they cause less attention so intent are all the bidders on making a good buy. A nine-month sucker revolves round and round, prodded by the owner and a market helper. Head up, it prances nervously. The bidding mounts slowly but steadily, the excitement increases, the dealers have arrived in force; it will be a good and profitable sale. People will go home contented, patting their full pockets.

The ponies meanwhile, chameleon-like, have lost their spirit, or so it seems. They stand with their heads drooping, a nondescript enough bunch of all sorts and colours. The pure moorland breeds have long since vanished, given way to larger and more profitable stock.

'Twenty pounds I'm bid. Twenty pounds. Any advance on twenty? Thirty on the right. Thirty, thirty, thirty pounds for the bay sucker in front of you. Any more bids, gentlemen? *Ladies* and gentlemen, I should say . . .'

Helen whispers to Caroline who has edged her way on to a step just beside her, 'Doesn't it make you sick?'

Caroline nods but her concentration is elsewhere.

'Can you see the number? I hope Patrick's haven't been sold.'

'Forty-five pounds. Have you all done at forty-five pounds? Fifty pounds, fifty I'm bid. Beautiful sucker – property of Mr Adams who you all know. Fifty pounds – I'm selling at fifty pounds.'

The hammer goes down. 'The gentleman on the right' – the auctioneer cocks his head with the inquiring beady eyes of a bird.

'Tucker' – a grey-haired aquiline faced man who is not local speaks up.

'Mr Tucker. Thank you, Sir. Lot 305. Black mare, suitable riding pony. Three-year-old. Unbroken but quiet to handle. Who'll start me at ninety pounds? Seventy then' – the auctioneer looks round hopefully. 'No one at seventy pounds? Please, gentlemen? Do you want me to give it away? A beautiful pony there anyone would be proud to see his daughter on.' He waits, looks around him searching for the lead that will set the money flowing. 'Fifty pounds then.'

A woman in jodhpurs leading the pony stops by the auctioneer and says something inaudible. He nods, continues, 'Ladies, aren't you tempted by a pretty pony like this? Beautiful trekking pony it'll make.'

In the silence that follows only the pony snorts and continues to pace round and round while the auctioneer persists in his herculean efforts to start the bidding.

'Thirty-five pounds?' No response. He gives up. 'Make your own price, then.' The market is completely silent, the tension has become unbreakable, a sort of joke.

'Will no one give me an offer for this riding pony?' Briefly it seems the auctioneer must weep such is his dejection. His standards, his very life depends on getting bids, seldom is he so defeated.

A voice from the crowd breaks the conspiracy of silence. "Taint broken. Get on an' ride, will 'ee?'

This comment is followed by loud and ribald laughter. The woman in the ring, whose face has stayed grave and passive throughout, whispers again to the auctioneer.

'Withdrawn. Lot 305 withdrawn. Right. Next one.'

Helen leans forward, touches Caroline's shoulder, 'What's wrong with it?'

Caroline moves into a space vacated beside Helen. 'It's because they want to sell it for riding.'

'What about the rest?'

'They mainly go for meat.'

Helen is shocked. 'All of them?'

'Just about.'

To Helen the romantic vision of the wild ponies galloping over open moorland earlier in the week has all been brought to nothing. Although she has known something of it before she can hardly believe the majority will end on the butcher's block. Caroline nudges her. 'Let's go for a drink. I don't think I can face watching Patrick's sold. I'll come back after and ask the auctioneers what they fetched. Stay if you want.' But Helen can't wait to absent herself. It has been interesting, informative, she has gained material for her article but there is something cold and inhuman about markets for the sale of flesh. She shivers involuntarily.

Patrick pads along the passage in his dressing-gown and slippers to the communal room where he can watch television. Since he has been in the hospital, along with his passion for Vanessa he has developed a passion for horse-racing – a thing that up until now he has never dreamed of indulging in. He lowers himself down on to the hard imitation-leather armchairs beside five other patients of varying ages, and fixes his eyes on the screen before him. In any case, this is the last week of his indulgence for he has been told by the doctor that he may go home on Saturday week. And about time too, for he has already been in six weeks instead of the promised three. Mentally he makes a vow never to get into the hands of doctors again – on the other hand something had to be done. He couldn't have gone on living with the seventy odd gallstones they'd found inside him, the alarming-looking microcosmic boulders they'd shown him in a glass phial.

The jockeys on the screen are mounting prior to going into the ring. Patrick thinks of his own brief history as a sticks rider. It had all come to nothing, he had sold the two horses and then Greytor had come up. He'd gone on going to race meetings though, enjoyed them until the stock had built up and he'd no longer time. Now he hadn't been in years. No – that was not quite true because he'd taken Caroline before they were married to a meeting at Taverston. As the day wore on she had become quieter and quieter in spite of there being a lot of other people he knew and could introduce her to. He recollected how she had almost totally submerged her charm, how his friends had looked at her first admiringly and then with reservations. What was Patrick doing, they must have thought, with a woman so dull, so uncommunicative. They had offered her delicacies from their hampers, hot coffee, even port with the Stilton, but Caroline had refused everything politely, stood a little away from the rest. Oh she looked the part alright, but then Caroline had a knack of looking the part, put her in a box of jumble sale clothes and she managed to shine in their shabbiness, their worn look, to make new clothes seem vulgar in comparison. On the way home he had asked her why she had been determined on disappointing everyone.

'Disappointing?' she had exclaimed startled, 'I don't know what you mean.'

'Well, you hardly spoke. You gave the impression you wanted nothing to do with anyone.'

She had been rather quiet until they had turned off the dual carriageway, then she had slipped her hand on to his thigh and said she was sorry, she hadn't meant to make people think that.

'So then what was it?' Sometimes her very silence irritated him beyond endurance.

'I suppose I felt quite alien,' she had said, 'absolutely not a part of them, or the sport. I don't think,' she had finished, 'I like horse-racing at all.'

The way she had said it had been somehow final, indisputable. From then on she had been eager he should accept invitations to other meetings but had always declined herself. 'It's a waste on me,' she said. 'I think I almost hate it.'

'Hate horse-racing?' Patrick was incredulous. 'I can't see how anyone could "hate" horse-racing. I can see they might be bored.'

But she had said it was more than being bored, it was an active revulsion and the fact that the royal family were so enamoured of it shocked her.

'You really are a prude,' he had said.

'Am I?' But she hadn't changed her mind, and gradually it had resulted in himself stopping going to race meetings too.

So in a sense the television racing he had recently discovered was a revival of an old love that had not quite left him. The fact that Vanessa liked it helped – she was always bringing him hot tips. He felt guilty about it, although he couldn't imagine why, and never mentioned it to Caroline. It was not that she ever tried to change his tastes, it was just the veiled expression on her face and the way she went quiet that made her unspoken opinion devastating. He found himself quite unintentionally always trying to live up to Caroline – which seemed ridiculous considering she was a lot younger and in many respects blatantly ignorant of the kind of everyday things most people know about. Take the farm, for instance, she let it blow over her like a dream – or rather a poem, for he was always finding scraps of her torn-up writing – never settled down seriously to tackle it for what it was – their bread and butter, or bread without butter . . .

The jockeys were mounting, they'd all been weighed in, any minute now and they would be going out on to the course. Patrick sits forward in anticipation, draws his dressing-gown over his pleasantly hairy bony knees. He might just as well make the most of this last week's racing.

Caroline and Helen edge their way through the crowded pub to the bar. On every side the faces are jovial, prices are good, drink and the money flows. Jim Thurley, a pint of dark liquid capped by foam held high, turns and sees them. He nods, raises his glass still higher. Caroline smiles back, at the same time giving Helen a little shove forward, they certainly don't want to end up talking to a rather drunk Jim Thurley. She has reservations about him at the best of times.

As they wait to buy their drinks, snatches of conversation float out above the general hum. Two farmers converse just behind them.

'A good market – better than expected.'

'A very nice day – better'n Taverston. They was giving 'em away back there.'

A woman's voice joins in. 'Do you know what Sedgewick got for his bunch of mares?'

'Now I couldn't say for certain but I believe 'twas somewhere in the nineties. 'Tis a good price for old mares.' Out of the corner of her eye Caroline sees the old farmer purse his lips almost in disapproval – a sudden rise in prices is a shock to those who have toiled for poor returns all their lives, they like to comfort themselves with the thought that ultimately 'weird' will bring all to nothing. For isn't that, after all, the essence of hill farming? If you want to grow rich you should be down in the valley, but if you want to tick along, get up late and drop asleep by the stove after midday, have time to enjoy the sun rise and set over Scarhill, if you want to have time to stop the tractor in the lane and grumble about the weather and prices to your neighbour, then hill farming is the right choice. Thirty cows and the milk cheque'll keep you going – just – and if milking makes too much slurry and hard work why then the subsidies for beef bullocks should just about allow you to manage without – provided you live a quiet life and don't go in for new-fangled buildings or any of that . . .

Caroline and Helen drink companionably but silently. They are busy taking in the company and general ambience. Later, as they drive back over the top, Helen asks if farming is what Caroline has expected. Caroline's expression at once grows serious, almost sombre.

'In one way, yes – it's just I've seen more now, a lot of things I didn't know before and no one lets out. Like how terrified the animals are of the smell of blood at the abattoir. That's the kind of thing you can't know till you experience it.'

'But you keep on?'

Caroline feels anger rise in her at the Catch 22 situation. 'What can I do?' she bursts out. 'What would you do? Once you go into it deeply the only answer is everyone vegetarian and the extermination of all farm animals – except a few kept in parks and zoos. That seems to me worse, probably. As farms go our sort gives animals the best lives possible till they're slaughtered.'

Helen has no ready answer. All in all it seems better to look at the panorama of sweeping hills and tors on either side. Most things of exceptional beauty have a darker side enabling them to exist, she comforts herself, you can't forever be insisting on reforms that might be doubtfully for the better. She does wonder though, how she will complete her article.

The agreeably soft velvet curtains Caroline has picked up here and there enclose her like a bird in a nest as she sits at the kitchen table in a bright oval of egg-shaped light. On every side the room recedes into friendly shadow, the fire glows red from the corner of the hearth. The shadow helps her to shut her mind off from the oppressive inanimate demands that beckon to her on every side – the pile of plates and mugs reaching dangerous proportions in the sink, the hole the kitten has made by climbing the curtain, the massive heap of ashes ever rising in the grate, the several milk-bottle tops that seem to have found a home beneath the table, and the catbox, for the old cat who can't make the door, that is in need of emptying – instead she concentrates on the farm diary and a little heap of brown envelopes that mount beside her as she pays the bills she daren't let go on any longer. From above comes the sound of running water and singing – Helen is having a bath. The stove has been well stocked up, hot water abounds.

She closes the farm diary in which she has written the pony prices and pulls her journal towards her. She writes: 'Sad we shan't be keeping ponies any more but the sales are sadder, and anyhow our grazing rights aren't enough to warrant going in for them on a big scale.' She pauses, nibbles her Biro, then puts, 'Helen goes on Sunday. Patrick *may* get home a week later if all goes well– that leaves one week of humouring Tom . . .'

Upstairs the bath is turned off and the singing comes up louder. She looks up, smiles to herself and switches on the radio. She turns it up full, by chance it is a contralto voice singing Schubert.

Helen, luxuriating in the hot water and Radox above, murmurs, 'The pig!' At the same time the voice wails to a halt and all the lights fade. Startled, she sits in the darkness. A small grey square slowly comes up in front of her indicating where the window must be. She shouts, 'The light's gone.'

Caroline beneath fumbles around the kitchen for the torch on the shelf. Her fingers alight on it and she switches it on, goes up the stairs. In the bathroom she flashes the torch on the bath and sees Helen's white shoulders rising out of the greenish Radox water, her head topped by a ridiculous frilled mob bath cap. The humour of the situation strikes both of them and Caroline collapses on the toilet seat, weak with laughter.

'Is it a power cut?' Helen asks.

'I suppose so.'

'Oh well, that's one thing I can't blame Patrick for.'

Their laughter dies down. Caroline hands Helen a towel as she stands shining with water, a pink Venus stepping from the white shell of her bath.

'Helen?'

'What?'

'Will you stop blaming Patrick?'

Helen wraps the towel round herself decorously. 'I'll try.'

'We haven't got children – I could leave him tomorrow if I wanted.'

Helen sits on the edge of the bath, lifts an elegant foot with coral toe nails and dries it carefully.

'That's what makes it worse,' she says frowning, her flushed face looking up at Caroline in the torchlight.

The lights come on as suddenly as they went off. Likewise the contralto singing. Both women laugh. Their laughter, mixed with the singing voice from beneath and the light from the torch in Caroline's hand that still shines ineffectually on Helen, gives the scene a bizarre reality that sets it both in and outside of time. The old granite walls seem to enclose them in an intensity of shared emotion that is the more powerful for its primitive inconsequentiality.

Rita is buying icing sugar and chocolate to make Tom's birthday cake. With one hand holding fast to Jenny she bends over the counter pointing at things on the shelf behind and talking to Christine. Christine collects a heap of things in accord with Rita's directions then starts to jot the prices down and add up. There is no one else in the shop, they are quite on their own. Jenny by degrees extracts her hand from Rita's and busies herself by emptying oranges out of the tray and putting them in the bag with the dog biscuits – but who cares if this allows a little peace and quiet in which to talk.

'Martin Weller had it coming to him, didn't he?' Christine murmurs as she adds up.

'Why – what happened?'

'He was walking back along the road from the Forestry two nights back when he got picked up. He was carrying his shot gun, see, and he couldn't get it under his jacket quick enough. Mind you he said he was only out after rabbits but it didn't make no difference. They want to see him along with Tom?'

'Tom?' Rita stares in alarm and disbelief.

'Didn't he tell you?' Christine looks suitably shocked. 'I thought he was bound to have said.'

Rita tosses her head proudly. 'He'd know better than to tell me a thing like that – he'd be ashamed.'

Christine starts putting the goodies into Rita's open basket on the counter. 'I didn't know you minded them having a bit of fun down the Forestry woods.'

'I don't,' says Rita tartly, 'I mind him getting caught. That's what I mind. He oughter known better after all the times he's been down there.'

Christine nods sympathetically.

'Where was Tom when they found him?' Curiosity has made Rita abandon her normal pride. She has to know, doesn't she?

'He was in his van, sitting right there on the track with the engine running.' Christine knows it all, she relates the whole unhappy saga, keeping the gem till last. When the moment comes she leans forward across the counter, revealing the lace on her Marks & Spencer bra, and says with a further giggle, 'And do you know what, the reason they were down there in the first place was because Mrs Ashurst had told Tom she likes venison' – at which point she leans backwards and sinks her double chin into her neck in riotous laughter.

Rita with commendable will, forces herself to join in. When the laughter has quieted down she says, 'That'll teach them to go poaching for a stupid woman's whim – not that I believe for a moment that was their real reason, it's more they can't leave nothing alone. Tom's very fond of rabbit himself.'

'Arch loves a rabbit. I always cook them with two big teaspoons of Marmite and they come out like chicken . . .'

Rita listens with her mind elsewhere. Wait till she sees Tom, she'll give him a piece of her mind. She won't let him know she's jealous, which of course she's not, but she'll tell him what a fool he is going and getting caught. And all because of that Ashurst woman – no, she won't say that. So absorbed is she in how she will make herself clear to Tom that she walks out of the shop without paying and Christine has the embarrassment of having to run after her. But she forgives her because she knows the reason why. Poor Rita, but then it was bound to happen sooner or later, wasn't it? The village have been predicting it since that day they first saw Mrs Ashurst at the Jumble Sale. After that it was only a matter of waiting. And now with poor Mr Ashurst in hospital Tom was up there more, so it stood to reason.

As Christine puts the money in the till she finds she has undercharged Rita but under the circumstances decides to forget it. Poor thing, she feels really sorry for her. And happily sad with her newly formed compassion and generosity, Christine turns the 'Closed' sign round on the door.

The big wheel revolves perpetually, its lights glitter like jewels set against a velvet cloth. Beneath it the fairground teems with people passing from stall to stall, collecting at the roundabouts, queuing for bumper cars. For this is the night-of-the-week at Goose Fair, the night the cheap-jacks have their stands set across the bridge and the card– and fortune-tellers wait in their kiosks like spiders. Even the schools have shut for the day so that many of the older children still hang round in sex-differentiated groups, licking candy floss and toffee apples, or sucking aniseed balls, each with one eye casting round hopefully for an approach from the other group. For the fair acts as a courting ground. Lives are joined temporarily or even permanently after a battle with the bumper cars or an empty seat suddenly filled on the big dipper. Money aside – for no one knows how much slips away shooting for a doll, or a vase that turns out to be chipped, or a goldfish that dies on the way home – a fairground is one of the last living places of 'romance' to be found in this country. The nomadic life of those who work with it and their apparent disregard of hours of sleep; the way in which a field during a day can be transformed into a miniature metropolis with a suggestion of adventure and mystery; the great motor-driven caravans waiting to move on at whim leaving no trace but the trampled ground, the rings where tents and roundabouts have been, and a smattering of litter; all combine to give the impression of a way of life more glamorous, more unpredictable, than our normal humdrum existence.

It is into this atmosphere of surface vitality and cheap goods that Helen and Caroline come by accident on their way to the hospital. Finding it irresistible they park the car and get out, clinging to each other like schoolgirls, partly because that is the effect the fair has on them, and partly because if they lost each other in the crowd hours might pass before they came together again. Having in their youth ridden on roundabouts and rolled balls for china dogs with chipped ears, they are more interested in looking at the variety of wares on the stalls, and listening to the bargaining between cheap-jacks and purchasers.

A man in a shiny pale-grey pin-striped suit is selling a blanket to a woman in a brown beret and coat tightly belted round her ample figure. Her apple face is bent with a frown of concentration on the blanket displayed in front of her.

'You won't do better, ma'am. You won't get blankets cheaper in the south-west – nor north-west neither. What do you want then, luv? Me to make you a present of them?' The vendor winks at the surrounding crowd.

'I want a fair price – something you never heard of,' she fingers the blanket, betraying by the sensual movement of her finger tips her disinclination to be parted from it. 'Wool, did you say? I ain't never come across a sheep with wool like that, an' I kept sheep all of fifty year' – she nudges her friend beside her, a small bespectacled little grey-haired woman who stands with hands folded over her shopping bag, her mouth pursed – "Tisn't wool, is it Mary? 'Tis synthetics.'

Whereupon the vendor's voice rises an octave with indignation. 'Look, my luv, this is wool. Feel it, if you don't believe me look at the mark . . .'

Caroline pulls Helen away from the riveting scene. They pass a candy-floss kiosk and a balloon-seller attached by invisible strings of different lengths to a vast pile rising into the air above, for all the world like bubbles. The next moment they are accosted by a fortune-teller who sets upon them with the familiar patter. They edge away, making excuses as they go, moving towards the main fairground. Caroline, who has bought, and unsuccessfully thrown, three darts for 20p is brought up short by coming face to face with Rita. For a moment they face each other in silence, then Caroline recovers herself and speaks.

'You gave me a surprise. Is Tom here too?'

'He's somewhere around – there's ever such a crowd.'

'It's a wonderful fair, but we've got to go unfortunately – we're on our way to see Patrick.' Caroline can hardly believe it's herself speaking, so unnatural does she sound.

Rita gives a murmur of assent, but her hostility is ill-veiled although she flashes a bright formal smile. They part and Helen who has waited at a little distance immediately asks who it was.

'Tom's wife.'

'She's a very pretty girl.'

'Yes.'

Helen at once perceives all is not as it should be. Caroline's mood has changed, she seems preoccupied and suggests it's time they went back to the car. It is not until they have driven several miles that she comments on the difficulty of getting on with the local people.

'You mean that girl?'

'Well not just her,' Caroline prevaricates.

'Why is it difficult?'

'Because they always think you're different – and the trouble is you are.'

'So then?'

'I wish we weren't. Class is supposed to have gone from this country but it hasn't. They – the real local people – hate us because they know it's not a question of money.

All the time the unions strike for more money, but really money is a substitute for class hatred. What they're really saying is they want to be as good as anyone else and if you can't be that, or convince yourself that you are, then you'll take all you can in compensation. It's like divorced people fighting over possessions – often they don't even want them, it's simply a manifestation of hate.'

Helen looks at Caroline's intense profile. 'You're waxing very eloquent tonight.'

'It makes me angry. It's such a mess and so difficult to get over – really get over. Oh lots of people profess to do so by all that camaraderie in bars and fraternization but underneath nothing's changed. It's a whole different culture.'

'Aren't you generalizing rather to explain why Tom's wife is hostile towards you. Isn't it more a question of her being threatened?'

Caroline changes down and pulls up at the traffic lights. 'I don't threaten her, that's just the point.'

'She thinks you do.'

'Well, it's rubbish.' The lights change. 'Anyway it's not just her. Tom's the same.' Helen says nothing but inwardly she thinks Caroline protests too much, and it becomes her turn to fall rather quiet in order to absorb the full implication.

Patrick sitting on the edge of his bed in his dressing-gown has been waiting expectantly for forty minutes. His temper and disappointment grows with every moment. Aren't they coming? And if not why not? On the other hand he's sure they will – one thing Caroline is is reliable. But supposing they've got a puncture on the moor? Helen may be a feminist but he can't see her making much of a job of changing a tyre, and Caroline is probably counting the stars in Orion's dagger . . . Bugger them. Rage is a way of Patrick shelving his genuine anxiety. Could they have had an accident? Of course not, he's being stupid. He cranes his head forward yet again in order to see the ward doorway. He blinks. They are there. Caroline sees him, waves and makes her way towards him across the ward followed by Helen. She reaches him, kisses his cheek. He pulls her to him, kisses her rather obviously as though to make a point in front of Helen. Caroline withdraws embarrassed.

'I began to wonder if you were coming.'

'You're looking better – I brought Helen.' She takes a bag of fruit out of her basket and puts it in the bowl at the foot of his bed. Helen moves off to find herself a chair.

'I think you'd better put the fruit in the cupboard.' He looks critically at the castle she is arranging. She stops, her hand containing an orange poised, looks at him.

'Why?'

Patrick lowers his voice. 'Some of these others haven't got anything – don't even have visitors, poor buggers.'

Caroline transfers the bowl and fruit to the cupboard. Helen returns with a chair and sits herself near the foot of the bed.

'How are you, Helen? I'm very glad you're keeping Caroline company while I'm away,' says Patrick heartily and falsely.

Helen returns appropriate inquiries about himself to which he answers that he could come out tomorrow if they could find an antibiotic which worked on him, but being a farmer he seems to have built up a resistance to most of them. Helen murmurs sympathetically and Patrick shifts his attention back to Caroline, still using the same hearty tone.

'Anyhow, everything's alright at Greytor is it?'

'Nothing much has happened since the new calf, and the pony sales – and I've told you about those.' Caroline sits stiffly, acutely aware of being the medium between Patrick and Helen, aware his rather aggressive manner is due to Helen's presence.

'Have you booked in the suckled calves with the auctioneers?'

'No – but I will tomorrow.' She fingers the shoulder-strap buckle of her handbag.

Patrick feels his animosity rise, though he couldn't exactly explain why. It is just something about Helen that rubs him up the wrong way, it's her assertiveness and aggression – or so he persuades himself. In fact it is because

Helen refuses to respond to him as anything but an equal, refuses to set everything in the perspective he would like by establishing through a sort of ritual of silent feminine responses and facial expressions that she is only Eve to his Adam. So he must meet her as a person rather than a woman, and this to Patrick is deeply disconcerting. Possibly he could have found room in his not incapacious soul to accommodate all this had not Helen, in some nether region of his consciousness, attracted and roused his desire. The fact that she did so yet refused to acknowledge it by any outward sign was unacceptable to Patrick and, if pressed, he would certainly have denied that she had any appeal for him whatsoever. Caroline was alright because he 'possessed' her, but in a man who did not she would most probably have raised the same antagonism. But her vagueness, her unconscious air of helplessness along with her long straw hair, did much to abate the male fear of inferiority, of loss of dominance. Be that as it may, the energy generated by the tension round Patrick's bed that evening could well have called up a poltergeist.

Patrick addresses himself pointedly to Helen. 'How about you, Helen?'

Helen keeps her voice carefully level, 'I've been hindering – as much as I can.'

They all laugh over-heartily.

Caroline, anxious to vindicate Helen's stay, joins in. 'Seriously, she's been marvellous – it's made such a difference.'

'You're exaggerating,' Helen hastily contradicts, 'but I have enjoyed myself . . . struggling.'

'Struggling? What with?' Sarcasm escapes in the tone in spite of Patrick's better intentions.

'Just generally.'

'And what did you "struggle" with today?'

Caroline can't bear it – she interrupts quickly, 'There was the feeding – we've started feeding.'

'Already?' Patrick raises his eyebrows, indicating both surprise and disapproval.

'Jim Thurley suggested I should. He said there wasn't much goodness left in the grass and a couple of bales of hay each day would help' – Caroline can't get it out quick enough to qualify her decision. Why is it she is so sensitive to Patrick's ridicule?

But Patrick is still worrying at the word 'struggle', the implication that there is too much work. He confines himself to saying, 'Later in the year it'll be fifteen bales a day to the bull's lot alone.'

But his tone has roused Helen. She says carefully, 'I know Patrick, but I don't think you realise what you're asking of Caroline at the present.'

Caroline looks across at her anxiously, steals a furtive glance at the next bed. Surely they are not going to get into a fully fledged argument here, in the hospital – now? She frowns at Helen. Helen ignores it.

'I honestly think she needs more help than she gets from Tom.'

'Do you, Caroline?' Patrick challenges.

Caroline gnaws the side of a finger. 'Not really. I can manage.'

There is a long and awkward silence. Patrick feels mildly triumphant, Helen feels let down, and Caroline a turn-coat and traitor to Helen. But it's really Helen's fault, she consoles herself, for it is her business not Helen's. Unfortunately Patrick, having got the upper hand, doesn't retire with magnanimity, but trots out the old cliché, 'I thought you feminists were as good as men – equal pay for equal labour.'

Helen's sense of humour has completely deserted her, and she batters on into the trough. 'There is a limit to physical strength. I doubt a man of Caroline's size would do much better.'

Patrick flings his head back and lets out a shout of humourless laughter. The others in the ward look across at them. Caroline feels acutely embarrassed and notices with alarm that Helen's face is rather red.

'Helen – you're wonderful. You never change.' Patrick's tone is aggressively patronising.

Before Helen can retaliate Caroline says quickly, 'Have they said any more about your coming home?'

'They can't keep me much longer – I shall walk out.'

His bluff falls flat. The women sit looking patiently depressed, until Helen stands up.

'I think I'll go back to the car now and let you two have a bit of privacy. I'll be quite happy listening to the radio.' She raises her hand to Patrick as she moves off, 'Take care – hurry and get well.'

They watch her make her way out through the ward in silence – a brisk figure in dark coat and high-heeled boots, her dark wavy hair bouncing in defiance with her step. Patrick seems to feel no need to speak, so Caroline sighs and says, 'It seems a shame you and she always have to argue.'

Patrick at once completely alters. He drops his abrasive manner and adopts his normal reasonable tone. 'I don't mean to – there's just something about her . . .' He reaches for Caroline's hand and takes it in both his. 'I've been missing you – really missing you. Perhaps I'm jealous of her . . . having you.'

'I've missed you too,' says Caroline enthusiastically, 'in fact all the time . . . almost' – a shadow crosses her face.

'When don't you?'

She hesitates. 'When I'm . . . very busy. Doing things.'

Patrick looks at her with anxious concern. Deep feelings of love stir within him – what is Vanessa in comparison to his beautiful wife?

'Is it too much for you, like Helen said?' he asks gently.

'Not at the moment. I'll be a bit lonely when she goes.' Caroline is amazed at her own sense of guilt. She feels dishonest, a cheat. She hasn't been missing Patrick half as much as she would have liked to, and to be truthful, since Helen's arrival she has hardly missed him at all – just as long as she has Tom. She feels the colour mounting in her face and neck as she recognises that Tom is the basis of her guilt, for Tom is concealed whereas Helen is revealed. Then immediately she vindicates herself to herself, for what, she argues, has she ever done with Tom to feel guilty about? Nothing. But is not the knowledge that should circumstances prove propitious anything could happen almost the same as an act? It was quite possible for an act to take place which meant so little it would not incur guilt – and yet the act was the offence.

Patrick is speaking, looking at her, ' . . . and it should only be five days before I'm home,' he finishes.

She puts her hand in his, grips his palm from which all traces of outdoor work have almost disappeared. Patrick following her gaze, looks at his hands proudly. 'I've got some proper nails for the first time in years,' he says, displaying them.

'Yes,' says Caroline, but thinks privately that it is the other hands she cares for and that a man is in part his outside skin, in so far as it denotes him; that a man and his labour are indivisible.

He reaches up, touches the curve of her cheek, pulling his fingers gently through her hair. 'I wish you could stay here with me.' He looks at her anxiously for a response.

She smiles, leans forward and kisses him, murmurs softly, 'I wish I could too.'

The first part of the drive back over the moor is slow and laborious, the mist encloses the car in a small pool of light as Caroline cautiously drives along, never daring to increase speed for the lack of visibility and the possibility of stock strayed on to the road. Then suddenly and unexpectedly they come through the mist and find themselves beneath a sky bright with stars and a full moon; the mist floats beneath them, filling the valleys like cotton wool, blacking by contrast the hills that rise from it. Caroline stops the car and they both get out, stand in this private world of perfection that isolates them. The mist shuts out the flickering lights of the towns beneath which, in normal visibility, stretch in a continuous chain along the coast. The Plough rears itself awkwardly over the dark hill ahead, Orion is directly behind them. In between the two familiar constellations more and more tiny stars appear, and as their eyes become accustomed to looking, the whole mazy path of the Milky Way shows itself. A sheep's cough comes up to them from somewhere down in the mist, otherwise the entire moor seems bereft of life by its total silence.

Quite soon the cold drives them back in the car, for the

temperature has dropped considerably in the past few days. They continue on their way without speaking, awed by the jagged shapes of the tors and the unreal silvery light cast by the moon. Small streams shine white as they slow down to cross them; the moon's reflection undulates at them from shadowy pools under the banks.

'He was quite different directly you went.' Caroline breaks their silence as they leave the higher ground and drive between trees.

'I'm very glad to hear it,' Helen answers with asperity. 'Why don't you tell him to let you have someone all the time – instead of Tom.'

Almost without thinking Caroline prevaricates. 'It would cause a disruption – and I'm alright. It won't be for much longer – we honestly can't afford it.'

'But even if he comes home soon he won't be able to do anything,' Helen points out.

Caroline feels defensive. Helen's criticism of Patrick is implicit. Both slip into their own thoughts, aware only of the division between them and the hum of the engine.

Sharon has brought Maggie to spend the day with Rita and Jenny. The two young mothers have pushed the push-chair containing Maggie, and the pram containing Ernest and Jenny, up to the playground and are sitting on the bench watching Maggie and Jenny in the sand-pit. All is well for the time being, the sand-throwing stage has not yet come and Ernest is tucked up and blissfully silent.

'So you see it is quite possible that she knew.'

'How could she?' asks Sharon flatly, being less inclined to believe the case against Tom than Rita.

'He could've told her.'

'As they meet every day he goes up there, then I don't see he's got any need.'

Rita mulls over the sense of this remark, while noticing a distinct smell of cat. Can it be the sand-pit? But as the girls are playing peacefully she thinks it's worth the 'cat' – there's always the washing-machine.

'If you ask me,' she says, 'I don't think they've got that far.'

'Don't you?' Sharon looks surprised. She wonders what all the fuss is about.

'No,' Rita goes on, 'I think if he were to stop going out there nothing would come of it.'

'But surely,' Sharon points out, 'with that other woman she's got staying, nothing much'll come of it anyhow. And Patrick Ashurst'll be back soon, won't he?'

'Oh, I don't know,' says Rita, 'I wish I did. If you want to know I think there was a lot more wrong with him than's ever been let out. He's old, isn't he?'

'Yeah, I 'spose.' Sharon puts her head on one side as though thinking deeply.

''Spose what?'

''Spose he's oldish. But he's ever so nice looking don't you think?'

This aggravates Rita for she wants to be able to pity the Ashurst woman rather than think her fortunate.

'Personally,' she says, 'I've never thought anything of him. I can understand why she's after Tom.' For this is the one thing that makes it bearable for her, that the Ashurst woman is after Tom and not the other way round. That way it gives her distinctly the upper hand. At this moment their conversation is spoiled by Jenny pushing Maggie backwards out of the pit. Maggie hits the back of her head on the ground with a dull thud and comes running, her face crumpling into yells. Sharon glares at the triumphant Jenny standing deep in broken sand-castle.

'Jenny,' yells Rita.

'There, there,' says Sharon, picking up the sobbing Maggie, 'it was a hard bump, wasn't it?' She rubs the tender spot thus exacerbating the sobs.

'It was only on the grass,' Rita comments, nevertheless she goes to the sand-pit and jerks Jenny from it, towing her back to the bench with her.

'Now you say sorry to Maggie for what you done.' Jenny sucks her fingers, turns her face away, hides behind Rita's skirt. 'I don't know what's the matter with you this afternoon, I'm sure.' Rita would like, just at present, to be able to blame Jenny for everything. Getting stuck with Tom for one.

She drags Jenny out of her skirts and comforts her with the now intermittently sobbing Maggie, who stares back a flat resentful stare.

'Kiss her then. Make up.'

Jenny remarkably does so, whereupon Maggie buries her face in Sharon and starts to sob again.

'For heavens sake!' Sharon laughs brightly to excuse Maggie's lamentable response. Rita feels she could scream, she really loathes Maggie, always grizzling and yelling. How can Sharon stand the child? She'd give her a good slap if she were hers, she's spoilt, that's what it is. Rita stands to relieve tension. 'Don't you think it's getting cold,' she says, shouts, above the din. Ernest who until now has been forgotten, joins in, high and agonised. Rita looks at the pram anxiously. Is he going to die? She seizes him up, rocks him vigorously to no effect. 'I suppose he wants a feed, I'd best get on back.'

'I'll come with you,' Sharon is also shouting.

They wind their way patiently back along the road, Maggie silenced by the push-chair, Jenny content to sit in the foot of the pram and gaze on the scarlet face of her screaming brother who pauses now and again and chews his fist, then bursts into fresh and more agonised paroxysms. There is no further time for talk, or even thought. Life as it clearly *is* has taken over.

The bullocks, varied in colour, follow a stream bed that stretches for about thirty yards across the valley bottom. Caroline walks ahead, a rapt expression on her face; Helen, concentrating on driving them, comes behind. The late autumn leaves are all colours and blend in with the colours of the herd. What with that and the murky stirred-up sand-bed of the stream, a pointillist could well have covered an entire canvas with spots of grey-green, ochre and brown – punctuated only by the mossy writhing trunks of half-fallen willow and the lichened stems of rotting alder. The swampy ground has increased over recent years, killing many of the trees and making those that remain lean dangerously as though uncertain of their grip on earth.

As the herd emerge on the far side, their hooves echo

over an old mudded-up clapper giving a clear indication of the course the stream once took. Stepping-stones also mark that it was a well-frequented route, taking the inhabitants of Greytor and Crype farms to church on a Sunday. For Caroline it is the most exquisite bit of Greytor's land; and, as the bullocks spread out over the wide flat meadow, she waits with a starry-eyed expression quite inappropriate to the muddy way that Helen, by being behind, has had to negotiate.

'Isn't it beautiful?' Her ecstasy appears to Helen ludicrous, but so not to do harm to her friend's poetic sensibilities, she only asks her to repeat again what it's called.

'The Frog's Parlour.' Caroline gazes at Helen incredulously – how could she have forgotten such a name?

'Why?' asks Helen, in far from excited tones.

Caroline shrugs. 'An old, old man who used to live here told Patrick. Lots of frogs, I suppose – I expect there still are.' She points out the Church Way, the clapper. Helen looks, listens, tries to take in and absorb Caroline's way of seeing things, tries above all to understand what she can get from such a life – and as she listens Caroline's enthusiasm does begin to penetrate almost in spite of herself. For as she talks her mind shifts to the summer, when the water curls silently through the trees undisturbed, purslane stars the banks, and tall foxgloves spring miraculously from round the edges of rocks already ringed by bird's-eye bluer than sky, than sea, than stained glass. The leaves of the alder flicker and dance delicate shadows over the rocks and water, from the sandy bed glint a thousand different minute stones . . .

She has written a poem about it she would like to show Helen if she can bring herself to, for her poems are something private that seldom surface for other people's eyes. Besides she feels rather embarrassed about the very fact she writes them. It is as though she has no right to trespass on such hallowed ground amongst names like Dante and T. S. Eliot – the thought of Emilies Dickinson and Brontë make her feel better, and Sylvia Plath better still. How silly it is that women, or anyway herself, continue to feel themselves unable to compete for standards except with other women. She says as much to Helen who firmly refutes it, but Caroline thinks it a long step from altering what you say, what you profess to feel, to what you actually feel – acquired from a vast accumulation of inherited or inculcated attitudes.

They walk through the flat low field past the cattle munching contentedly. As they go through a gate Helen acknowledges, 'I do begin to see . . . or feel . . . what it is you like about this place.'

Caroline turns grateful, joyous eyes on her. 'It grows into you. It's like ivy that pushes its feelers in through the windows and under the gutters.'

Yes, thinks Helen, it is.

'It's been so good having you,' Caroline murmurs with genuine feeling, clings to Helen as they wait the same evening on the platform. The long London train glides into the station, doors open to discharge passengers, others pile in and search for seats, wave from the windows to those who remain behind.

Caroline stands in front of the door, while Helen goes to put her case on a seat. She waits anxiously. Why doesn't Helen hurry? The train will go without them having exchanged those last essential few words, she suddenly feels desolate. Helen's face and shoulders appear filling the open window space.

'I don't want to go back – another week and you'd have converted me. Completely,' she says.

But Caroline knows she doesn't mean it. It's a question of Johnny town-mouse and Timmy Willy she tells herself sadly, and for a brief instant imagines herself going to Taunton in a hamper – but the trouble is she's not a proper country mouse, she's a sort of hybrid. 'You must come again, Hel – very soon.' Caroline's voice catches, she feels childish. Ashamed.

Helen leans out of the window, squeezes her hand. The train starts to move. 'Let me know how you're getting on – and about Patrick. I'll keep my fingers crossed he's home Thursday.' She sees the tears in Caroline's eyes with alarm. She is so emotional, such an unsuitable person to have taken on the life she has. She continues to lean out waving to Caroline until she turns and walks away towards the exit, then makes her way into the compartment, puts her case on the rack and settles herself by the window with her briefcase on the table. She opens it, takes out her unfinished articles – the one about 'country buses' she has given up and the one about ponies for meat that she is more than half-way through. She sits watching the passing countryside out of the window and thinking, not of her article, but of Caroline. What, she wonders, will happen to her? Does she care about Patrick enough to stay with him? Then there's Mr Pritchard – she can see his attractions but really, the whole thing is absurd. Caroline and he can't possibly have anything in common, he only communicates by grunts. And at this point Helen comes round to herself. Why is she determined to write off Patrick and Tom? Why does she like to make a mockery of Caroline's feelings? Is it not that she is at some deep level jealous of Caroline, jealous that her life though isolated is in some way emotionally richer than her own? Helen feels uncertain, for how can she be jealous of Caroline who she genuinely cares for, loves more than anyone, *wants* to be happy? She sits very still for a long time, not seeing the passenger opposite, not seeing the passing landscape though she looks out of the window. Finally, her honesty triumphs, gives her the answer she can hardly believe herself – yes, she can be . . . and is.

As the train slows down for Taunton, Helen tears up her article to which she has not added one word and drops it in the litter bin on the platform. She puts on her dark glasses behind which she feels much safer, and makes for the 29 bus stop.

The first thing Caroline sees on returning to Greytor is Jim Thurley's pick-up. It stands in the yard and Jim himself stands ominously by the back door. Her heart sinks. Were there any chance of evasion she would take it, but as it is she is fairly and squarely caught. Jim raises his hat to her as she gets out of the car.

'Good afternoon, Mrs Ashurst.'

She opens the back door and he follows her in. She feels exhausted, that she can't stand talking but must sit – so there is nothing for it but to invite him in. As she undoes her coat, hangs it up, pushes the kettle over on the hotplate, Jim pulls a chair out from the table, sits, folds his arms, inquires after Patrick. Caroline answers automatically, her head is aching. If only he would go but she knows he won't, not until he has conveyed the reason for his visit that she has already guessed.

Jim waits for his tea, stirs, then raises shrewd blue eyes. 'Problem is, I got my heifers just across the stream to your bull.'

Just as she had thought. But why shouldn't she put their own herd in their own field? It was always the same, Jim always got his way and so their bottom field was losing its fertility for lack of grazing.

'Mr Ashurst generally makes sure he puts his down his bottoms when mine is up top.'

Caroline keeps her voice carefully level. Pleasant, even. 'This morning when we moved our bull your heifers weren't opposite. We'd have heard them.'

'They been down my bottom meadow since Friday.' He looks Caroline in the eye, who for her part is dumbfounded. She is sure he isn't telling the truth but can't prove it. Neither will it do to upset a neighbour though she's not sure she'd care if it wasn't for Patrick . . .

'You didn't bring your dog today, then?' she asks innocently, glancing out of the window.

'No – I left him back at the house' – but Jim has shifted his glance. He looks round the room, the clock ticks away the minutes, it is getting dark or perhaps it is just a dark cloud gathering to precipitate on Greytor. She moves across to switch on the light, returns to the support of the stove, and says, 'You mean you want me to move our bullocks?'

'I'd be grateful if you would.'

He is standing up, taking his hat. Now he moves towards the door. Caroline follows him automatically. As he turns the door handle he nods, asks for himself and his wife to be remembered to Mr Ashurst, expects to see him soon. Caroline forces a smile on her unwilling face, wonders if it looks like a smile to Jim Thurley, reads the expression on his face and knows she's made an enemy. Oh well, she did try. She turns back into the kitchen, sits down to her going-cold cup of tea and finds that her hands shake as she lifts it to her lips.

'*25 November*. The second week of frost – the ground is hard as concrete. Wood – I must get some in, ask about chain saw. Suckled calves go on Tuesday. We're putting four steers in for the prize – it ensures a better place in the market. Ring auctioneers.'

Caroline breaks off from her journal to drink from a cup of coffee beside her, at the same time pulling a small and tatty hardbacked book towards her. She opens it where an old envelope acts as a marker and starts to copy some lines half-way down the page: 'I begin to think there can never come much happiness to me from loving – I wish I could make a world outside of it, as men do.'

She looks up, sits with chin in hand gazing at nothing, for the intensity of her inner world quite precludes her from seeing the litter of washing-up surrounding the sink. How she agrees with George Eliot, or rather Maggie Tulliver. A world outside of loving seems to her the only way to any sort of true independence. Too often a woman's life becomes a sort of three-legged race, eternally bound to another whose stride is out of time. The trouble with many of us women – Caroline hops mentally from three legs to the Sphinx's riddle – is that we go on three legs all our lives instead of only in old age . . .

She looks at the clock, which says eight-fifteen, frowns – Tom is late. A moment later she hears the tractor start up. Hastily she gets on her boots, jacket, scarf, woollen hat and gloves – for the frost on the windows and the whiteness of the ground outside leaves her in no doubt as to the temperature – and goes out. The tractor stands over night at the top of the drive so it can be started by running it down, the battery being old. But by the time she gets there all that remains to show where it has stood is an oblong clear of frost and two skid marks lower down the drive where the engine has picked up in its run.

Caroline bites her lip in frustration. Trust Tom to go off like that without even bothering to say, though he knew she liked to go with him, see all the stock and help him – she added this last more doubtfully, for given the chance Tom seemed to prefer to get on alone, or that was the impression he gave. Like now, for instance.

Ten minutes later she stands on top of the hay in the central bay in the Dutch barn, looking down at Tom beneath who loads the heap of bales beside him into the link-box. The tractor which has to be kept running because if it stops it won't start again, prevents communication except by shouting or gesticulation. She tries the former: 'Enough?'

But Tom either doesn't hear or chooses to pretend he doesn't, so she slides and slithers down until she is on the ground beside him. She stands watching the ease and speed with which he lifts each bale, making it futile for her to join in. He finishes, looks round.

'Alright?' she asks.

'Couple more' – he looks up at the rick, making it clear she has come down too soon, then walks round the side and comes back with one in either hand to pile on top of the others. He looks at her expectantly, she takes it he means her to drive and gets into the driver's seat. As she lifts the load with the hydraulics, puts it in gear, Tom jumps up beside her, standing, squeezing his head under the cab roof. Caroline's face remains expressionless but she is acutely aware of his thigh which perforce presses against her when the tractor jolts over the hard ruts. Tom puts out his hand to protect himself.

'Trying to kill me?' – but it's good-humoured and Caroline relaxes. From day to day she can never tell how his mood will be.

'Sorry.' She glances up at him, sees he is smiling and so smiles back, then looks away. Looks at the white landscape that surrounds them, the pale, pale transparent blue of sky, the numerous small animal tracks leading in inexplicable trails across the frosty fields, the patches of emerald that begin to show as the sun thaws sheltered corners. All around the hedges glisten and drip, but any sound is drowned by the tractor. Caroline feels inexplicably happy, the whole world to her appears almost perfect. But hard too, hard and unrelenting as the robins tell, hopping along the hedgerows with drooping wings. And the tiny ruffled wrens that have long since ceased their ticking.

They cross a further field and come into the one with the cattle. No sooner are they through the gate than they are set upon, Caroline still driving but now no faster than walking speed, while Tom cuts the strings and spreads the bales from the back in a long wake of hay. By degrees the cows stop trying to seize it from the back of the tractor and spread themselves out in a long line, munching, picking at heaps, pushing another out of the way, or being pushed themselves, shifting hastily on to an unoccupied area. The bull, slower to arrive, now approaches the link-box ruby-eyed and belligerent. Tom jumps down to cut the string on an unopened bale dragged off by an impatient cow, and confronts him. The bull doesn't stop but comes straight on, horning a cow out of his way. Tom shouts at him, shoves at his head with his boot; the bull tosses his head with an angry shake, Caroline on the tractor holds her breath. Why can't Tom leave him alone, get back on the tractor? Tom continues on down the line eyeing up the stock, counting the calves. Caroline turns the tractor, meets him back at the gate. As he climbs on the tractor a thrill, a tingling passes through her entire body. She's met it before but not often. It's unmistakable. She sits lost in the sensation, the momentousness of the discovery that it is caused by Tom's proximity.

'What are you waiting for?' Tom looks at her curiously.

For answer she drives forward letting out the clutch too quickly, the tractor jerks. Tom's good humour to her surprise doesn't vanish, in fact he's quite remarkably good-tempered.

Still in their thick clothes they sit over the table holding mugs with curls of steam rising from them. Caroline has a form in front of her, a frown on her face. Tom also leans forward looking at it. The farm diary is open beside her with a heap of papers and forms scattered all over the table. Tom stands, moves closer to Caroline to see better – or so he tells himself. Actually it is because he gets a better view of her fair hair spreading over her shoulders, the back of her neck, the scent of her rising up to fill him with want. This way too, he can stand close, let his thigh almost touch against her shoulder so the sensation between them can pass across the gap – too far apart and it doesn't work, closer and . . .

'I hate doing paperwork,' Caroline is emphatic, perhaps unduly so. What is she really saying? She starts shovelling the papers back into the diary; then stops at another form. On it is written 'Less Favoured Areas Capital Grants Scheme', beside it she unfolds an Ordinance Survey with the field numbers.

'It's the woman's job,' says Tom on purpose to make her retaliate but she lets it pass, says calmly,

'Why do you say that?'

'Stands to reason. They can't do much outside, can they?' Caroline ignores this, partly because of the truth of it and partly because they have argued the issue before. But mainly because she is not in a mood to argue, Tom's presence is too pervasive for her to want to destroy it by words. It is like a lamplight burning between them that a severe gust of wind could put out. Tom also becomes silent, watches the bent head, moves a little away. 'Not having that friend of yours out again, are you?'

Caroline looks up. 'Helen? She's probably coming for Christmas. Why?'

'What she says might go for the town – it doesn't do out on a farm.' Tom feels firm, the closeness, the electricity has gone – he walks over to the stove, leans against it, folds his arms. In its wake desire has left aggression.

'I didn't know you'd talked to Helen,' says Caroline, surprised.

Tom gives a kind of grunt that could be described as a laugh. 'She was the one done the talking. Told me she was one of them at Greenham Common.'

'I'd like to have been there.' Caroline's honesty in this instance is unfortunate.

Tom glares at her, his dark eyes make clear his contempt. 'Trouble-makers – all of them,' he says putting down his mug in the sink, then starting to move towards the door. 'I won't be back till the end of the week, then. Think you can manage the feeding?'

'Of course,' says Caroline, standing too. In actuality the thought alarms her very much; since the cold weather set in, Tom has been coming in to do the feeding but the next few days he's on full-time down at the Mills. The seething, pushing cattle and the red-eyed bull flash across her mind. But nothing would make her express her anxiety to Tom who has his hand on the back-door handle prior to letting himself out.

'Right then. I'll drop out one evening, see how things is going. And don't go shaking that tractor to pieces over the ruts.' He smiles at her to take the edge off his reprimand. He doesn't think she'll manage for a moment but he might as well let her try – he likes the idea of her coming to find him. Begging. She moves forward as he opens the door, the cat in her hands. She puts it out, lets it jump free of her, watches it go off up the yard. As she moves back from the doorway she brushes against him, she can't help it. The sensation comes again, passes through her – imperative, demanding. She looks up and with a shock sees he is looking down on her, recognises the expression in his eyes. For a few pregnant seconds it seems that Tom must bend his mouth to hers – indeed she invites it, not exactly by anything she does so much as all the things she might have done rather than remain still as though a figure in a frieze; a timeless figure caught in an act of spreading its wings to the sun like a new-hatched butterfly.

Tom gazes at this creature for a full moment, then pushes open the door over her shoulder and goes out as she moves to one side. Through the glass panels she watches him walk away up the yard.

Patrick has been told absolutely and conclusively that he will be going home on the Friday. This last month in hospital has taken its toll on his and Caroline's relationship, visiting hours being but a poor compensation for shared life. Caroline has continued to visit regularly, bring him books, papers, magazines, clothes, fruit, anything he could wish for. But talking, the verbal intercourse that is supposed to cement relations between thinking individuals, has suffered a decline – partly because Caroline talks about the farm with which he is increasingly losing touch and partly because he senses in her a reticence. The fact that he feels secretly guilty over Vanessa does little to help. It's not that he's *done* anything or even seriously considered such a thing. How could he in hospital? It's just that the times during the day when she stands by his bed and chats, bends over him, meets him in the corridor and speaks to him, have come to mean more to him than his wife's visits. Of late he has even taken to walking almost non-stop up and down the corridor between the ward and the television room in the hope of catching a glimpse of Vanessa in the nurses' retiring-room – or whatever it's called. The sight of her back bending over a temperature chart fills him with an indescribable longing; if she turns and sees him a flush creeps up his neck and his legs melt and weaken beneath him. Before now he has been forced to reach out to the window-sill for support. Once Vanessa came rushing out, thinking him ill.

Patrick is frankly amazed at himself and puts it down in his thinking moments to the incessant drugs they have been trying him out with, but deep down he feels guilty. And guilt does nothing to ease his relations with Caroline on her visits, on the contrary it makes him formal and inclined to a tiresome self-defensiveness. Caroline is both pained and puzzled at the difference in him and thinks it must be due to him having gleaned by psychic means a knowledge of Tom's attraction for her.

Another thing that has come between them is Patrick having all the time in the world to read the newspapers and become well informed. Caroline, by being fully occupied as well as wrapped up in a private world of her own, has little idea of what is going on in the outside world, and the only way she has kept up with current events is by listening to the radio at odd times. Patrick, secure in his reading, derides her for her ignorance and unworldliness until she becomes resentful and hostile, pointing out that she has other things to think about. And certainly she has.

So when on the occasion she comes to visit him and is told he is quite definitely coming home on Friday, her feeling of pleasure is less instinctive than in obedience to her will. It is different for Patrick – Vanessa has never been more than a projection of his own need, so he has no alternative but to put her behind him. Outside hospital hours she has another 'friend', she's told him.

As Caroline places her basket of goodies like Red Riding Hood at the foot of the bed, draws off her wool gloves and scarf, her face is serious and thoughtful.

'You don't seem very pleased,' Patrick challenges.

'Don't be silly,' Caroline rejoins, 'it's simply they've promised so often, I shan't believe it till you're home.'

'I will be' – he is firm. Having made up his mind that he *is* going, *is* leaving the hospital, Patrick has regained some of his former energy, his excitement. Nothing can prevent him now.

Caroline sits. 'What shall I say to Tom?' she asks.

'Don't say anything,' Patrick looks at her wonderingly.

'He's coming in a lot at the moment – well there's an enormous amount of feeding.'

'Well I shan't be able to do it – they won't let me out unless I promise not to for at least a few weeks.'

'So then you want him to keep on coming?'

'Of course.' It seems to him Caroline is being very obtuse. 'Tell him I'd like it if he can keep on for another six weeks.'

Caroline pulls a *Farmers Weekly* from her basket and hands it him. 'Alright,' she says, 'I'll try to persuade him but I don't know if I'll be able to.'

Really, he thinks, she's very odd. Why all this fuss about Tom? He'll probably be glad of the extra pay at this time of year when there's not much work around. He says as much but Caroline continues to look dubious and point out that Tom likes to have time at home.

Feeding, says Patrick, losing his patience, is only two-and-a-half hours – that allows for the rest of the weekend at home. And she has been managing on weekdays on her own, hasn't she?

Caroline nods, she doesn't add that recently Tom has been dropping in quite often on weekdays as well, and not for pay. She doesn't know why and Tom hasn't said, but she supposes it's because he likes working with her out at Greytor and that's all there is to it. She twists a piece of hair round and round her finger until she sees Patrick frowning. 'If he doesn't want to,' she says, 'I can manage.'

Patrick sighs, this conversation is becoming boring. He hopes, he really does hope, Caroline isn't going to be difficult when he gets back. He feels irritated by how compulsorily dependent he will be to begin with, but it shouldn't be long before he's back to the old routine.

'Heard from Helen?' he says to change the subject.

'Yes – she's hoping to come over at Christmas.'

'So are my parents,' announces Patrick, 'my mother said so yesterday.'

'Are you serious?' Caroline's heart sinks.

'Of course. They always come. They only missed out on last year because my father wasn't well.'

'Yes,' says Caroline meekly. There seems awfully little else to say. Patrick however seems unusually talkative and tells her at some length how much he dislikes the Conrad stories she has got out of the library for him. Caroline indicates the extent of her disagreement by looking round the ward. All in all it is a bad visit, and she springs up with alacrity to leave at the first bell. He draws her to him and they kiss and part with the understanding that she shall drive in to fetch him at midday on Friday, with extra cases for the accumulation of things he has acquired during his stay. People have been very kind, as he puts it.

Caroline makes her way from the hospital not joyously, as might have been expected, but weighed down by guilt and depression. Later that evening she opens the door on the now cold and lonely bedroom that she and Patrick share and asks herself what it will be like back in bed together after so long? She feels slightly afraid, afraid that Patrick will not be able to awaken the response in her he has done in the past and that it will be her own fault. At the same time her nature rebels, declares it's not her fault and that she cannot help, or direct her feelings. They are stronger than she is and far more wilful. How easy life would be if you could select with your reason and then press a button to make sure your feelings matched! She calms herself by lying at length in a hot bath before going to her own relatively cosy room and continuing a letter to Helen.

Your last letter, as no doubt you intended it to, disturbed me, made me ask questions. What for instance, does being 'a person in your own right' mean? Does it mean living without men? – or living alone? – or being in some meta-physical state where you are both with others but contained and independent? Are you suggesting I'm less of a person now than before I married Patrick, because if so I simply don't agree. Neither am I 'half a person tempered by another'. And what kind of action or gesture is it necessary to make for you to believe me 'a person', as you put it?

If you could come out at Christmas, Helen, as you say you might, it would be the greatest imaginable treat for me. The thought of Patrick's return on Friday will certainly shift a great weight of responsibility off me – but there's the rub – I was beginning to positively *enjoy* it, feel that my knowledge of the farm had grown vastly so that, for instance, I'm now able to choose the right moment to sell the right animal – I have the confidence, and confidence is all, or so I am learning. I'd make mistakes, I'd be bound to, but I realise now that if I was left alone with the place I could continue – as long as the set-up was the same as at the moment, Tom, or someone similar, coming part-time – and make a go of it. This realisation is very valuable to me . . .

By degrees the pad slips off her knees and the Biro from her fingers. She is asleep, exhausted on every count.

In the morning she wakes to rain driving against the windows – the chimney booms and the house quakes. She lies with her quilt pulled up beneath her chin, dreading the need to leave its cocoon-like warmth. It is a day when Tom has said he will not be out and she must tackle the feeding alone, which is not in itself alarming for she has been doing it for some weeks now. But not in this weather! She swings her feet to the floor and goes across to the window. The yard is awash, rivulets of water run down the cobbles from every quarter and the drain appears to be blocked outside the back door; the water is rising in a dangerous brown pond.

She wastes no time but gets into the clothes she has taken off last night and hurries down the stairs. As she had thought water is already flooding through the scullery and into the kitchen, as she watches it pours down the step. She pulls all the furniture to one side, gets up the carpet that is already sodden in one corner, then goes back and opens the back door – a deluge falls on her from the blocked gutter. Crouching she fumbles to free the drain of sticks, leaves and old milk bottle tops. Thankfully, she sees the water level begin to recede, but the rain doesn't let up and ever more rivers converge on the ineffectual grating. She goes back in the house shutting the door, stands dripping. She gets the mop from the dairy and mops frantically trying to divert more water from going into the kitchen. After a bit she notices it is following its own course irrespective of her endeavours and running across the room and out of the door on to the lawn at the front. She consequently abandons her mopping, rolls the carpet back further and goes to change.

Half an hour later in black sou'wester and raincoat she drives along the road with the tractor loaded with hay. The rain still comes down solidly, limiting visibility. At the gate into the field she stops, gets off to open it. Such is the force of the wind that it is almost beyond her strength to open the gate against it and she is almost knocked off her feet as it pushes her backwards. While she does this she keeps an eye both on the tractor blocking the road and on the cattle advancing ominously across the field. She rolls a heavy boulder to prevent the gate blowing to, gets back on the tractor, drives forward. As it mounts the muddy, slippery incline to the rising field above, the front wheels rear up unbalanced by the heavy load on the back, at the same time it swings sideways frighteningly. For a moment it seems as though it will swing too far and stick itself against the hedge, but by good fortune it rights itself as the incline reduces and the front wheels return to the ground.

She has no time to recover from her doubtful entrance before she is beset by the herd on every side, seizing the bales, dragging them neither cut nor spread from the link-box. She drives on regardless with the intention of going back and spreading them later, the tractor is not easily controllable and slips sideways on the steep muddy ground. The quick thaw and heavy rain have reduced the ground to a quagmire through which the cattle plough up to their hocks in mud. On reaching drier ground she stops the tractor and goes round the back to spread the remaining bales. But the bull reaches it at the same time as she does. She jumps in quickly and makes to throw out a bale but before she can he jerks it out of her hands, then for no apparent reason lowers his head under the link-box and starts lifting it sideways, forcing it down the hill. Caroline, her face white with fear, clings to the side, then with more presence of mind, kicks her foot at him, shouting. At the same time she heaves out another bale. But the bull, apparently delighted by his own strength continues to raise the link-box till the tractor rocks and it seems for a horrifying moment that it will go over, tipping the tractor with it – or break. Then suddenly, for as little reason as he began, the bull retracts, ambles round and starts to tear at a bale. Caroline takes her chance, gets back in the driving seat and drives to the far side of the field. The cattle still follow but now she has time to get out the hay ahead of them.

Rather than return past the bull in his present frame of mind she decides to go out by another gate. It is a bad decision, just before she reaches it the tractor sinks to its axle in mud, the wheels spin. Caroline persists, reverses, opens the throttle, pushes rocks under the wheels, but nothing avails – it is completely and hopelessly stuck. Getting off in despair she abandons it and makes her way back across the field opening up the bales as she goes. She gives the bull a wide skirting, counts the calves and settles for walking home along the road. Leaves whirl past her, even the big oaks bend dangerously before the wind. Water drips from her clothes, trickles down the back of her neck. Quite definitely the elements have got the upper hand and when she eventually turns into the front drive it is to see that it has become an impetuous torrent hurling stones and sand into the garden and flooding the sheep-dip.

Caroline murmurs a prayer of thanks she is not in a flood area and paddles into the house where the stream from back to front is still running.

A short while later, dressed in dry clothes, she noses the car along the front of a row of unprepossessing, cement-rendered council houses. She knots her scarf over her still wet hair and gets out. The wind remarkably has dropped, but it still rains although the sky has lightened. She hesitates at the gate of the third house, looking at its soulless post-war windows. She tries to imagine what it must be like to live in such surroundings . . . even shared with Tom . . . She puts the fanciful thought from her mind and walks up the paved path. The door is dark maroon – she presses the bell and waits. She hears a door close and footsteps approach, then the door opens and a face she recognises as Rita's peers round it. At the sight of Caroline no friendly smile takes the place of the first expression of curiosity, rather the mouth sets sullenly and the eyes look at her with distrust and suspicion. Only the door is opened fractionally wider.

Caroline smiles the best she can in the face of such a reception and explains the reason for her visit. From the inner recesses of the house come the cries of a child. Rita cuts Caroline's explanations short. 'I've left Jenny alone with the baby. Come in if you want.' She turns her back and goes off down the passage. Caroline takes off her boots inside the door and goes down the hallway tentatively in her socked feet. At the open door through which Rita has vanished she pauses. Rita is sitting on a settee opposite her changing a baby whose yells redouble at the indignity. Rita looks up, a safety-pin in her mouth. 'In here' – she gives a kind of quick indicative nod of her head and goes back to the business on her lap.

Caroline enters and sits delicately on a chair that seems free and not piled with extraneous objects like the others. She doesn't speak because it is nearly impossible to be heard above the baby's yells, and because she doesn't like to interrupt Rita's concentration. Instead she examines Rita. This is only the third time she has set eyes on her, and the first time for more than a glimpse. Rita's dark head bending over the baby, the flush of her cheeks, seem to give all the more colour to her eyes that flash at Caroline a breath-taking blue. Her rather heavy sensual lips set firmly as she grapples with the kicking legs and writhing body that threaten any moment to leave her lap for the floor. Not wishing to be found staring, Caroline forces her gaze away from Rita to the chaos that surrounds her. On the carpet at her feet is a mixture of small lumps of anthracite, toys of brilliantly coloured plastic and women's magazines. To add to the impression of a great deal going on, the carpet has a boisterous floral pattern and the curtains yet another similar one; above the stove are a series of washing lines strung from mantel to wall, supporting small bright clothes, pale pink nappies, numerous shirts and jeans. Some Caroline recognises as Tom's. Out of this wealth of colour unexpectedly appears the small elf-like face of Jenny, staring, finger in her mouth, from behind Rita's chair.

Caroline absorbs as much as her eyes will allow while the baby is rolled up in a yellowish cloth like dough and tucked into his pram, then pushed out into the passage and the door shut. Jenny rushes after her mother to the door, clearly terrified of being left on her own with Caroline which does nothing for Caroline's confidence. Most surprising of all she feels a kind of humbleness before Rita – in some strange and profound way she senses that Rita by having experienced the most normal and fundamental process on earth, that of giving birth, has a deeper knowledge of life than she has herself. As a result Caroline sits there feeling in some sense a lesser person. Even arid. Rita's round, fine face, her breasts that confidently ooze milk through her thin blouse, combine to make her a mother-figure which has both an upsetting and startlingly disconcerting effect on Caroline. Her own confidence spills from her like melting wax. In halting fashion she explains for the second time her stupidity in having stuck the tractor and that she can't shift it on her own. 'I've tried all the neighbours without much luck – it's market day, I suppose,' she finishes.

Rita gives her a sidelong glance, aligning herself with all the others who don't want to help. Caroline falters on. 'Anyway I thought perhaps Tom and I with some rollers could get it out. It's just by the road . . .'

'Tom's not back,' says Rita with some satisfaction. She equally is taking in Caroline – her hair, her skin, her old waterproof jacket and baggy jeans. Nothing much to look at when you come down to it, she thinks, but nevertheless she can see she could appeal to men. A bit of fluff, if you asked her opinion . . . She reaches out a hand and draws Jenny to her who eyes Caroline distrustfully, still sucking her finger.

'Could you give him a message?'

Oh yes, thinks Rita savagely – what will the woman ask her next? To fix up a date for her with Tom, most like. She indicates the table behind Caroline. 'There's a piece of paper there if you want to write it down – that way there'll be no misunderstanding.'

Caroline notices that Rita speaks with hardly a trace of dialect – that her voice is sharp and quick. She goes to the table, sees the paper and looks helplessly round for a Biro. Rita offers no further help so she is forced to ask for one, explain she hasn't brought her bag.

'On the dresser,' says Rita with patronising patience – she has taken up a hairbrush and is brushing the protesting Jenny's hair.

Caroline looks among the heaped shelves containing every object other than the plates it was designed for. She can still see no Biro.

'Second shelf,' says Rita tartly. 'No – next one up.'

Caroline finds it, thinks for a moment, then writes:

Tom. I've got the tractor stuck in Homer Meadow. Haven't been able to feed the cows on the top – nor the steers. Caroline Ashurst.

She looks up. 'Shall I give it to you?'

'Leave it on the table, I should.'

'Will he see it?'

'I'll tell him.'

Their eyes meet in mutual distrust, but as there is nothing further she can do, Caroline thanks her. She starts to move towards the door. 'I'm sorry to have had to worry you,' she says.

'It isn't me, it's Tom,' Rita points out acidly. At the same moment a cry comes from the passage. Rita goes out and returns with the snuffling baby in her arms.

Caroline swallows this last insult and peers at Ernest. 'It's a lovely little baby,' she says, looking at it with mixed feelings not least of which is the desire to have one herself.

Rita softens fractionally at the compliment, she sits on the settee, unbuttoning her blouse. 'He's a little devil, he is,' she coos. 'Aren't you a little devil, yes you are!' She pushes her large dark nipple into the hungrily snuffling mouth, the small hands clutch and knead the breast with rapacious passion – if Rita could have purred she would have. Caroline watches fascinated, she has never seen a small child behave in such animal fashion, never seen a mother revel in giving the breast as Rita does. Neither is she immune to the beauty of the young mother with the child at her breast, the great classic symbol stretching back beyond history, through time. She also feels slightly embarrassed and uncomfortable, as though Rita is making this display for her on purpose – a kind of triumph. No, she corrects herself, that's not fair – the poor girl has to feed the child if it's hungry. Trying a final desperate attempt to bridge the chasm between herself and Rita she says, 'I'm longing for one of my own – but you must be terribly busy with the two of them.'

'Jenny goes to play school two mornings, so that gives me a bit of time,' she says flashing blue from under dark lashes and eyeing Caroline.

'I'm sure Tom's good with them,' says Caroline hopefully.

Rita's mouth hardens. The baby loses the nipple, lunges with frantic rage, its face crumpling as it claws at air. Rita shifts the nipple back just in time to avert the inevitable noise. 'He didn't do much for Jenny when she was a baby, but they get on really well now. She hangs round him all the time when he's home.' She looks up, her eyes hostile again. 'You won't expect him out your place tonight?'

'No,' Caroline stammers, 'I mean . . . as soon as he can manage.'

'It won't be tonight,' says Rita, leaving no doubt in Caroline's mind that it is so, 'I didn't want you to expect him tonight.'

After this oracular prediction there is a decided lull in the conversation.

'I ought to be getting back.' Caroline glances at the door longingly, but it seems impolite to leave until Ernest has completed his meal, at least the first side. She prepares for the moment by buttoning her jacket. 'It's pouring with rain,' she says by way of explaining her actions. She gets up off the arm of the chair. Rita eases her nipple out of the baby's mouth.

'I hope he's satisfied,' says Caroline, looking at the bloated cheeks with some distaste.

Rita looks at her curiously, full of suspicion. ''Course he is.' She sees Caroline's eyes stray back to the note on the table. 'I'll tell him,' she says.

Outside the rain has let up. Caroline gets in the car and sits for a moment staring through the windscreen. Rita has set loose a turmoil of feelings in her, one of which is antagonism. Caroline wants the tractor out and she needs Tom to get it out – she's pretty sure Rita won't give him her note till tomorrow morning, if then, so there's only one thing for it and that's to go in search of him herself. Without more ado she sets off as though going home but as soon as she is out of sight of Rita's windows she turns sharp right for the Saw Mills.

Fifteen minutes later she drives in through the big double gates and parks beside one of numerous heaps of neatly sawn planks. She gets out looking at the dark green corrugated building before her, stretching long and low and appearing conclusively shut. She goes to the office, finds it locked. In frustration she turns away to search the outhouses, in one of which she finally detects a light. As she nears it she hears a rhythmic sound from inside; she tentatively pushes wider the corrugated door, already ajar. In front of her is the solid back of a man in cap and apron working away at planing a plank with long sweeping movements. She stands arrested by the sweet smell of sawdust, the solitariness of the worker – his total absorption in his task. It calms her agitation. To attract his attention so as not to startle him she coughs then steps inside, approaching slowly between the heavy benches. The tools are in neat heaps or hooked up in their places on the wall – everything signifies the methodical orderliness of a craftsman of the first order. The carpenter hears her, and straightens up.

'Good morning, ma'am.' He touches his cap.

Caroline returns the greeting equally politely. 'How beautifully you keep your workshop,' she adds, looking round still further. The joiner beams. His workshop, his tools, are his joy, his love, his life out of which he creates objects so finely wrought as to outlast him by centuries, God willing. The fact that he has only just met Caroline worries him not at all, that she admires his work is all that matters and this is exactly what she proceeds to do, moving from new made door to window to table, examining each object with delight and enthusiasm. For a few minutes the pressures of Greytor lift from her shoulders and all is forgotten except what she sees, the thick heavy wood that not only complies to the old man's will but seems the finer for it. Presently the thought of the hungry animals comes back to her and she turns to the joiner and asks if he knows where she might find Tom Pritchard. He takes off his cap, scratches the back of his neck, tells her Tom is working for the Forestry people today and that he should be down in Water Woods. Caroline frowns, she doesn't know their exact whereabouts but the joiner walks to the door with her, gives her full and detailed instructions which she memorises to the best of her ability.

He stands watching as she walks away to her car. What a nice young woman, not many of that kind around today who know a good bit of workmanship when they see it. He settles his cap back on his head, closes the door and resumes his planing with even greater enthusiasm. Caroline is to him like the morning star that continues to shine long after the rest have faded into the grey dawn sky.

The deluge of rain in the morning has let up by the afternoon, a watery sun slants into a clearing in the trees. Tom pulls his orange helmet down over his ears, adjusts the shield and picks up the chain saw. Things down at the Mills haven't been going too well recently, a lot of them have been put on a three-day week, including Tom, so he has had to seek work elsewhere. He hasn't said anything to Caroline because although he's been out once or twice in the week, he doesn't want her to ask him to do more days permanently at Greytor – the pay doesn't compare and he finds the feeding routine boring. Let her manage and him drop out there when it suits him, on the way home, for a cup of tea – make sure she's alright and not got herself in trouble. Well that was the agreement, wasn't it? He'd go out there when he could.

A shout of timber and crash of a tall tree going down, makes Tom jerk on the string starter and advance purposefully on a tall spruce towering about forty feet up into the damp grey sky. With confidence and skill he saws a wedge from the foot of the trunk in the direction he wants it to fall, then stands back to look at it. Yes, it should fall neat as they come down between the two trees ahead. He goes round the other side and lays his saw at a forty-five degree angle into the tree. The wood resounds to the high-pitched deafening noise. The tree sways and tilts in the direction Tom had hoped, he springs back, waits. No, it hasn't gone. Cautiously he approaches, reinserts his saw. This time, within a few seconds, the tree with a rending crash of its few remaining fibres plunges through its standing friends and lies prostrate on a bed of its own needles. Tom tilts back his shield, examines his saw and goes forward to look at the stump. He doesn't bother to try and count the rings but there are a good few there – a pretty tree. He looks with satisfaction at its long tapering body, goes forward to prune off the green-needle branches at the top.

He has all but completed his task when he catches sight of something unusual moving along the path through the trees on his right. He straightens up. Is he seeing things? No, it is her – it's the Ashurst woman come after him down in the woods. He takes his helmet off to hear better, glances round anxiously. Shit, he thinks, what if someone sees her with him – it'll be all up with Rita, someone'll tell her for certain.

So when Caroline, hot from walking for she has had to leave the car some way back, approaches glowing with the sort of blonde beauty that would make most men's hearts quicken, she receives from Tom a gaze full of dark menace and hostility. She is so taken aback, that she becomes quite tongue-tied and stammers self-consciously in trying to explain her very simple reason for being there. She has got the tractor stuck and the animals are unfed.

'How did you know I was down here?' Tom positively glares.

Caroline now begins to realise her error in having been to Rita. She becomes even more confused. 'I . . . I went down to . . . to ask Rita,' she admits in shame. Of course she shouldn't have, Tom's eyes tell her, but at the time she hadn't thought . . . she'd only thought about not being able to get hay to the rest of the stock . . .

'You never been down there?' Tom looks at her as though she's done a murder.

'Yes I have. I had to get hold of you.'

Tom stares at the silly bitch standing there, her wet jeans clinging to her legs, pushing back a long strand of straw hair self-consciously, and gradually his heart melts. Perhaps it is the whiff of cocoa-butter reminding him of ice-cream that now blows his way. He picks up his chain-saw and starts to walk down towards the forestry pick-up, saying as he goes, 'You get on back and I'll call in soon as I've finished here.'

'Thanks' – but she still hangs around. Tom despairs, anyone could come at any moment. He climbs in the pick-up, shuts the door and winds up the window. If that's not final what else is? He takes out his thermos and sandwiches packed for him early that morning by Rita and starts to eat.

Caroline looks at the pick-up uncertainly. Does it mean

he's coming now? Has she conveyed to him fully the seriousness of her predicament, that the unfed cattle on the top are wandering up and down the hedge ceaselessly, bellowing continuously, and the young bull, normally quite quiet, is eyeing up the gate? This final thought gives her courage. She picks her way down through the dead stumps and taps on the closed window. Tom, his mouth open to receive a bite of fruit cake, turns glowering eyes on her. He waits for her to go but she doesn't. Worried she may shout and attract attention he unwinds the window a crack. Caroline, uncertain whether to speak through crack or window, puts her fingers through in hope it will prevent it being shut.

'If you come to the house I'll show you where it is. Will you be long?'

'I got to eat my dinner,' says Tom belligerently, biting his cake in half.

Caroline nods, removes her fingers and goes. As she is getting in the car, Martin Weller, whom she doesn't know and has never seen before but who knows her, emerges in his usual fashion from the dark forest. As she starts the engine and reverses down the track, he grins and thwacks his axe into the stump beside him. Tom's got it coming to him.

Helen sits at her desk during the mid-morning break munching a health-giving apple and reading a letter from Caroline with some alarm:

' . . . I should have been depressed at my painful inadequacy when confronted by anything going wrong, but all I could feel was a sort of ecstasy, a profound joy that buoyed me up like a butterfly crossing an ocean. Do you understand me?'

Helen does and doesn't. She reads on.

'I don't know why I keep a diary, it doesn't seem to me that if you do more than describe the facts as they happen everyday, that it can remain strictly honest. *Are* people ever honest when they write them? Virginia Woolf, Elizabeth

Webb, Marie Bashkirtseff? It must be impossible if you know they will be read by tens of million eyes when even I find it impossible to write down my true feelings which almost certainly will not be read except . . . except by . . .'

Helen spits out a pip but otherwise eats the core, she frowns as she reads and lays the page down to think. What is Caroline up to? What *is* all this talk about secret feelings suddenly pouring forth? Caroline who has always before been disarmingly open and honest as though there is no thought or feeling she would not eagerly share in the certainty that all experience is beneficial if seen in the right way. So why all of a sudden this dissertation on the inevitability of secrecy?

'. . . Patrick is really truly coming home at the end of this week so I shall move out of here into our bedroom . . .'

Helen can hardly continue reading, so much unsaid is packed between the lines. The suffering, the interior conflict comes through to Helen with unbearable force. She notices the page she holds is not quite steady, she is afraid she'll cry and yet crying does not begin to convey what this controlled page from Caroline makes her feel.

Helen folds it, puts it back in its envelope in her handbag. Pulls herself together. No one else at present is in her room but at any moment now her secretary will return, sit with fingers poised above the typewriter keys for the two articles Helen is about to dictate; one for the arguments in favour of starting a campaign to support the Greenham Common women by a rota of others to relieve them on a regular basis; the other on the need for a bigger Government grant to enable water supplies to be repiped to workers' houses on the edge of the Quantocks, many of which still retain the old lead pipes. She adjusts her reading glasses, opens her file, looks at her watch. What is Wendy doing?

Wendy is in the canteen telling a lengthy and sad story about the bus she always catches having been rerouted, she now has to walk three hundred yards to catch another every morning and evening. Helen waits impatiently, studying the anti-nuclear posters on the wall before her, regarding the huge familiar mushroom of Hiroshima, and wondering if her own life, indeed any life, is worth living and what she should write back to Caroline? Is not the greatest pain in life, the one most impossible to alleviate, watching those you love suffer – and suffer more often than not from things anyone close to them could have predicted and advised against? Why, Helen wonders, staring down from her window on to the stream of slow-moving traffic beneath, does life have to be so destructive of all that is most tender and passionate? Is it concerned only in selecting against the vulnerable in favour of that which is shell-like in its resilience? Instinctively she feels she should go and see Caroline, but she can't do that with Patrick returning, it would only exacerbate the situation. Perhaps she should drive over on Christmas Day – just for a few hours.

Caroline is sawing wood when Tom drives down the front yard in his van. It is late afternoon and as the days are at their shortest, dark falls early. She picks up an armful and walks ahead of him into the house. In the kitchen he opens the lid of the stove, stands warming his fingers over the plate. The weather has taken a sudden change as only English weather can do; the weathercock has gone round, the wind is coming from the north and the sky is clear.

'Snow's forecast,' Tom comments.

'Thank heavens you've come,' Caroline says with feeling. Tom immediately looks offended.

'Haven't I been doing it often enough lately?' She detects his surly tone, her heart sinks. She makes him tea, hands him a cup with saucer as she has learnt to do, amazed and relieved at the placatory effect it seems to have.

'What about this tractor, then' – he looks full at her.

'Will we be able to get it out tonight?' She looks at him anxiously.

'I don't know till I see it, do I? It's nearly dark.'

They both look out of the window at the dark line of the hill against the clear sky. Caroline sits down and pulls on her boots, still soaking from the morning.

'I took some hay up to the others in the car. Four bales.' Tom nods.

'We'd best get out there right away while us can still see,' he says, 'else it might get froze in for the winter.' He looks down on Caroline's alarmed face with amusement. Smiles. She returns his smile, she feels as though she could smile forever if only Tom is there and in a good temper. He closes the lid of the stove, looks at her small heap of logs.

'What's that?' he nods at it.

'Wood – I just sawed it.'

'I can see that.' His humour is wry.

'I'm right out.'

They move towards the back door.

'Remind me after an' I'll cut a bit up with the chainsaw.'

Ten minutes later he squats in the mud shoving rocks under the tractor wheels. Caroline stands holding a further rock which she hands him. It is almost dark; the clear sky that stretches to their left with a fiery orange tint is intruded upon by menacing violet clouds that gather behind the leafless trees.

'Shine the torch,' orders Tom who, undeterred by the mud, has almost disappeared beneath the tractor. Caroline does so. He re-emerges.

'Let's try that then.' He wipes his hands on a rag from the tool box, gets on the tractor, turns the starter key. Caroline stands back to avoid the spray of mud from the spinning wheels. Skilfully Tom manoeuvres it forward until one wheel grips on the rocks beneath it. He jumps off, resets the other rock, tries again with a rocking motion. The tractor grips, reaches hard ground, moves forward out of the field. Caroline shuts the gate behind it. Looking up the hills she can just make out the dark shapes of the bullocks grazing in the field above. With a jubilant feeling of joy and relief out of all proportion to the circumstances, she follows Tom along the road until he stops the tractor, lowering the link-box for her to climb in. She sits huddled on its cold tinny floor amongst the remains of wet hay and baler-cord while they rattle back along the road. The banks on either side stretch out branches which meet above their heads to form a tunnel, the sky still shows light against the darker foreground shapes. Everywhere she looks stars are appearing.

Tom slows down. She clings to the sides as he turns into the steep drive and pulls up outside the back of Greytor.

Patrick is packing with the help of Vanessa. She has brought his large leather suitcase left by Caroline the previous day, and has it open beside his bed. Patrick who is perfectly capable of doing it on his own, sits complacently on the bed fully dressed and gives her orders. To keep her at it longer, thereby keeping her near him longer, he becomes excessively dictatorial, fussing about the placing of each object, the wrapping of some. And as the ward is almost empty due to no one wanting operations just before Christmas if avoidable, and the nurses all feeling more rested and in a festive mood, no one, not even the Ward Sister, complains about the inordinate length of time Vanessa is taking to pack nice Mr Ashurst's bag. For Patrick has become a great favourite with the nurses. When Caroline comes to visit they watch her pass with curiosity and, in some cases, envy. Amongst themselves, they discuss whether or not she is right for him and are divided in their opinions, but by and large Caroline comes in for as much criticism in the hospital as she does everywhere else. It never occurs to the nurses, the younger ones at any rate, that the brightest lights have the darkest shadows. And it is Patrick's shadow Caroline has to deal with. More – live with.

So as Vanessa bends over the suitcase, her dark hair curling wispily round the nape of her neck, Patrick gazes at her with longing and desire. His better self is so much more agreeable than his other self, why can it not always predominate? But he knows that when he gets home Caroline will look at him with puzzled eyes that demand he shall be more than he is or feels capable of becoming. And as a result he will become bad-tempered and aggressive and she will withdraw, go about rather quietly, slip upstairs to her bedroom . . . And yet there are the other times, the times when they hold hands for no good reason and walk across the fields together, both partaking of a deep and uncommunicable satisfaction, a joy in each other's presence, the capacity for enjoyment all the greater because the other is sharing it. But still there is that gnawing fear, a fear that he does not fully satisfy Caroline and she is looking for something else. But she has chosen hasn't she, chosen him — for no other reason than that she wanted him? He feels uncertain and only Vanessa's glowing face, as she looks up at him to ask if he had more than one hot-water-bottle cover, gives him comfort. For the hundredth time he imagines the joy of being inside Vanessa, of clutching her to him like a soft, soft doll. He imagines her big dilated pupils looking at him afterwards, drowsily satisfied. With discomfort he feels himself growing big with desire and thinks despairingly of the unpredictability of sex with Caroline — she is never the same twice. It seems to him that he is always the same but she is sometimes responsive and at other times recoils into herself like a sea anemone, rolls away, lies as far apart from him in feeling as if she inhabited another planet. Yet the times when he *does* reach her . . .

Vanessa is shutting the lid. He realises with alarm that their last minutes together are near. For Vanessa is off for the next three days and on the Friday he goes home. On Saturday when she comes in again, someone else will be in his bed receiving gentle solicitous attentions from her small hands. He pulls out his notebook, writes down his name and address on one sheet, tears it out and hands it to her, takes down hers in exchange. Yet all the while he knows he will never see her again. Why should he unless he runs into her in a supermarket sometime in the unforeseen future? Vanessa pushes his address into the pocket of her apron, it will be something to show the others. They shake hands formally, she bends forward and with a giggle gives him a little kiss on the cheek, having made sure the Ward Sister is not about. Patrick returns it, tries for her lips, but she pulls away, walks out of the Ward, and out of his life for ever. At the doorway she turns and waves. Patrick lies back on his pillow one knee up and indulges in a deep nostalgic fantasy in which he and Vanessa take a cottage in Cornwall for three weeks. Why don't they? No one exactly knows. Is it because at the back of his mind he thinks if he does he'll lose Caroline? Isn't it his very faithfulness to her, his new-found dependence, that spins an invisible web round her harder to escape than any other?

Six o'clock comes and goes. Rita pulls Tom's 'tea' out of the oven and slings it across the table. If he's late he can eat it cold and serve him right. She sits at the table, chin in hand, looking round savagely to see what else of Tom's she can wreck to annoy but not enrage him, for she is rather afraid of Tom enraged. Also she is too thrifty to break anything he's likely to go and waste money on replacing. It's not easy to decide exactly how to vent her feelings and it takes some time. Jenny is kneeling at the table beside her, painting. Ernest has been removed from pram to cot for the night.

All at once her eyes alight on just the thing, his Ford Escort instruction book, with which he is rebuilding his rally car, but she won't tear it up – that would really cause trouble. No, she'll hide it. She picks it off the dresser, makes sure Jenny's not looking and shoves it as far back as it'll go under the settee. When it is found she can say it got kicked there. So impotent is a woman bound to the house by children in the face of her man's 'fancying another', that she will sink to the most futile tricks of spite to retaliate. In this case Rita was typical rather than the exception. If she could have hit and slapped and punched Tom she would have, but she couldn't – because Tom would have hit her back much harder. Her frustration boils and foams inside her with no outlet other than the petty deed just performed. But relieved by having accomplished *some* act of vengeance, Rita feels able to turn her energies to coaxing Jenny towards bed. To do this she has first to make a painting of Tom at the Saw Mills, then a picture of him coming home in his car. After this Jenny still demands more but Rita's patience expires, she picks her up and carries her upstairs forcefully. Fifteen minutes later Jenny peacefully sleeps and Rita tiptoes down the stairs. She looks at the clock again, 6.48 – if Tom isn't here by 7.15 she's going and that's an end to it. In the act of drawing the curtain she looks with longing eyes at the lighted windows of the pub two hundred yards down the road. Why not go down there? Let Tom come back to an empty house, that'd do him good, give him a shock. She could pop back every fifteen minutes or so, make sure the children were alright. With a guilty glance up the stairs, she combs her hair in front of the mirror on the dresser, picks up her best jacket and lets herself stealthily out of the front door. Seconds later she is hurrying up the road to The Fox. She pushes open the door to the public bar and lets herself in to the cosy warmth and conviviality.

Several people greet her, including Sharon who serves behind the bar most evenings. A group of Tom's acquaintances are playing darts down one end and a fire burns in the corner. Rita goes straight to the bar and orders herself a half-pint of brown ale. Glass in hand she feels able to look round properly, while at the same time talking to Sharon. Sharon admires the way Rita has got her hair. Rita explains she wanted a change, she's getting so dull from staying in with the kids. Sharon asks after them, assumes Tom is at home with them. Rita doesn't disillusion her, she doesn't want it to go round the village she's the kind to leave 'hers' on their own. Tom won't come in here, that's one thing she's certain of – he never does, he can't abide pubs.

Shortly Sharon has to leave her to serve a party of strangers who've just come in, and Rita turns her gaze on the darts foursome. No sooner has she done so than Martin Weller, who is watching rather than taking part, moves her way.

'Hello, Rita.'

'Hello, Martin.'

'How's things, then – how's the kiddies?'

'Fine. How's Doreen?'

Martin Weller moves in closer, orders himself a drink and another one for her. He leans closer to her, beery, tousled but not unattractive with his mop of curly hair and air of confidence. 'To tell the truth I think we're going our separate ways.'

'You're never?' Rita expresses more shock than she actually feels for it has long been rumoured that Doreen is having it on the side with Jimmy Bayes.

Martin shakes his head, looks into his glass. 'I think we are.'

Time passes. Rita thinks guiltily of the children, then Sally Bowden says she's going back past Tom and Rita's so she'll put her head in and if she hears anything she'll come back for Rita. Rita thanks her joyfully, she is on her third glass and having a good time with Martin who is chatting her up the best he knows how – and that's good enough for most. Sharon at the bar watches Rita and Martin but keeps her own counsel – for the present. Finally, at the time he judges ripe, Martin brings out his ace of trumps.

'Know who I saw down Water Woods today?'

'No,' says Rita, all innocence.

'The Ashurst woman.'

'Oh,' says Rita surprised for she hasn't grasped the significance, imagining Tom to have been in the Saw Mills.

Martin sees with disappointment his trump has been thrown away, tries to salvage it by over-trumping. 'Didn't you know Tom was working out with the Forestry today?'

'No,' Rita stares at him, comprehension dawning. 'When was that?' she asks sharply.

'About half past three.'

'She was down worrying me at three. She'd got her tractor stuck.'

'Oh,' says Martin Weller, but in a tone that makes clear he doesn't believe the excuse. Rita hardly hears him, she's frankly puzzled.

'How would she know to find him in there?'.

'They say not even a thorn hedge'd keep her away from Tom' – Martin chuckles, too insensitive to see Rita has gone rather pale. She asks him to fetch her another drink but when he returns a few minutes later, she has gone. He stands there foolishly looking round the crowded bar with a drink in either hand. Eventually he drinks both alternately and has to be 'helped' out when The Fox closes at ten-fifteen.

In the light of the opened workshop doorway Tom is sawing up firewood. Between them they have carried a heap of ill-assorted lengths from the woodshed for Tom to reduce to stove-size. Caroline stands clear to avoid the flying chips, but every time he pauses she moves in and loads the logs into a barrow which she wheels away and unloads on to the benches thoughtfully built into the porch during its construction. The noise of the chainsaw precludes speech, seeming to slice through the darkness and echo off the buildings with even greater violence than in daylight.

After three or four barrow loads it cuts out. Tom straightens up, pulls the starter cord to no avail, looks inside. Empty. He looks round.

'That's it.'

Caroline nods. 'It should last me. Patrick's coming Friday – though I shan't believe it till he's here.'

She goes off across to the porch with her last barrowful. Tom puts his chainsaw in the workshop and follows. He stands lighting a cigarette, watching her unload.

'He won't be able to do much, will he?'

'Nothing at all to start with, except walk.' She continues stacking up the logs in silence. They make two shadowy figures beneath the electric light that nestles over the porch entrance, snuggled among strands of old briar rose, its light diffused and intermittent. Less than a hundred years ago it would have been a lantern giving a warmer, softer light. The first electricity had come to Greytor in 1947 in the form of a primitive generator proudly installed by Patrick's uncle. In 1964 the mains had come through and the old farm's ways had kept abreast of the times. In fact it had changed very little in the last four hundred years, a north wing at an early stage had been dug back into the hill, adjoining lean-tos had been first added then incorporated into part of the house, partitions and staircases had been added and taken down, chimneys blocked up and unblocked and more recently lofts had been turned into bedrooms. But the basic layout of farm and surrounding yards, walled garden, ash-house and buildings had clearly stood as they were for a great length of time. So as Caroline unloaded her logs and Tom watched, they were not much different outwardly to their forebears. Tom's family had been in the area no one knew how long, Caroline's could have lived in some such district in the past and moved to the outskirts of the city during the time of the Industrial Revolution – no one knew that either. All that was known was that Caroline's family had prospered and grown relatively rich over the years, whereas Tom's had continued in a peasant way of life that until the present had changed little from generation to generation. The resulting difference between Caroline and Tom's cultural background was a chasm awkward to cross, and yet in other ways they were surprisingly compatible.

Caroline in her enthusiasm allows a heavy log to roll down on her thumb and squash it. She sucks it with an exclamation of pain.

'Hurt yourself?' Tom's concern is both gentle and genuine. He takes the hand she is nursing, tilting it to the light to see the better.

'No' – indeed it was no more than a momentary pinch. She looks down on his working hand, brown, ingrained, acutely aware he has never held her hand before as he does now.

'It's alright,' she says, then on impulse, unable to prevent herself she kisses his cheek. The rough hairs that have grown on it since the morning meet her own lips with a shock of pleasure, his male outdoor smell is to Caroline like fire. The blood leaps through her veins.

'Thanks . . . Tom,' she says, drawing back.

He turns his head, their mouths meet very gently, briefly. For a moment it seems as though more *must* follow, but Tom shifts a little, draws on his cigarette. Caroline watches him, her hands clenched. She can't believe he does not want her as she wants him, but as he makes no move towards her, pride forces her to turn her back, continue with the unloading.

If truth be known Tom has forgotten time. He seldom forgets time unless something happens to throw him badly off course. On those occasions time seems to stop, and the realization that it is still ticking forward comes with a shock. Now as he switches on his car lights it glows at him from the clock face in startling fashion. He can hardly believe it, nearly nine o'clock, He drives from the yard in a roar of exhaust and without remembering to wave at Caroline who stands anxiously watching him inside the back door.

As he swings round the sharp corner at the top of the hill that takes him down to the village, his car swerves curiously, the steering pulls to the bank, becomes heavy. Tom swears, hardly believing his ill luck, mutters 'bloody thorn' and gets out. Sure enough his front left tyre is flat. With no more ado he sets about changing it, but in the dark it takes time, and time is exactly what he's short of. At almost exactly nine-thirty he pulls up outside his house, locks his car and goes up the path to the front door. He is surprised that there are not many lights on but perhaps Rita is trying to economise . . . Inside, again to his surprise, there is no one in the kitchen and it is in a state of more than usual disorder. He pulls open the door of the lower oven, looks inside, no tea, nothing. Anger mounts in him, he's been working for everyone except himself hasn't he? Sawing wood for the Ashurst woman for nothing, getting her tractor out of the gateway – that won't be for nothing, he'll see to that – working all day in the woods to bring home a pay packet for Rita to spend and she can't even leave him something to eat when he comes in. He goes to the bottom of the stairs, shouts up.

'Rita?' Silence, no answer.

Even more enraged Tom mounts the stairs, switches on the light in the passage, pushes open the door to their bedroom. But the bed is empty, it remains rumpled and unmade from the night before, and the night before, and the night before that. Rita doesn't make beds. Tom stands taking in the full impact of the empty bed, then goes along to the next door, opens it stealthily, switches on the light ready to switch it off again swiftly if he sees what he hopes.

But what he does see is a nasty shock even worse than the first, the cot is empty and the pram has been taken off its wheels which remain in the far corner. Tom swallows, his anger is rapidly vanishing to be replaced by alarm and fear. Has Rita left him and if so when will she return? That she might never return is beyond Tom's imagination. He has no doubt he can get her back, it is just a question of finding her. He slowly makes his way back down the stairs to the kitchen and cooks himself an egg while he thinks, but the harder he thinks the blanker his mind becomes. He considers Sharon. Could Rita have gone up there? He thinks it unlikely with the two kids, there wouldn't be room. Christine? No, it would get all round the village and she wouldn't want that. Finally, as he pushes the last of his badly fried egg into his mouth he hits on the answer – down her parents, but how?

No sooner has he made up his mind where she is, than he rakes the stove, puts a few sticks in it and a log hoping it'll draw up, and goes back to his car. Half an hour later he opens the gate of his in-laws' house and walks up the path. Lights, he is relieved to see, shine from the downstairs window. Rita's father opens the door, looks at him, mumbles something and stands back. Tom enters, his confidence not quite what it was before he left the smoky blue interior of his car and the comforting pop of Radio 2.

'They're in the sitting-room', says Rita's father.

Tom opens the door, suddenly conscious that he is still in his working clothes and has not changed into the smarter and cleaner clothes he normally wears to visit his in-laws. He stands looking down at Mrs Hunnicot, who looks at him with owl-like eyes through pale-rimmed glasses, and Rita who sits opposite on the other side of the imitation coal fire. Rita, after the first glance, looks at the glowing red and black coals and not at him. Tom sees no point in preliminaries, he never did like it down here, he doesn't want to stay and the sooner he gets Rita out the better, so he plunges straight on.

'I came to fetch Rita and the children.'

Mrs Hunnicot edges herself forward in the chintz-covered chair, settles her fluffy slippers more firmly into the deep-pile nylon carpet, and stares straight at Tom. 'I'm not at all sure Rita wants to come with you.'

Silence. Tom eyes the rows of Hunnicot relatives in frames of various sizes on the mantel shelf, lets his eyes wander to the shiny dull-gold curtains drawn across the bay window. He sees it all but doesn't take it in or make any judgement – he has been there before, sat on the chintz chairs in his best suit, in fact he was down here quite a lot when he was courting Rita, had to be. But now he continues to stand in the doorway.

'I understand from Rita,' says her mother, 'that you don't come home at nights, and that isn't fair or right is it, with a wife and two small kiddies?' She regards him severely.

'I ain't aware I ever been away a night,' says Tom with some accuracy.

Rita chips in. 'You may not a'been gone *all* night, Tom, but that don't mean you haven't been gone the half of it.'

Mrs Hunnicot takes off her glasses, polishes them. 'I don't know I'm sure,' she says, 'but if Arthur hadn't been home of an evening when Rita was a baby I'd have gone straight back to my family, but then Arthur was as fond of Rita as ever I was.'

Tom continues to stand. After some minutes when no one has said anything further and Arthur can be heard coughing in the kitchen having seen fit to make himself scarce, Tom says boldly, 'Do you want to get the kids and come back with me then Rita?'

Rita looks up at him coldly. 'I think they've been moved about enough for one night, don't you? I planned on staying down here for a bit with my parents till you mend your ways. Then if you want you can come down here and fetch me and them home.'

Tom nods, he backs out of the room and walks back down the passage. As he goes he hears Mrs Hunnicot say, 'Well, I never, not so much as a goodnight.'

Outside in the porch he looks at the stars and moon that shine over his head and remembers they have also shone at Greytor. Bugger the Ashurst woman, now look where she's landed him. But his outer anger with her is indicative of other emotions she rouses in him at a deeper level. He walks down the path between the miniature cypresses and lets himself out of the ornate wrought-iron gate that Mr Hunnicot has made himself.

Rita sits holding out her hands to the falsely glowing coals and listening with inward longing as his car engine recedes and silence returns to the street. She hopes and prays Tom will come back for her tomorrow.

Patrick sits with the farm herd book and diary open on his lap, by a blazing fire in the sitting-room. He feels cross, edgy and surprisingly disorientated, not helped by the fact that Greytor has obviously ticked along quite satisfactorily during his absence. He feels slightly superfluous in his own home and not particularly well – in fact not nearly as well as he thought he would. It's alright when he sits, but when he stands his legs feel weak, he finds it quite difficult to keep his balance and is very conscious of the distance between his head and the floor. In fact his head feels only balanced on his body instead of being a part of it. Also he is missing Vanessa. Caroline is doing her best but it is the attitude. Vanessa seemed to enjoy attending to him, Caroline does it rather like a martyr. The door opens behind him, he knows that she is there but doesn't turn round. Instead he says before she has hardly entered, 'I can't make head or tail of these calvings. You've got one cow written down as giving birth six months after the previous calf.'

Caroline flushes, bends over beside him looking at the page. She points. 'You're looking at the wrong line – that goes there. This one . . . here.'

'You mean you've marked it up in the wrong place? Couldn't you have done a bit better? If I don't get the calving dates right I stand to lose a thousand pounds or more in subsidy.'

Caroline pushes her hair back nervously, she must stay calm, keep her temper – everyone has told her it will be difficult when he first gets back, and it is. Unbelievably so.

'I'll go through them with you later, it's just . . .'

But Patrick interrupts impatiently, the male desire to dominate, establish himself, strong. 'Look, this is important.'

Caroline says in a doggedly controlled voice. 'Tom's waiting for me to help with the sheep.'

'The sheep?' Patrick sounds suitably incredulous.

'He said you'd talked about it. He said you told him to go through their feet because a lot of the ewes are lame.'

'Why doesn't he use the foot bath?'.

Caroline is gradually moving behind him towards the door.

'I don't know – I supposed you'd told him not to' – for since his return Tom has been coming into the kitchen most days for lengthy discussions with Patrick as to what he should or should not do.

She now waits, her offence conveyed by her silence. As Patrick seems unforthcoming she eases her way out by saying, 'Well, I'll go and help him . . . and we can go through the calvings when I get back.'

But Patrick hasn't finished. 'Listen to this then,' he says quickly before she can get the door shut, '"W. R. Stevens – repair to hedge-trimmer – one hundred pounds." You've run up a bill for a hundred pounds on a piece of machinery that isn't worth fifty.' He cranes his neck round to look at her. 'Who do you think is going to pay?'

Caroline is finally insulted. She turns on him in defiance, comes back. 'What else was I to do? It's not my fault you have such useless machinery.'

Patrick smiles in despair, his gesture enrages and belittles her.

'We managed, didn't we? The suckled calves got really good prices, better than last year. We kept everything going – nothing died.' Emotion does not help her articulacy.

'We?' Patrick looks at her superciliously.

'Me, then,' Caroline shouts, going out and slamming the door.

Patrick sits gripping the arms of his chair till his knuckles turn white. He can't bear rows and yet he engenders them. He feels slightly sick. And jealous. Because though he has no possible reason for suspicion, there is a kind of unity of purpose, a sharing of the farm between Tom and Caroline that he finds hard to take. Also . . . but he checks himself, for that is ridiculous. It is simply his own past feelings for Vanessa that makes him suspect Caroline might feel the same for Tom. He quickly puts such a thought from his mind for, he tells himself, with some accuracy, Vanessa is altogether different to Tom . . . He doesn't qualify this conjecture, instead he gets up awkwardly, crosses to the window seat and looks out. Caroline, well wrapped up for a fine sleety snow is falling, makes her way across the garden to the gate. In the leaden grey light the buildings look particularly oppressive and dark. She lets herself through the gate, crosses the yard and halts in the workshop doorway. In a few seconds Tom emerges, says something to her, turns up his collar and they set off up the drive together, walking well apart, quite unaware they are watched.

Patrick continues to sit staring out, desperately in need of the three things that can give him security: territory, authority, and the undisputed possession of the woman he has chosen. Yet he is no fool and as he sits watching the ground whiten, he argues with himself to be more sensitive, more reasonable. Has he any right to expect Caroline to be more ideal, less human than himself.

The noise of the barley mill disturbs the silence of the cold, dark December afternoon. Caroline stands beneath it holding a sack to catch the crushed barley as it trickles through the shoot from the half-floor above. Bent forward in her hooded jacket in the pool of electric light she resembles nothing so much as some strange moorland gnome. As the bag fills she replaces it with another and, swinging the first over her shoulder, struggles out from beneath the overhead floor. The barn resounds to the engine's chug cancelling out all else. She reaches into another bag standing by the door, adds a handful of mineral the colour of paprika, mixes it in thoroughly then heaves it into the back of the tractor along with a bale of hay. Leaving the mill running she drives to an adjoining field, the chill numbing her fingers and toes. The sheep clamour round; she climbs down and, pushing her way through them, grasps the bag before they upset it. Half carrying and half dragging it to their troughs she tips some in each – they barge and butt in their eagerness to get at it, nearly knocking her off her feet. That done she takes up the bale and shakes it out in the two hayracks. As she does so Tom appears in the gateway, shoulders hunched, collar turned up, his hands deep in his pockets. His dejected stance at once alarms Caroline, and his exaggerated slouch as he comes towards her confirms her fears – he is undoubtedly in ill humour.

Since the evening of the wood-sawing Caroline has lived more than ever in two worlds, one of dream and the other of fact. Each day she has hoped Tom will call, and as each day has passed without his coming her disappointment has grown. When at last he came she hoped for some sign, even the smallest indication to show they were on more intimate terms than before, but Tom has relentlessly kept his distance, taking instructions from Patrick and working alone as far as possible.

She found herself filled with longings that she recognised as childish but could do nothing to dissipate. During the days she struggled with her tasks alone and in appalling weather conditions, only returning to the house to cook the meals; each night she stayed up a little later than Patrick to write her journal, her letters, and struggle with a poem she was endeavouring to bring to fruition. Her relations with Patrick since his return had been difficult. For the first time in the period they had known each other she had stood back from him, seen him as a stranger – more, seen him as a person she could live without. At the same time she had strong feelings of guilt and duty. Patrick was ill, he needed her, depended on her, there was no-one else, she must do it. Yes, well she would, but could she, would she, learn to love Patrick as she had before? As a result her longing for Tom was both fantasy and escape as well as being, for her, agonisingly real. At nights when she lay in the double bed beside Patrick and he stretched his hand out beneath the covers to touch her, she lay still, gave no sign of response. Patrick, equally sensitive and touchy in his own way, would withdraw his fingers and lie silent in the darkness. After a few such incidents he stopped touching her and she perversely asked him why.

'You don't want me to – I can feel,' he replied.

'I do' – but her tone had carried no conviction. So the nights passed for both of them in tense isolation until out of sheer exhaustion they fell asleep and woke on their separate sides the next morning.

So now as Caroline goes over to Tom she takes with her a sense of loss, a lack of identity – her dream world, centred on him, prevents her from being herself or relating fully to anyone else, very much like a creature long tethered that though the string is cut cannot comprehend its freedom.

'I didn't think you'd be out today,' she says in as unemotive a voice as she can muster, heedless of the rain which suddenly turns to hail and lashes her face viciously.

'You won't be seeing me much more.' By comparison to his words the sting of the hail is nothing. She watches it patter and drum on the roofs of the nearby buildings.

'Tom – why?'

'I've had enough.'

In the silence that follows they both acknowledge the superiority of the elements over their personal lives.

'Well don't let's stand out here,' Caroline says, 'Let's go in the barn.'

She walks ahead and Tom follows. In the sombre interior of the Great Barn they stand side by side, shoulders hunched, heads hanging – everything about their aspect expressing the dejection to which the numbing cold has reduced them. Both gaze outwards, watching the ground becoming covered with small white balls.

'Poor sheep,' says Caroline feelingly, then goes on in the hopes of a response from Tom, 'the mill jammed earlier, I sorted it out.'

Tom nods disinterestedly. Caroline looks at him curiously, something must have happened for him to be this bad. 'What's the matter?'

'What do you think?'

'I don't know.'

Tom glances at her contemptuously as though for her not to know is a sort of crime, and indeed it is for persons like Tom who are a great deal more aware of things unsaid than the more sophisticated people Caroline has been used to moving amongst.

'Coming out this place,' he says.

'But you always have.' She feels as though she has been hit in the face. 'I thought you liked it.'

Tom speaks as brutally as his turmoil of incomprehensible feelings suggest he should. 'I did once, but I don't any longer.'

The silence that follows is interrupted by a wild and violent gust of wind that bursts open the double doors on the side of the barn behind them. It lifts a polythene bag off the ground which bowls over and wraps itself round Tom's legs. He picks it up, folds it with the deliberate care and precision normal to him and places it under a stone on the storage bin. He then closes the offending doors, cleaning the earth out of the vertical bolt hole so they shall hold better. Caroline watches and waits till he comes back.

'So you want to stop coming out here?' she ventures.

'It's gone on too long, hasn't it? He said three weeks and it's gone three months.'

'He didn't know. It wasn't his fault – it wasn't anyone's fault' – she defends herself in defending Patrick, for though Tom is criticising Patrick she correctly reads it as herself.

She sighs. 'Shall I tell him you've had enough?' But Tom has climbed up to the mill, is examining the belts and hopper, his back to her.

'Tell him what you like.'

'I think you should tell him.' They have arrived at an impasse so she tries a new line. 'Apparently I filled in the herd book wrong.'

'That'll give him something to do then, won't it? Sorting it out.'

She tries desperately to joke, raise this intense and terrible conversation on to another plane. 'He's not very pleased.'

'I don't blame him' – Tom doesn't really care who he attacks as long as he attacks, and the more viciously the better. Caroline's depression mounts, there seems no point in her saying anything for everything she says will be chopped off abruptly like a child cutting off heads of bracken with a stick, so she remains silent while Tom continues to fiddle with the mill – it as though his interest, his action belies all he has just said. When at last he jumps down and returns to the doorway, turns up his collar again as though to go, she says, 'Quite a lot of the sheep are lame.'

'They never oughter have feet like they got.'

'But what could we have done to prevent it?' She feels deeply the injustice of his remark. She, after all, is not an expert shepherd and doesn't pretend to be.

'Put 'em through the bath a month back.'

'But you didn't say.'

'I'm not the manager round this place,' Tom's pent-up jealousy and resentment build one on top of the other like thunder clouds. Caroline's face is tragic at his discontent; that she'll take so much from him is a measure of the amount she cares for him. It begins to dawn on her that something is very deeply wrong, something still unspoken. She has a sudden moment of insight.

'Is Rita alright?'

'She doesn't like me coming out here.'

'But that's ridiculous. Surely you've told her?'

' 'Course I told her.'

Caroline absorbs the information with concern and alarm.

'What will you do?'

'I'll have to stop coming out here.'

She says nothing but in a sense things have taken a slight upward lift. She knows now the trouble, knows that the anger Tom vents on her is in part frustration, his inability to deal with Rita. More alarming is the implication that she has caused the disruption, for though she has done nothing – well nothing that could constitute anything – hasn't she been wanting to? And will not her wanting have got over the psychic grapevine to Rita? Or even more probably, people will have been gossiping. She has been unwise and foolhardy, she recognises that, but the belief that Tom means to leave lessens so that she can say with more asperity. 'I'll have to find someone else, then.'

As Tom doesn't reply she pushes her advantage. 'Do you know anyone?'

But Tom is too quick to allow her the upper hand for

long. 'That's part of the trouble – you don't know anyone round here. You're close, you are.' He comes back at her.

'Close?' She is insulted and uncertain, quite knocked off her balance.

'You keep to yourself – don't mix in.' Metaphorically Tom has rolled his sleeves up, is getting down to business.

'That's completely untrue . . . and unfair.'

He sees she is upset and hurt, that he has scored irrevocably.

She looks up at him, 'So I won't see you any more?'

From his hard-won position of superiority Tom starts to relent. 'I'll go on coming out when I can, but I can't keep on like I've been doing.' He looks with satisfaction at her sad face; almost in spite of himself he stretches out his hand, draws her to him, presses his mouth into her damp silky hair that glistens with moisture. She turns her face up to his but Tom is carried away, impelled by every sort of emotion as well as desire. He is holding in his arms a woman he thought never to attain, on top of which she is Patrick Ashurst's woman, making Tom in his own mind Patrick's equal. Added to this Caroline's physical response suggests a passion he hasn't met before – sex, yes, but not this. So his hands almost before their lips have met start to draw her body in to his. Unexpectedly the limp, compliant form suddenly stiffens and she pulls away, turns her face from him. Equally to his surprise she pushes his hands off her, frees herself, steps a few paces from him, stands in silence quivering, her back to him. Tom moves to recover her having been taken off his guard by the sudden change in her and regretting the ease with which he has relinquished his hold. But when he touches her and she turns to face him, something in her expression, her eyes, checks him. She backs away, presses her back to the heap of stakes waiting to go in the creosote bath. They wait, facing each other. Finally she says.

'Is that all you want?'

Tom's gesture has a pathetic honesty about it, a helplessness. 'What else is there?' he asks, but as he says it he knows it's not enough. He knows his moment has come and gone, that had he kept hold of her in the first place things would have turned out very differently. But he didn't and they haven't, and now the distance between them is growing with every moment. Tom is as frustrated, as bitter, as disappointed as Caroline. Had he been Samson he would have pulled the temple columns towards him, brought it down on his and her heads, smashing everything, killing them both. As it is he takes the only other alternative, leaves her without a word, goes out of the darkening doorway into the oncoming night.

Caroline stays in the barn as though crucified on the stakes she leans against. Her anguish is extreme – she both knows and refuses to accept that Tom has gone. Only when she hears the sound of his car start up in the lane does she take in exactly what has happened, what her own idealistic nature has done. Dramatically, as though an actress but yet not acting, she allows herself to sink on the barn floor, moaning and rocking, her hands over her face, beating her forehead on the hard cold metal of the feedbin. Had anyone entered the barn at this moment the scene could not have been stranger, this woman wailing and rocking herself in the half-dark like some tragic figure from outside time; what might have been most surprising was the contemporariness of her dress.

Tom doesn't stop outside his home, he drives right past. In fact he doesn't stop till he's left the moor behind and is outside the door of his dreaded in-laws' house. They haven't actually been dreaded till just recently, but since Rita has run off down there, ganging up with them against him, they have become more dreadful. He retraces his steps up the paving that he last trod that night five days ago, and knocks on the door. He's having Rita back or they'll know what for. He has let one prize slither through his fingers and common sense tells him not to lose another; he is also fully aware of the finality of what happened this afternoon. The whole thing had been tempting fate, he'd been a fool, now he was seeing reason, or if not reason, Rita. He knocks on the door with the brass knocker and presses the bell. There is a total silence from within. Tom curses, kicks the iron doormat, raises his fists – he would like to break the door down . . . At this moment it opens, and Rita's mother fills the hallway. To his amazement she smiles at him in most friendly fashion, a great contrast to last time, and ushers him in.

'I'll go and call Rita,' she says, walking ahead of him. Tom following behind hopes Rita won't get so fat. There's fatness and fatness, it's not that he minds a woman on the plump side, but . . .

Rita appears from behind some other flush door. He's only ever been in three rooms in this house, the sitting-room, the bathroom and the kitchen-diner. She is looking rather strange he thinks, but by and large better than he'd remembered and he prides himself on a good memory. Her strangeness is probably accounted for by a new hairstyle; her naturally wavy hair, on her mother's insistence, has been 'shaped'. Her father now comes out of the sitting room and says 'Oh, Tom', in a relieved tone of voice. If the truth be told Rita's parents have had a bad week of it, their bungalow is much too small for Rita and two children as well as themselves, and they had begun to despair of Tom ever coming. Rita for her part has held out with admirable courage. She has ignored the hints from her parents to ring Tom and the offers to drive her 'back up there' to 'talk it over' with him. Instead she has remained adamant that if Tom wants her back he can come and get her otherwise she's not going, so her tender-hearted parents have had to endure it unwillingly. In the quiet of her bedroom at nights she has looked up to the moor with longing and dread, dread that she has miscalculated and that Tom won't come for her. And sometimes when the moon has been at its fullest she has thought herself unable to stand it and has cried herself to sleep with love and rage. So now Rita has difficulty preventing the joy that she feels expressing itself in her face as she stands looking at Tom.

Tom feels it incumbent upon him to say something, for even his mother-in-law seems to have become mute.

'I've come to take you back,' he says, finding difficulty in looking at her.

At this Rita's mouth crinkles into a wide smile of joy, as indeed do those of both her parents. Tom smiles too. The small hallway is more smiled in than for many months and only a slight shadow crosses Tom's unclouded face at the sight of Rita's dress stretched over her breasts as she reaches over the pram to pick up Ernest. It reminds him of another happening no more than an hour ago but already seeming a thing of the past. Well, just at the moment it does.

On the way home things sink back to a more normal level. A bird caught is never so tempting as the one still in the bush and Tom finds his mind wandering in spite of his good resolutions. Rita sits with Jenny on her lap, while Ernest in the pram along the back seat utters perhaps the wisest comment for he yells every moment of the way.

In bed that night, Caroline lies sleepless, afraid to move for fear of disturbing Patrick who needs his sleep to get strong – or so his mother has rung up twice to remind her. After watching clouds scurry before the moon through the gap in the curtains till one a.m., she can stand it no longer. She furtively slips out of bed and, reassured by regular breathing that Patrick is still asleep, steals out of the door and along the passage to her bedroom. She closes the door behind her in relief, switches the light full on and then the bedside light. Her tense face relaxes as she looks round the small familiar room and then climbs beneath the duvet. She opens the drawer in the table beside the bed and takes out a writing pad on which a letter is begun. Knees bent up, she crouches forward over it and drawing a jersey round her shoulders for warmth, writes: 'He was right of course, I was the fool who'd not outgrown a romantic ideal. He saw things realistically, understood the only part of each other we had to peddle was sex.'

She bites her polythene Biro splitting the end, stares at the barred blank window, the blackness beyond, murmurs to herself with a stricken expression, 'Why not, why not?' For she is suffering the unacceptable and deadly anguish of sexual loss – and more. Because in an intense and limited way she loves Tom.

A few moments later she rips the page from her pad, crumples it and throws it at the wastepaper basket. It misses and slides across the floor-boards, a complex rigid paper shape. She continues to sit staring at it for some moments, then starts again:

Dearest Helen,
No need to say I miss you. I have got Patrick back which is wonderful – though not being able to do anything is making him quite edgy and difficult to get along with. The same goes for Tom – he's very moody lately . . .

She stops, looks at the white bars across the black squares of window, seeing them and not seeing them, then goes on:

If only you were here we could laugh about it together, but on my own I do get low, even depressed at times, but isn't that part of living? And when the sun shines I rise out of it like a phoenix.

For the second time she gives up. Nothing she can write to Helen seems worth saying because she can't bring herself to tell her the truth: that she is isolated in her own bottomless misery which she cannot share or even communicate to anyone, and it is at least in part due to her obsession with Tom. She lays her pad down and buries her face in her clasped knees. Should she leave Patrick? Admit her failure, her mistake – simply go? But how can she, how can she possibly? He is still unwell, still totally dependent on her, leaving him before he is completely recovered is out of the question. It is not that she has any illusions about Tom, she assures herself, it is simply that he has shown her a part of herself she did not know existed . . . For five, ten minutes she sits staring at the blank, soulless aspect of the window. Finally she sighs, and seeming in part to shake herself out of her despair, reaches a book off the table beside her – Virginia Woolf's *A Writer's Diary* – reads to herself:

Oct. 29 1932. I will go on changing, opening my mind and my eyes, refusing to be stamped and stereotyped. The thing is to free one's self: to let it find its dimensions, not be impeded . . . October has been a bad month; but might have been worse without my philosophy.

She reads on wishing that she had a philosophy such as

Virginia Woolf apparently had to sustain her, and is soon arrested by another passage:

If I could catch the feeling, I would; the feeling of the singing of the real world, as one is driven by loneliness and silence from the habitable world; the sense that comes to me of being bound on an adventure.

The real world? Does she by that mean the unreal world? The intangible world that it is possible to sense in mystical moments? The habitable world to her must be what Caroline would describe as the real world, so even if their philosophy has a resemblance their linguistic usage of words is far, far apart so that it might have been difficult for them to understand each other. She suspects it is more the climate of concepts that has changed; people now are less metaphysical, more concrete, and she herself is no exception . . .

A cough and pad of feet sound in the passage. Caroline stiffens and in an instant has pushed her writing pad under the pillow, closed her book and slid down the bed. Patrick's head comes round the door.

'What are you doing?' His hair stands on end, his face has lost its normal angular quality owing to inactivity and stodgy hospital food, he wears a long T-shirt leaving his thin legs bare beneath it. Yet something about him impinges on the distance Caroline has felt from him ever since his return from hospital. At the same time she can't look at him properly for fear he will notice her red-rimmed eyes. She lets her hair fall forward, raises herself a little.

'I couldn't sleep – I was afraid of waking you.'

Patrick hovers uncertainly in the doorway. She looks at him anxiously, 'Are you feeling alright?'

Patrick still seems in two minds whether to join her in the narrow not-too-comfortable bed or return to his own.

'It's cold in here' – he looks at the blank blackness of the windows, the undrawn curtains. The ceiling is low, it bears down on him. He has never particularly liked this room with its north and east windows, except perhaps when the sky spreads red behind the piggeries and the sunrise strikes the church tower gold. 'Can't you come back to our bed?' His demand is direct and straightforward, like that of a child. It awakes the same kind of response in Caroline that a child might – her own indulgence, emotional self-pity, is forgotten. Life stretches ahead of her in a series of demands from others, others' expectations, hopes. She pushes back the duvet and gets out. Patrick stands to one side holding the door as she ducks under his arm and goes through, walking ahead of him down the lighted passage. I've taken the easy way out, she thinks, gone back – but then how could she have done otherwise? Oh easily, easily – she could have hardened her heart and followed her own instincts unfailingly, seen where they led, seen who she was, *is*. As she climbs back into her side of the double bed it becomes clear enough who she is – a woman whose life is played upon by others, a sort of Aeolian harp for men, a woman like 990,000,000 others but in her case, and perhaps, in some cases, theirs, it's no one's fault but her own. She lies stiffly, depressed at having given in, for that's how she sees it, yet knowing she could not have lain alone in the other room aware that Patrick was miserable.

Patrick switches the light out, gets in beside her, lies separate and away from her. She makes the slightest move, her foot almost by accident touches his, his hand steals across the bed, reaches for her, pulls her to him. She turns towards him and his arms go round her, she stops thinking, feels only the comfort of his chest, his warmth, his protective arms encircling her – trapping her? She has ceased to care. The burden of being a thinking woman builds up a dichotomy that seems at times insuperable, for a woman has not the facility for persuading herself her own ego is all important in the way a man can – and does. It is a side of her she must work at if it is to be developed. No doubt it is this in-built altruism designed by nature to enslave her to her children that has placed her in the position she now finds herself.

Over breakfast next morning Caroline nurses her mug in both hands elbows on the table, sipping the hot liquid; Patrick sits sideways to the table, the *Times and Gazette* on his lap, going through the farm sales in search of a buck-rake and any other likely buys. Occasionally he drinks from his going-cold mug.

Caroline suddenly says as though she has been working up to it, 'I thought I'd ask a few people in for Christmas Eve.' Then as he doesn't answer she adds in support of her suggestion, 'I thought it would be nice to do something – have an ash faggot*.'

Patrick drinks the last of his cold coffee, makes a face. 'Don't forget we've got my parents for lunch.'

'I couldn't forget.' He looks across at her, detects an edge in her voice, or is he imagining it?

'Won't it be rather a lot? Both.'

'I was only going to give them drinks. You won't have to do anything . . . except sit,' Caroline adds carefully, but she does want this party. Since it came into her head in the early hours of this morning it has gained in importance. She can ask everyone around, all the local people who've been a help in Patrick's absence – and some of those who haven't, she thinks of Jim Thurley – and one or two other friends she's met around and in the village, and . . . and Tom and Rita. Which'll show Rita there's nothing between her and Tom and never has been . . . Caroline's imagination fails her at this point; the point of the whole party. She says, 'I think it would be nice, anyway.'

'It seems rather a waste when I'm not able to be part of it in any full sense. I'm not even supposed to touch alcohol for six weeks.'

'You can have orange juice,' she says, making a mental note to buy a crate. She can see Patrick thinking who's going to pay so she says before he can, 'I'm paying – my father's sent me a Christmas cheque.' However, Patrick's expression quells her enthusiasm and she says in a subdued voice, 'I won't do it if you don't want.'

'No, do as you like,' replies Patrick perversely. The idea has more appeal now he doesn't have to pay.

'Then I'll go and get the ash. Will you tell me how to fasten the ties?'

'Get some long hazel – I'll come out and do it.'

* *Faggot:* bundles of ash bound together with hazel or willow.

'You're not supposed to,' says Caroline standing, 'not for another week.'

But Patrick is taking his coat off the peg, getting it on. He's feeling better. He tries the light in the cobbled passage, finds the bulb's gone and blunders his way down to the hefty front door. Pulling it open he looks out on the ground that glitters with frost, breathes in the cold air with satisfaction; hospital memories recede. He looks at his watch, Tom should be out today. He must get him to mill up barley for the steers, separate them out into the linhay field to bring on for the spring sales. He himself must ring up for a mineral block. At this thought he goes back into the house and does so, only to be told rather firmly it is two days before Christmas and they are not taking any more orders till after New Year. Patrick swears and clumps the receiver down.

Caroline meanwhile has got the tractor started by running it down the drive. Patrick catches her in the yard, tells her not to be long because of the feeding.

'I'm doing it,' says Caroline coldly, resenting his interference. He treats her, she feels, as though she has learnt nothing during his absence.

'Tom'll do it for you,' he says.

'If he comes,' she replies with bitter irony, and drives off.

Once away from the house her spirits rise. The sun is warming up the land, the birds flitter along the hedges. The white-patterned ice on the puddles cracks and vanishes beneath the tractor wheels; the ford flows in its normal curved sweep over sand and pebbles, the stepping stones, now grown over with moss, push themselves up out of the frosty ground beside her. Ahead of her, on the far side of the ford, the lane stretches up between granite walls lined on one side by immense beeches that stand motionless and leafless in the still air.

She turns in a gate on her left, lurches through ruts worn deep in the wet weather but now frozen hard, and comes out in the field opposite the farm. Above and on her right are tumbledown buildings of Crype farm that fifty years ago stood solid as Greytor; now only the big barn remains in use. Across the field she opens the throttle, missing as far as possible the frozen molehills. This side of the valley which faces north remains largely in shade, and will do so until the sun gets high enough to look down over the top of Crype Down which rises sharply to the south.

Caroline, who hates shade, makes for the far left-hand corner where a hedge trimmed two years ago has sprouted tall and slender hazel, ideal for ties and full in the sun. The sky above her is quite dark blue, but as it descends the blue fades into a grey haze. Looking behind she sees the emerald double wake the tractor wheels have left on the otherwise grey-white ground.

Leaving the tractor running for fear it won't start again, she sets about the hazel with her bill-hook. Soon she has ten or more straight, unforked lengths which she lays across the link-box and secures with baler-cord. That done she goes up the field to where Tom has sawed up an ash for firewood. On the ground remain many small branches and numerous twigs. These she gathers, piles them in along with the hazel and makes her way home. In spite of her activity, her business, the expression on her face is distinctly wistful.

As she reaches the yard she sees that Tom has indeed arrived and stands leaning on the wall, talking to Patrick. Her heart, over which she seems to have no control, leaps – or in any case makes her well aware of its presence. She pulls up beside them, Tom nods to her briefly and she smiles back. She goes round to take out the wood, but Tom is there before her and lifts out the ash while she unknots the cord to free the hazel, her fingers clumsy and numb from cold. Tom sees her difficulty and slashes the cord with his knife. Caroline feels as though her feet are not quite touching the ground, she floats, is disembodied as long as Tom is close. All her good resolutions mount as directly into the clear air as does the smoke from the great kitchen chimney.

'Will it be enough?' she inquires, addressing her remark to neither in particular.

'Should be' – Tom's expression indicates more than enough.

'Tom'll make it.' Patrick's voice is unusually firm.

'But . . .'

'My mother rang,' he interrupts, 'she wants you to ring her back.'

'What about?'

'Christmas lunch I imagine – she didn't say.'

'Shall I help Tom first?'

But Patrick is alerted by Caroline's unusual desire to help in a tricky and cold task. It seems perfectly fair to him, in fact only sensible, to prevent it.

'I think you ought to ring right away,' – he stands waiting by the gateway making it clear he expects her to come. And she comes, however unwillingly. As she passes him he says in a low voice, 'For godsake let Tom get on with it. He knows what he's doing.'

Caroline hates him then, hates him as it is only possible to hate someone who prevents you doing what you most wish to. It is the blind hate of the child for the authoritative adult, but Caroline is not a child and under her emotion she is forced to see reason in Patrick's attitude. The whole thing is ridiculous and she is behaving like a lunatic. The position of the older woman with the younger man is never very edifying, the woman being generally besotted and invariably ill used. There is little to recommend it except the doubtful value of passion of which there is undoubtedly a great deal. So although Caroline opens her mouth to answer Patrick back sharply, she changes her mind and walks on ahead, biting her poor frozen lip instead.

Tom glances after them, betraying nothing by his face, then bends down and sets about sorting through the ash for the faggot.

When Tom gets home that evening and announces to Rita they have both been invited to the Ashursts' party on Christmas Eve he is greeted with a worse reception than he had anticipated.

'*Her!*' says Rita with venom. 'Who does she think I am?'

They are sitting at the table while Tom eats his tea – eggs, bacon, tomatoes, baked beans and fruit-cake – and drinks a cup of tea made from a Red Label tea bag. Rita has forgotten it and left it in too long, so it is extremely strong.

Tom blinks. 'I reckon she thinks you wouldn't a' liked it if I'd a' been asked without you?' He lapses into comfortable dialect to express himself fully, if tactlessly.

'You mean she doesn't want me?' Rita's indignation, her hurt pride explodes.

'It weren't her as asked.' Tom gathers the baked beans on to his upturned fork, shifts them with steady hand towards his mouth.

'Him, was it?'

'Yes,' Tom says after he has swallowed and wiped his mouth.

'I don't suppose *she* would want me, that goes without saying,' says Rita, slightly placated.

'They'm asking all the wives by what I hear tell.' Tom is doing better.

Rita falls silent for some time. Jenny fortunately is out to tea with Maggie, and Ernest obligingly sleeps in the front room. Rita examines her leg and foot thoughtfully, replenishes Tom's tea with another bag and the kettle. Sits again, chin in hand, elbow on table.

'Who else is going?'

'Thurleys – Robbins – Hawkins – Harrises – Christine and Arch – Ben Carter—' he stops. 'I don't know that there is any others. Maybe that woman that come out and stayed with her back in the autumn.'

'Who?'

'Helen something or other.'

'Is she coming to stay again?'

'I dunno.'

Tom takes his cup and cake to the chair by the stove, puts his socked feet up. Rita watches him dropping crumbs with distaste, but the five days spent with her parents is still clearly enough etched on her memory for her to hold her tongue. Instead she says, 'I haven't got anything to wear.'

'What about that dress your mother gived you?'

Rita shrieks, 'What are you talking about, Tom? I wouldn't be seen dead in that thing.'

'Blue – I liked the colour,' says Tom hopefully. He doesn't in the least care what Rita wears, his only dread is she will ask him for money to buy something new. He closes his eyes, hoping the subject is concluded.

'I saw some really nice dresses in Dorothy Perkins in Exeter last Friday.'

Tom keeps silent but the tension mounts.

'Tell you what, if you were to give it me for Christmas then it would save you having to go down the shops tomorrow. I done the shopping for Jenny and Ernest and my parents an' your mother.'

Tom's eyes open unwillingly. 'How would you get in there?'

'I could take the van.'

'So how'm I getting up to work?'

'Don't tell me you're working again tomorrow?'

'In the morning I am.'

Rita looks vindictively at him, certain of the reason. But this is not the moment to argue because Tom is about to fork out the cash – well he knows what'll happen if he doesn't.

'I'll drop you off,' she says, 'drop you off and drive on into Exeter. I'll pick you up after.'

'Twelve-thirty?'

'Alright. Twelve-thirty,' she has to agree to this if she's to get the last concession.

'Can I take twenty-five pounds?'

Tom's eyes open wide, he takes his feet off the stove and puts them squarely on the ground. 'For one dress?' – he expresses his amazement.

'That's cheap – some of them are fifty.'

She gets his jacket containing his wallet, dangles it in front of him. Tom, every inch of his person resenting being parted from his hard-earned wage, silently fumbles in his pocket and withdraws his wallet. Laboriously he counts out five notes, hands them to Rita, then resumes his former position, feet back on the stove. Rita counts the notes with satisfaction, puts them in her purse, hums to herself the current number one in the charts as she dreams of the green dress with sequins she has seen on the stand – cut straight with a belt knotted at the waist. She crosses her fingers it won't have gone by the time she gets in there.

Greytor sitting-room is looking at its best. Caroline has taken advantage of time gained owing to Tom's having taken over the feeding, and used it for decorating. She has cajoled and persuaded Patrick to join in with the putting up of mistletoe and holly, the strewing around of yew. Candles stand in the niches thoughtfully built into the massive walls; drinks and tit-bits to eat are set out on the sills and the table, along with draught ale and cider. Caroline glances round her, pleased with the results, puts another log on the already blazing fire, and goes up to get herself ready.

Twenty minutes later her bed is strewn with clothes – clothes she has had since the time she lived with Helen and that now look oddly dated and unsuitable. What shall she wear? She swallows guiltily at the thought that her main concern is to please Tom. For now it is all over, the door completely closed on anything that ever happened between them, why should she still care? It is all humiliating and shaming – she wishes Helen were here for Helen somehow helps her to see things as they really are, keep a balance. And Patrick? Doesn't she want to please him? Yes of course but he never notices. When they get into bed after everyone has gone and she asks him the colour of her dress the chances are he won't remember. Or is she being unfair? Again guilt flushes her face. She puts Tom from her mind, or thinks she has, and looks round for a dress to please herself. She lights on one in shades of burnt sienna and ochre that has a tiny old-fashioned leaf pattern and drops from the square neckline to a deep frilled hem below her knees. The sleeves are long and full, buttoning at the wrists. Round her neck she fastens an amber necklace and slips a gold bangle on her wrist. Her face she leaves alone except for darkening her eyelashes. The problem remains of what to do with her hair – something special or leave it as usual? In front of her mirror she holds it back from her face. Up? Alter her parting? No style satisfies her. Finally she shakes her head so it falls naturally, brushes it till it shines and shimmers like pale straw, and leaves it loose around her shoulders. She thinks she hears a car. Seizing the heap of clothes from her bed she shoves them in the cupboard and shuts the door, runs down the stairs.

But it's a false alarm. Patrick is in the kitchen mulling wine, the pungent smell of cloves pervades the rooms.

'Oughtn't you be sitting down?'

'No.'

No, of course he doesn't need to, why doesn't she sit down instead of fussing around? And why, oh why, does she have to feel so nervous? It will be a strange enough gathering, that's true – only one or two people she could genuinely call friends and the rest people round the area who Patrick has known for years or who know them because of work connected with the farm. It's not that there are many coming because there aren't, it's more that although she is the hostess and the festivities will take part in Greytor at her instigation, she knows she will still feel an outsider – people will look at her rather than into her, talk about her rather than to her in any real sense. She sighs and bites the sides of her nails, wishing for the second time Helen were here. It seems strange she has heard nothing from her for over a fortnight . . . A car! Yes, this time quite definitely someone has arrived. She hurries to the backdoor – for the front is too muddy and could never be attempted at this time of year by any who know the farm – holds it open as two people descend towards her out of the darkness.

'Tom?'

'What is it?'

'Can you do up my zip?'

Tom obliges. Rita with a sinuous movement manages to elongate and narrow herself as the zip proceeds up her body.

'Now the hook.'

'I can't see no hook.'

'There's one at the top. Take care, mind. Don't tear the material.'

Tom, whose fingers though broad have an amazing daintiness and precision, fastens the required hook. Rita pushes back her hair and turns round.

'How does it look?' She has none of Caroline's uncertainty but smiles with conscious pleasure in her own appearance. And well she might, for the emerald green lights up her eyes so that they shine sea blue, her skin looks more white and her hair even blacker. The dress indeed fits like a glove and as Rita moves it undulates with her body, the sequins glitter.

'Alright,' Tom says, and means it.

She now looks at him critically. That he doesn't look quite right she is aware but is not quite sure what is wrong. Perhaps that maroon jersey she got him should have been a size bigger, certainly it gives him a rather barrel-like appearance. Also Tom's neck doesn't seem to have been designed for a collar and tie. Oh well . . . She picks up her sequined handbag to match, puts a white shawl round her shoulders and trips down the stairs in her high heels for all the world like an understudy for the young Elizabeth Taylor.

In the van there's a fuss. Tom has had his tools on the seat which is not very clean and Rita is understandably anxious about marking her dress. 'How can anyone go out with you, Tom? If I was anyone else I should simply refuse to sit down on a seat like that. You wouldn't ask any other girl to.'

Tom wipes it off with the palm of his hand, spreads his own coat for her to sit on. What greater gesture can a man make? Rita is moderately soothed, her life after all has taken a turn for the better since lunch time today when they left Jenny and Ernest with her parents to be collected again after the party tonight. It means Tom'll have to lay off the drink, but all in all the gorgeous peace has been worth it. Her mother has been given a bottle to pacify Ernest who is in the process of being weaned . . .

Rita slams the door, puts everything but the party from her mind, and asks Tom what he's waiting for?

*

'I thought she was older, from what you said,' Angela, the vet's wife, murmurs to him as she leans forward to help herself to a chipolata on a stick.

John Robbins, about to reply, sees Mary Thurley and Rita approaching out of the corner of his eye. To warn Angela from further comment he clears his throat and says loudly, 'Magnificent fireplace – the same kind of scene as this must have been going on for hundreds of years.'

Rita, who he has had his eye on all evening, stands in front of him rippling with sequins a-glitter like sun catching the waves. She sips her drink daintily held and murmurs reverently, 'It's a beautiful house.'

She's alright, thinks John Robbins, more than alright but has she got a slight squint? In fact it is just Rita keeping one eye on Tom, or trying to, while she flashes the other at Mr Robbins. Right at this moment Caroline is filling Tom's glass. She says something to him in what Rita considers an insultingly intimate manner. Tom smiles, she laughs and goes on to fill the next person's glass.

John Robbins is about to make an attempt at chatting up Rita, having observed Tom to be on the other side of the room, when Bob Haines moves over.

'Hullo, Bob,' says the vet unenthusiastically, 'How's things?' He compensates himself for the loss of Rita by taking from a passing plate an egg with a dollop of mayonnaise and an anchovy on top.

Caroline reaches Angela with her jug of mulled wine.

'I've never seen an ash faggot before' – Angela, who is about the same age as Caroline and a member of the up-country middle classes, flashes a display of white teeth at Caroline. 'Of course, you need a chimney like yours to have one.'

'Yes,' says Caroline, glancing anxiously at the fire. Faggots either don't go at all, or go with a fearful flame that fills the room with heat and sometimes smoke, depending on the wind. This one is just beginning, a tie flips free as she watches, everyone cheers and drinks. 'Patrick must be getting roasted,' Caroline murmurs mainly as an excuse to abandon Angela who will almost certainly try and pin her down for a CND meeting – not that Caroline is anti, in fact she is pro, but it is the meetings she particularly dreads. They are interminable and never seem to get further than what could be done in five minutes' talk on the telephone. Another tie goes, and during the resulting hubbub and drinking she moves in Patrick's direction.

Angela Robbins watches her go with some envy. It is not, she thinks, that Caroline is in any way smart, nothing could be simpler than her dress; it is more that she has an innate sense of what suits her, a sort of style which makes her the odd one out. Well . . . different. She was a funny wife for a man like Patrick Ashurst to have chosen, she agrees with John there. They'd always assumed he'd stay a bachelor . . .

Caroline bends over Patrick who looks hunched and rather red on one cheek.

'Don't you want to move back?' She has to raise her voice above the considerable level of noise in the room to enable him to hear. He looks at her with a bright smile she knows is forced, answers, 'I'm alright at the moment – I'll go in the other chair when it really gets going.'

They both view with some trepidation the ever-increasing flames that leap and curl up the blackened chimney. The only other light in the room is from the candles which gutter and drip, drawn by the draught of the fire. The conversation lulls as everyone watches with some awe. Do the Ashursts really know what they're doing? May not the chimney catch fire?

Jim Thurley however is well fortified by ale. He roars with joy at the flames, claps Bob Haines on the shoulder, helps himself up on the table, and raises his glass for a toast.

'Here's to the New Year – in case us is snowed in by then . . .' – he is interrupted by protests and laughter but goes on undeterred, 'and a good lambing, good prices, and let's hope the hill farmers don't get forgotten by the EEC . . .'

He jumps down amid applause, whispers something to the vet and they burst into loud laughter. Caroline watching presumes the general level of noise means the party is 'going'. She glances round and sees everyone is talking to someone else except herself – she, on the contrary, stands quite alone nursing an empty jug. That's as it should be at your own party, she reassures herself, but it does nothing to help her overcome the acute sense of isolation she suddenly feels. Behind her she hears Rita and Bob talking.

'How's the family, Rita?'

'Coming on fine thank you Bob. Jenny goes in play-school now.'

Caroline slips down to the far end of the room to replenish her jug. Bob sees her going and moves in closer to Rita. He indicates with a slight nod Caroline's receding back view, lowers his voice. 'I've only met her once back in the summer – is she settling in here alright?' His tone makes it quite apparent he doesn't think she will.

Rita pops her mince pie and cream delicately in between rosebud lips and murmurs equally low, 'I really couldn't say. She's not like one of us at all but Tom seems to get on with her.' She licks the cream from the tip of a small finger with a healthily pink tongue.

'I shouldn't wonder if he does,' says Bob grinning.

'No,' says Rita tartly, 'but then you don't wonder at much, do you, Bob?' and she turns on her heel with a sinuous undulation and walks towards poor Mr Ashurst.

Patrick who has moved back to the sofa, blinks. Who the hell is it?

'You don't recognise me, do you Mr Ashurst? I'm Tom's wife.' Rita leans forward so that the sea green dress reveals depths that remind him instantly of Vanessa, so does the scent. He blinks again.

'Of course I recognise you, Rita – I'd have known you anywhere,' Patrick lies. He has had quite enough drink to be convincing and Rita, though not convinced, feels her ruffled feathers calmed by something admiring in his expression and sits down beside him crossing her legs. Soon their heads lie back on the soft cushions and both bask balmily in mutual admiration. Rita recedes and glows in the firelight before Patrick like a emerald dragonfly, her fishnet tights criss-cross before his eyes.

On the other side of the room Caroline's eyes meet Tom's

for a split second – she drops hers quickly, turns to the young doctor who has recently taken up a practice. 'Robert – your glass is empty.' As she fills it a final hazel tie flips out over the granite flags. There is a roar of joy from the gathering followed by an awed gasp as the flames redouble their height, vanishing behind the lintel which is some four foot six inches from the floor. Caroline bends over the back of the sofa. 'Are you alright?' She addresses Patrick but smiles into Rita's glowing face that is either reflecting the fire or suffering from it. 'Why don't you move back?' They do, perching themselves on the window seat, Patrick saying to Caroline before she leaves them, 'You did remember to ring my mother?'

'Yes,' she says, carefully keeping emotion out of her voice, 'she only wanted to know if I knew how to make the stuffing.'

For a moment their eyes meet in a shared knowledge of his mother's tiresomeness. They smile. Caroline drinks herself for the first time, begins to relax. People round her mellow, dissolve. Smoke begins to creep back under the lintel but no one worries – drink and warmth have got the upper hand. The plate of mince pies is empty, she notices, but feels no further desire to replenish it. Let them help themselves, let everyone help themselves. She drops on to the hot sofa someone has dragged back, lets her head sink into the cushions. Not far away from her she recognises Tom's legs. Then, quite suddenly, she becomes aware something has happened. People in front of her have turned, are looking at something over her head. A kind of hush falls on the room. Caroline, with an immense effort of will, raises herself from the low position to which she's sunk, as she does so she looks over the sofa back.

'Helen!'

For indeed it is Helen who stands imperiously in the doorway which is a step above the level of the room, and frames her to perfection. Dressed in black jersey, velvet trousers and boots she is an arresting figure and Caroline's heart gives a little leap of delight at the sight of her friend, which is sharply tempered by an acute sensation of embarrassment that Helen should find her in the centre of this ribald and rather drunken company. Who for instance, Caroline asks herself as she hurriedly makes her way across the room, can she introduce her to? Her head reels – it's because she's eaten nothing and Patrick must have fortified the mulled wine.

As she reaches her, Helen steps down into the room. They embrace each other and kiss, Caroline with a passion released by drink and stimulated by Tom, Helen with more restraint.

'Here I am,' she says triumphantly, 'I said I'd come.'

Caroline pushes her hair back with an unconscious gesture of nervous excitement – she can feel the whole room is watching them.

'Why didn't you let me know, but it doesn't matter. It's a wonderful Christmas surprise. Come and meet everyone.' And resting her hand on Helen's arm she boldly leads her towards Angela Robbins. Out of the corner of her eye she sees Patrick wave and acknowledge Helen in the hearty and aggressive fashion he normally adopts towards her.

'Angela,' says Caroline, looking at her with such intensity that Angela takes a step back, 'this is Helen Baxter who I used to share a flat with – you must remember my talking about her to you? Helen – this is Angela Robbins who organises all our CND meetings . . .'

Caroline looks at both with imploring eyes. Talk, she thinks, oh, do talk. Speak to each other that I may be relieved of this terrible burden of being hostess and taking upon myself, even for a few short hours, the need for all of your well-beings. Oh yes she is happy Helen is here – it has made her Christmas. But how unfortunate to have her at this truly awful party. Why did she ever dream it up? Why couldn't they all go home? The ash faggot, she notices with some relief, has died down to a huge heap of red embers and a few flickering flames; unfortunately the same cannot be said of the smoke which has thickened, so that a fair number of her guests are openly weeping. She flings open doors and windows, lets in icy air, suggests people should move through to the kitchen. There is an unmistakable surge for the door except by those who are on the floor or low chairs beneath the smoke level, Patrick and Rita who have moved back to the sofa seem quite unaware of it. Tom, she notices, is one of the worst affected. But there is nothing she can do, absolutely nothing. Caroline replenishes her own glass from the jug and makes her way to the kitchen in pursuit of her guests to offer them coffee. They sit around her, dabbing their eyes, and repeating what a wonderful evening it has been. Caroline's own eyes begin to water – is there nowhere in the house the smoke has not permeated?

Helen has been frankly amazed to see such a gathering surrounding her friend, but not wholly dismayed. Is not this, after all, how life in the country should be – convivial, bucolic and classless? Yet she sometimes wonders. Have all these people gathered here out of affection for Caroline and Patrick, or is it not rather because only few human beings can resist the offer of another's hospitality and the chance to nose into other peoples' houses and private lives? No, she is being cynical she tells herself firmly as she stands beside the sink, drying-up cloth in hand polishing the umpteenth glass. Patrick, having helped them clear, is in his usual chair by the stove. Caroline has her sleeves rolled up and her hands in the sink. Helen looks across at Patrick, says, 'You must be quite tired,' which translated means 'why are you sitting watching us – you can't be that ill?'

'I am rather,' says Patrick modestly, as though unwilling to complain, 'but more from socialising than physical strain. It's only because of the doctor's insistence that I'm not back on the job.' Then he returns her sally at expressing a false interest in his health. 'How is the career?'

Helen refuses to rise to the ill-veiled sarcasm in his tone.

'Actually, I've got some news,' she says.

'Helen – what?' Caroline looks back over her shoulder from the sink.

'Tell us,' Patrick looks as though he has sucked a lemon.

'I've got a new job. I'm to be assistant editor on a new literary mag. in Bristol. They haven't settled for the name yet, but it's definite.'

In the pause that follows Caroline absorbs the information with mixed feelings of which envy and loss of her friend are the two uppermost. Oh, it's not that she doesn't want it for Helen because she does, it just makes her wish that she could do something as exciting and useful. She suddenly feels like bursting into tears, perhaps it's the drink. She hears herself say with only the faintest tremor in her voice, 'Helen, that's wonderful. I'm terribly pleased for you,' but can't help adding, 'but you'll be further away.'

'Yes,' agrees Helen, 'but I'll be paid more and have my own car so I'll be able to get down here much more often to see you.'

Caroline dries her hands slowly and methodically on the roller towel while she regains full control of herself for she knows what Helen says cannot be true. Helen will be busy; occupied by new friends; have a new, stimulating environment and life style, a responsible position . . .

'That's the best news I've heard this Christmas,' she lies with fortitude and self-possession, 'tell me more.'

But Patrick interrupts – 'So you're . . . launched on your career?' There is no mistaking the sarcasm now.

Helen picks up his phrase, flings it back at him like a challenge, 'Yes – launched.'

'Well, I congratulate you.'

'Thanks.'

But the interchange could hardly have been less friendly or more two-edged; Patrick's attitude has completely taken away the pleasure Helen had anticipated in sharing her good news with Caroline. She feels deflated, flat. She turns her back on Patrick and speaks pointedly to Caroline, 'Perhaps you'll be able to get away an occasional weekend, Caroline, come and stay with me in Bristol?'

Helen, for the first time, openly and in front of Patrick endeavours to make a bid for Caroline's continuing friendship, to openly ask that she shall come to her even if only for such a short period as a weekend. Implicit in the invitation is the secondary one – that of course Caroline can stay longer, even indefinitely if she should choose to do so.

Patrick gets up, says with ill-disguised resentment, 'I'll leave you two to talk.'

Caroline looks at his rather drawn face guiltily – he does

look tired. She tells him she'll join him soon – just as soon as she has helped Helen make up a bed.

Tom and Rita leave the party just before midnight with the others – their van, skilfully parked by Tom, would not have proved any trouble had not some other guest in their enthusiasm to make a quick getaway, run it down the field. As it is, Tom tries without success, then puts Rita behind the wheel to steer while he pushes. By this means they traverse the muddy field till they reach the stony track.

Tom brushes his hands, looks regretfully at his muddy best trousers, tells Rita to hop out and let him drive. But to his surprise and annoyance she stays where she is.

'Move over,' he repeats.

'No – you get in the other side.' Rita is obstinate. Tom, fed up with hanging about and not liking to seize hold of Rita in her new dress with his dirty hands, obediently goes round the other side. He has quite forgotten they will not be just returning to the village, but must journey nearly to Taverston to collect the children. So ten minutes later when Rita flashes past their house driving rather fast, he exclaims, 'What do you bloody think you're doing?'

'Trust you, Tom,' says Rita who is feeling the effect of numerous glasses of mulled wine, 'to forget all about your own children. I don't know what you wanted them for. You really aren't fitted to be a father.'

Tom agrees but refrains from saying so, he is too concerned with the way Rita is driving.

'Stop,' he says, 'and let me drive. You're drunk.'

His lack of tact at this crucial moment is a serious error. Rita feels annoyed, rebellious – and full of confidence. If anything she thinks she drives rather better after a few drinks, her eye is better, the van seems part of her, an extension of self. She ignores Tom, only slowing down fractionally.

The road ahead proceeds steeply down off the moor by a series of hairpin bends; it is narrow and requires careful driving at the best of times, let alone at night when the air is cold enough to have formed the dreaded invisible black ice on sections of the moist tarmac surface. Even Tom cannot know this, though he suspects it and says, real fear in his voice, 'Go slow, Rita. There may be ice us can't see.' He is in two minds whether or not to grab the wheel but at the speed they are going it would almost certainly mean disaster.

Rita, arrogant from drink, answers firmly, 'If there was frost it'd show up white . . .' but as she speaks something happens. The van no longer responds in predictable fashion but drifts sideways across the road, there is a sickening thud as they hit the iron railings set as a weak protection between travellers and a drop into an oak wood. The next instant the rails give, the van goes over. Tom is miraculously flung clear and rolls virtually unhurt down through the leaves till he stops with a thud against a tree trunk which knocks all the breath from his body. Rita is trapped in the van which pitches over and over down the steep incline till it too is stopped by a tree.

It is some moments before Tom can get breath enough to stand, as soon as he does he leaps down through the darkness to the van. The lights have gone off but the red glow of a rear light shows clearly enough where it has stopped, tipped over on its side, the bonnet open and crushed in. Crawling up on the passenger side where the door has ripped off Tom sees Rita pinned between seat and steering wheel. His heart seems to stop, he feels sick with terror and dread. But the smell of petrol and his fear of fire forces him to act. Somehow he climbs in, grasps Rita and drags her free, aware as he does so that he may be doing her further damage. What choice has he? He lays her in the leaves, he can see almost nothing in the pitch dark of the wood. He shifts her well clear of the now overwhelming smell of petrol and flickers his lighter. What he sees fills him with even deeper horror and fear. He looks down on her for a full moment, then takes her in his arms and struggles up the steep incline towards the road above. As he does so car lights approach, but continue past the broken railings. In despair Tom thinks they have gone on but no, a few seconds later it stops, and then reverses back till it is above him, its engine still turning over, lights blazing.

Tom shouts. A man's figure gets out, starts climbing down the hill towards him.

Caroline bends over the corner of the bed, lifting it to make the neat hospital turn-unders she has been taught when young and does unconsciously like so many habits formed in childhood. Helen is talking and has been talking during most of the bed making, ' . . . so I'll have to find somewhere to live,' she finishes – oh, anything'll do me – a bedsit. If I can get cheap enough rates. I've simply ceased to care about how and where I live – it's what I'm doing that matters.'

'Yes,' agrees Caroline. A kind of numbness has overtaken her. So it is when someone else's extreme good fortune rivals very closely your own less happy stars, for if Caroline had not opted for Greytor and Patrick, her own path might well have taken a similar direction. And Caroline not unnaturally regrets the path she did not take, the gate she never opened. That is not to say that given the same choice in the same given circumstances she would not have chosen the same again, it is rather that at this particular rather low ebb in her life and with the hindsight she now has, her confidence in the choice she has made is shaken. Had she been a seer and able to look into the future, most probably she would not have suffered the regrets she does at this moment. At the same time Helen, who until now has been slightly blinded by her own happiness, has begun to realise how her news must seem to her.

'It's completely different for you, Caroline,' she says, awkwardly, 'I mean, this house and . . . Patrick.'

Caroline sits down slowly on the end of the bed. 'Yes,' she says in a small voice.

Helen at once becomes very silent, a look of consternation replacing her former one of happiness. 'I haven't got anything else, have I?' she says helplessly, 'only my work.'

Caroline looks up at her with eyes full of doubt and questioning, 'Only?' She waits but as Helen doesn't answer goes on, 'Have I got . . . everything else?'

Helen deliberates before replying, then looks at Caroline

and says with more faith and confidence than she feels, 'Yes.'

'And that's enough?'

'That's for you to decide.'

Caroline takes up the tasselled bedspread, pulls her fingers repeatedly through the tangled fringe, combing it.

'It's not enough – but I am . . . rich. Oh, not in money . . .' She breaks off.

Helen answers with even more doubt and hesitancy, 'Yes. I see that.'

'Do you?' Caroline leaps at her friend's words like someone trying to keep their balance by grasping at blown gossamer.

Helen feels a fraud and yet realises how deep is Caroline's need of her understanding. To be ruthlessly truthful at this moment can only be destructive.

'I think I do,' she compromises.

Caroline sighs as she realises that that is exactly what the normally blunt Helen is doing. It forces on her the need to explain herself to herself as much as Helen, launch into a desperate attempt at analysis.

'I've learnt a lot about myself. You could say that I am cut off – dead – but in another way I'm alive and absorbing.' Does she really believe this, she wonders, or is she just saying it? 'In the last two years, I have resisted and resisted because I thought I was "someone" already. But I wasn't. I am no more able to retain the person I was – thought I was – than a sponge dropped in water can remain dry. I feel myself malleable – in a process of reshaping . . .' She hesitates, begins to plait the tassels, 'and it's frightening because I know as soon as the shape forms it must go again – what's there is never more than an idea for what's to come . . .' She breaks off, looks up at Helen who leans against the bookcase with her arms folded, looking not at Caroline but beyond and through her and back to her own thoughts about her. Caroline goes on, 'I'm sure it's impossible to understand a word I'm saying – it's more what I feel but can't formulate. Before I came out here I knew – or thought I knew – what I wanted. Now I'm sure – for me – that's *not* the way – the way I used to think the way . . . Oh I know I took a step into the dark and like most such steps it was not, is not, all roses. But if you want to know if I'm the better for it, why yes I am. I want the experience of roots that go right down into the earth – it's always easier to take home a bunch of cut flowers, I know, but it's not my way.'

This time she doesn't look at Helen, but waits, shoulders hunched as though afraid, as though even anticipating some sort of physical blow. Helen sees Caroline's suffering, her doubt, and is moved to compassion and an equally profound sense of inadequacy.

'So you'll be alright,' she says awkwardly, aware of the futility of her own words. 'You . . . and Patrick?'

Caroline turns her eyes to meet Helen's; there is no doubting her sincerity, the truth of her conclusion, 'Ultimately, it's me. I don't think I'm able to relate except in part to other people. Part of me relates to Patrick, to you . . .'

'To Tom?'

There is a tense pause in which Caroline drags undone the plaits she has made in the counterpane fringe.

'To Tom,' she admits finally.

Impulsively Helen drops on the bed beside her, slips her arms round her shoulders, kisses the silky hair that falls either side of the small and shapely ear.

'I do understand you – just.' They look at each other, laugh. Caroline for the relief of having at last confessed and confided; Helen for love of Caroline, for the shared intimacy. Urged on by their closeness Caroline exclaims with passion, 'And then this place – it's *so* beautiful – it's almost like relating to another person, or it seems so to me.'

Looking at Caroline's flushed face and eyes that seem to have grown larger with intensity, Helen's love amounts to a sort of adoration for her coupled with an urge to protect. Why, oh why does Caroline have to live in this lonely place among these alien people – no wonder, with the undemonstrative man she has chosen, she feels a need to fill in with Tom – but what a waste, what a terrible waste! She lets her arm slide away from Caroline, shifts herself a little.

'How far has it gone – you . . . and Tom?'

'Oh, not far at all,' Caroline is evasive, 'and anyway what little there ever was between us is finished . . . now.'

But Helen is not satisfied. 'Are you sure?'

'Oh yes – he made me realise.'

'He made *you* realise? Realise what?'

'That it was simply not possible.'

Good for Tom, thinks Helen, but looks extremely dubious. 'But you still care for him?'

'Oh yes, I *care* for him.'

And all at once there seems no more to say. Caroline looks at her watch. 'I'll have to go, or Patrick'll be angry.'

'He has no right to be,' Helen's own jealousy bursts out of her in righteous wrath against Patrick.

'I'm the same,' admits Caroline mildly, almost apologetically, 'I get angry if he doesn't come to bed.' She leans and kisses Helen's cheek, smells her pleasant familiar scent, gets up and goes to the door where she pauses, 'I hope you'll be warm enough.'

'Oh, I shall – I've taken the precaution of bringing my hot-water bottle. Don't bother about me tomorrow because I'll be gone before you're awake – I've promised to be with my mother for lunch.' Helen makes a final bid to cling to their friendship for she senses it slipping away, slipping through her fingers perhaps forever, perhaps to be kept together by meetings, not how it was before but like a broken vase restored to its natural shape by glue. It might look well enough from a distance but not on close inspection, and certainly it will leak. 'You'll send me some poems?' She asks like asking for a remembrance card, a forget-me-not.

But Caroline is already three parts out the door. 'If I think any are worth sending,' she says diffidently. The door closes.

A sense of desolation settles on Helen. She looks round the room so dear to Caroline, and shivers. Then, with the habitual courage that allows her to live her own life, she limits her vision to the immediate, the things she can cope with, gets up from the bed and takes her bottle downstairs to fill.

*

Caroline wakes, lies on her back looking at the ceiling. There is something about the room that is different, unfamiliar. She continues to lie in the half-sleeping, half-awake state of comfort and warmth and examine the strange light round her, the difference – ponder on its cause. It bestows on her an unusual feeling of contentment, a lulling. There is something restful in the wonder of it. But as she becomes more conscious she frowns, sits up sharply. The roof outside the window is white. Instantly she is out of bed and breathing on the window to clear the miraculous tracery made by the frost. She clears it as a child might, looks out as a child might on the virgin world undulating away for her in whiteness. The trees, wet the day before, are covered in thick rime, the transformation of the familiar landscape is complete right down to the icicles that hang from the gutters tapering to sword-like points.

For some moments Caroline gazes out in rapturous wonder, lost to all but the sensuous beauty before her. Then she remembers Helen, sees the shallower patch in the snow where her car has stood. Surprised she has been able to leave at all she hopes fervently that her journey down the tricky road from the moor will have been safely negotiated – it must have been snowing when she left and snowed more since. A glance at the clock tells her she and Patrick have slept unusually late.

'Patrick?'

No answer – she tries again. 'Patrick?'

'What?'

'Snow – masses of it.' Caroline's voice rings with an excitement she is unable to subdue. Patrick raises himself on an elbow, looks out. 'Hell.'

'Come and look – there's ice on the pond.'

'Wait till you try getting through it on the tractor.'

'Will it start?' A note of anxiety creeps into her voice for Tom will not be here today, the onus of feeding falls on her. She starts to dress. At that moment the telephone goes. Semi-dressed she runs down to the office, wondering if it will be Helen in need of help. She picks up the receiver, speaks. But all she hears is a crackling noise, the faintest sound as of a voice talking, far, far in the distance, the words indistinguishable. Then the line goes completely blank. The weight of snow must have brought the line down somewhere. Slowly, almost fearfully, she lowers the receiver. So they are completely cut off, this Christmas will be spent entirely alone with the animals. She cannot help but feel a small sense of relief that Patrick's parents won't be able to come.

Half an hour later, plunged up to their thighs in snow, they endeavour to locate sheep in a drift that has mounted along a bank. In parts the snow has been driven directly against the bank so that the top is almost submerged, in others it lies a little out, shaped like the fin of some great fish. Along this fin Caroline and Patrick make their way probing into it every few feet with their sticks. Most of the flock stand out in the field where the ground is swept bare, but five are missing. Presently Patrick feels his probe alight on something soft and moving, he calls Caroline who brings the spade and digs. It is exhausting work but fortunately all the ewes are together so once one is freed the other four follow behind. That done, they gather the flock together and drive them into the yard, for further heavy falls of snow are forecast.

Next they shift the cattle to fields beside the grain-tower buildings; Caroline drags out hay bales to them while Patrick, cold and frustrated, watches. As she cuts the string and spreads the hay over the snow-covered ground small birds gather round for hayseeds, tamed by the sudden cold. Pink-faced and warm from her work, she looks with concern at Patrick hunched in the yard doorway.

'Why don't you go in? You look frozen – I've almost finished.'

'There's the blackface.'

'Shall I take them up a bale?'

'You can't get it to them – the snow plough hasn't been through.'

Caroline shades her eyes against the glare, stares up at the moor. 'I could drag one up on the sledge to the hunting-gate.'

'You'll never do it.'

'I will.'

*

As she struggles over a drift where the snow has blasted off the moor through the narrow gate, the bale slides off the sledge for the third time and has to be put back and the sledge righted. She is escorted by tiny birds who track her along the hedgerows, fluttering out behind her wherever the hay spills. With only another twenty yards to reach the gate she rests to get her breath but a gust of icy wind whips up a twister of snow into her eyes. She half covers them with her hands, looking back on the Christmas-card farm beneath her, then struggles on surmounting the last of the drift and getting through the gate itself which is mercifully clear of snow. Out on the open moor she takes a wide zig-zag across the hill until she comes out on the bare ground near the rocks at the top. Here the snow has almost entirely blown off and the frozen turf surrounding the tor is visible. She cuts the string, spreading the hay amongst the gorse to prevent the wind snatching it up before the sheep find it. Even so, the wind catches some and rolls in away over the ground – up here without shelter she herself is propelled forward by the force of it. Once it is done she wastes no time but grasps the sledge rope and sets off down the hill towing it over the partially concealed rocks and bracken. From time to time she catches sight of Blackface lurking with hopeful eyes; she wishes she had seen them earlier and fed the hay lower down, begins to think they will not find it and her effort has been wasted. Should she fetch another? But her fingers and feet are numb and by the time she reaches the farmhouse it is snowing afresh with blinding thickness. Flakes cling to her cheek like tiny starfish and only dissolve in the warmth of the kitchen.

Inside she drags off her frozen clothes, suffers the pain of the circulation flowing back through her frozen toes and fingers. As she stands warming herself by the stove, she wonders yet again what time Helen must have left to have got away before the roads were blocked.

So certain was Tom that Rita was dead when he dragged her from the car and carried her up the hill that he can hardly believe it when the woman in the stopped car corrects him. Rita's heart still beats, she insists, after helping the two men to lay her flat in the back of their estate car. She is a nurse and to Tom an angel sent by the god he doesn't believe in. His new companions sit in the front while he crouches in the back, protecting Rita's inert body from moving as they go round corners or sway about. It has been agreed better to proceed in such a fashion rather than leave Rita lying out suffering shock and exposure while they search for a telephone to ring for an ambulance. She is covered in all their coats and another slid beneath her head.

The descent off the moor is necessarily slow because of the treacherous road surface, but once on the flat the driver puts his foot down and they are in Taverston less than thirty-five minutes after the accident. Rita is rushed on a trolley straight into the emergency operating theatre. Tom thanks his benefactors, bids them goodbye, and then sits on a black plastic chair in the waiting-room his head bowed and his hands clenched between his knees. After he has waited in this fashion, in complete isolation and silence, for two and a half hours, a nurse of commanding appearance comes to tell him that they have done all they can for Rita and hope to be able to give him better news in the morning. They suggest he goes home and gets some sleep and rings them then. Tom points out it *is* morning and that he would prefer to stay in case Rita asks for him. She replies that she is expected to be unconscious for some time yet so the chances she will ask for him before mid-morning are minimal – it would be better if he went.

So Tom goes. But he can't face Rita's parents and has no car, so ends by wandering desultorily round the cold streets. An hour or so before dawn it starts to snow – wet slushy flakes that thaw as they touch the ground. Tom instinctively looks up to where the moor would be if he could see it – they'll get it up there, he shouldn't wonder! He thinks dismally of his van from which he might possibly have extracted parts though most will be fit for nothing but scrap. At dawn he wades through the now knee-deep slush and with dread rings Rita's parents. Tells them. They will come instantly. He tells them not to – can they keep the children? Fortunately, the pips go whilst they argue. He dials again, this time Greytor. When he hears Caroline's voice the other end he asks for Patrick but the crackling of the wires and her repeated 'Hullos' soon make him realise the lines are damaged and he is inaudible. Almost with relief he puts the receiver down. He returns to the hospital which stands up on the hill in the grey light, silent and forbidding.

The first fall of snow has been followed almost immediately by a further and much more violent blizzard. Five days later the outlying farmhouses are still cut off from all exterior communications. The telephone lines are down and Greytor exists in a small world of its own. By some miracle the electricity, usually one of the first public services to go, has not failed so the actual house, apart from frozen pipes, is little affected. Caroline looks at Patrick anxiously from time to time, wondering what she will do if his temperature should suddenly rise again, otherwise their main concern during daylight hours is the well-being of the stock. The chickens never venture from their house, the door of which was buried and had to be laboriously dug out; the garden gate is drifted over and the drift has frozen so it is simpler to walk over the top of it. The ducks and geese attempt the snow, forming a single-file track down to the frozen pond where they slide about comically and swim in the one unfrozen patch of black sinister water. Their normal whiteness changes to yellow against the snow backdrop, and their beaks show up as dabs of orange. In spite of the immense difficulty and physical strain of keeping everything fed, Caroline is not immune to the fabulous shapes of the world she suddenly finds her own, for only her prints mark its virginal covering, along with numerous animal tracks and criss-cross claws. She keeps the cat in as far as possible to prevent it molesting the birds in their weakened state, hangs out fat and puts crumbs on the sills brushed clear of snow.

In the evenings she and Patrick, who is now of necessity helping her more than he ought to be, sit on either side of the log fire they keep burning night and day, and wait for a thaw. On this particular evening Patrick has his eyes closed and is dozing and Caroline is at the table writing:

My dearest Helen,

I have never spent a more isolated New Year. We are still snowed in – that is to say the snow plough has not yet got as far as Greytor so the roads are impassable – no telephone and no post. The kitchen, as you know, is sunk into the hill and with the snow drifted over the windows it is very much like a cave. I enclose a poem I wrote yesterday – all of a sudden there's a lot of time because once the feeding's done there's nothing much else I can do, except bring in wood. I don't suppose it (the poem) to be good but I thought you'd be interested. How much one needs just that – someone who is interested.

Certainly living in this white world is an experience I wouldn't miss – the cold cleanses, jolts me into seeing – I look round at the mauve shadows tucked in the curves of drifts – the shapes of them have an immaculacy that asks to be disturbed – I like plunking my feet in their perfection. I touch one as though making love – its iciness comes as a shock – repels. The glare dazzles . . . Oh, but you know it all, there's no need for me to keep on and anyway I have said it better in the poem, I *hope*.

I must admit, in spite of what I've said, I'm beginning to feel a sort of apathy from long hours of darkness and being indoors. It was exciting when it first came, but now it's more endurance . . .

The wind booms threateningly in the chimney, making her look up, and a big puff of smoke billows back from under the lintel into the room. The smell of smoke stirs Patrick to open his eyes.

'Wind's changing.' He stretches his legs out, sits up. 'I feel better,' he says unexpectedly, looking across at Caroline's bent head. Something in his tone makes her look up – wait. A wet bit of wood sings on the red embers, Patrick grips the arms of his chair, fiddles automatically with a fray in the velveteen. 'I know you've had a hard time of it,' he gets out at last. 'That this place isn't all you expected and I'm not all you thought I'd be. I know you feel isolated and cut off out here . . .' He glances at her, then away. She makes no attempt to help him out. He struggles on. 'The isolation used to drive me mad – it doesn't any longer. I'm used to it. That's not to say I've forgotten what it's like to feel what you're feeling.' He looks at her again, hopefully. But Caroline is no longer looking at him but doodling on her writing pad. He makes a helpless, frustrated gesture with his hands, says not untinged with bitterness, 'I did warn you it'd be like this.'

'I know.' Caroline's lip trembles slightly. She can't meet his eyes, the curtain of her hair hides the side of her face nearest to him.

'I'm better now if you want to leave?' He looks at her again, then away. Why can't she look at him, give some indication what she's feeling? But instead her head is still bent, her doodle is beginning to cover the pad.

Then, as awkwardly, with as much difficulty as he has just had, she says, 'I . . . wanted to tell you . . . about with Tom when you were away.'

Patrick stares at her head, sees the way the hairs fall forward from her parting, watches her fingers twisting round and round the Biro.

'I don't want to know,' he says, jerkily.

But Caroline ignores him, persists relentlessly. 'I wanted to tell you there's nothing to tell – of . . . importance.'

Patrick stares at her for some moments, then the corner of his mouth twitches into a half smile. 'Well, good,' he says at last. He stands, goes over to her and kisses the back of her hair.

She turns her head, looks up at him intently. 'Patrick?'

'Yes?'

'I wish you'd talk to me more.'

At this he withdraws, moves round to the fire, stands with one hand on the lintel as he pushes the burnt ends of logs in with his boot then turns to face her. 'I don't trust words,' he says.

Caroline methodically crumples up her doodle. And that's that, she thinks – there we are. Yet she can't help but respect his view. For hasn't she just uttered words of extreme equivocation? She has told the truth but it's not the truth – Tom *was* important. Anyone who affects you deeply must be – must have been, she corrects herself.

Patrick opens the stove, feeds it with logs. 'If this cold goes on much longer we'll be short of hay.' He shifts a little uneasily. 'I'm surprised Tom hasn't got here today – I saw Ron out looking for his sheep, he said the snow plough's been to within a mile of Thurley's.'

Caroline kneels and, taking up the bellows, blows the embers, watches them glow and finally burst into flame. Then returns to her letter.

I've had time to think too – about us. Our time together was essential – both of us were exploring our own and other minds, our thoughts, our attitudes and beliefs – but it couldn't go on for me like it could for you. You were always more down to earth, more positive. Perhaps I chose to come out here for the wrong reasons, but my instinct was right, I know that now. It's as though it was necessary to push myself into experience I'd always resisted – force myself to my own limits. And when I did the other side of myself began to live. Alone here, all my illusions slipped away and I saw things as they are – perhaps for the first time in my life. I stopped forcing things into the mould I wanted and accepted them. Someone like me needed to drag away a dead sheep and bury it in the pouring rain. Try doing that and see if you can keep on rose-tinted spectacles at the same time! If the writing is the person then I'll write better, I am so close to things; animals and insects and plants are as much a part of my daily living as people. When I cut and lay a hedge in winter, watch it shoot in spring, thicken in summer, I too grow and am enriched. Looking at that hedge gives me a sense of achievement that is more than material – that to me is as much success as I think the kind you mentioned . . . I see now that if I had gone on living in a town, working in an office, had got a successful job like you, I shouldn't have had the necessary introversion to form from myself something that might otherwise have remained unformed. By taking me to live a relatively lonely life, Patrick has given me the impetus, forced me to face myself.

She stops writing, looks across at Patrick, 'Shall we go to bed early?'

'I'm ready when you are.'

'I'll just finish this.' Caroline bends her head forward over her letter, the silky straw hair slides forward covering her cheek but Patrick's eyes are closed and Caroline is oblivious of her appearance. Rather she is intent on a superhuman effort at explanation.

Isn't being as important as becoming? What *is* important? I don't know – I absolutely don't know . . . And yet just sometimes it seems to me I feel what it is, and the feeling is so strong – for life, I mean – that that's all there is to it, that and working to prevent the whole of this planet destroying itself. But then a reverence for life is part of it, it must be.

A knock comes on the door. They look at each other in startled apprehension. Patrick gets up slowly, glancing at the window but can see nothing beyond it. He opens the back door. Tom, who has the habit of responding by appearance whenever thought about, stands in the doorway. Five minutes later he is sitting in the corner of the fireplace relating all. Rita, it seems, is recovering slowly, her face and head by a miracle completely undamaged except for a small cut above one eye. The main worry has been the extent of internal injury caused by three broken ribs.

Caroline listening, feels a confusion of horror, shock and guilt – could she have had anything to do with Rita's intake of drink on that evening, her reckless driving? At the same time Tom's presence revitalises her like a tonic – it as though she is only fully alive when he is there. She tries to conceal the change in herself by keeping silent, but presently gives up – it is completely harmless, she assures herself. If it hasn't been before it will be from now on, and as she firmly licks and sticks her envelope to Helen she equally firmly renounces Tom and resolves to visit Rita in hospital just as soon as she can get the car out of the drive.

Tom has not been cut off in the village in the same way as the higher and more isolated Greytor; he is about to purchase a second-hand van to replace a borrowed pick-up. To reach them tonight he has walked the last half-mile but, he tells them, the snow plough should push past them tomorrow – unfortunately it has progressed more slowly than it might have owing to losing track of the road and pushing walls down instead of drifts. But then the Council has employed drivers who don't know the area and are not used to the work.

Talk and silences mix with the hiss and crackle of the fire; the evening passes in sympathy, consolation, and the peculiar intimacy thrust upon them by circumstance – all things of which Tom has had little enough lately, for gossip has held him entirely responsible for the accident. And so, naturally, have Rita's parents. The fact that she was driving has only gone to show. Exactly what, no one has said in so many words because, as gestures and hints imply, it is self-evident – poor Rita had no alternative. And Tom himself thinks that fate has been kind to him in preserving Rita – for who else is to look after the children? He resolves not to tempt fate again by any monkey business with Patrick Ashurst's woman. But ultimately it will be Caroline who decides and Caroline has already decided – that to be an independent being, a person she can respect, her will must conquer her impetuous body. Mustn't it? So that evening in the kitchen horror and shock are followed by resolve and good intentions.

Exactly five days later Caroline goes to visit Rita. She has debated with herself earnestly whether she should or shouldn't and decided conclusively that she should.

The hospital is Taverston General, much smaller and more modest than the great impersonal building in which Patrick had his operation, but nevertheless, its very smell is enough to awaken in Caroline her dread of hospitals, and remind her of the dreariness of prolonged visiting.

Rita is in a small room with three others. A curtain half drawn at visiting hours gives an illusion of privacy. She does not look unduly surprised to see Caroline, and wears a bright expression to cover her instinctive antagonism. She looks ready for a honeymoon, being dressed in a nightdress with numerous ruffles of lace out of which rises her young and shapely throat. Caroline, never visually immune, cannot help but admire its unlined perfection. She wonders that necks are so out of fashion, so little admired these days. While doing so she smiles equally brightly at Rita and sits herself on the provided chair. 'I hope I'm not being a nuisance,' she starts, 'and that you're not expecting anyone else' – why does she always have to excuse herself, be over-humble? It really is quite out of place.

Rita assures her she's expecting no one else and it is very kind of her to find time to visit because she knows how much there is to do on the farm, Mr Ashurst not being right yet. This is followed by a slightly awkward pause which Caroline breaks by asking Rita how she is feeling and how much longer it will be before she is allowed home? Rita tells her she hopes to be allowed out in another two weeks.

'How are you managing over the children? I did say to Tom I'd be only too willing to have them any time if it would be a help,' Caroline says with more goodwill than fervour.

Rita looks at Caroline calculatingly, as much as to say she can't imagine Jenny and Ernest in her hands, but says politely, 'That's very good of you, Mrs Ashurst.'

'Please call me Caroline.'

Rita makes a slight indication of assent.

'I must say, you're looking wonderful – no one would know you'd been in an accident.'

'They say I was very fortunate,' says Rita, acting a demure innocence quite alien to her nature. The time, Caroline thinks, has come to establish that the main purpose of the visit is to form some kind of understanding between them. 'I wanted to talk to you about . . . about Tom coming up to us – to work,' she begins.

'He won't be doing it much longer,' Rita says sharply.

'Oh?' Caroline is taken aback.

'We've decided. He's leaving the Saw Mills and going down the Forestry – just as soon as ever I'm home and got my strength back.'

'What . . . what made him decide to do that?' Caroline feels shattered, knocked quite from her position of confident magnanimity.

'I dunno – wanted a change, I 'spose,' Rita looks at her with narrowed, mocking eyes.

Caroline plunges on. 'I hope . . . I hope it's not because of the insidious gossip in the village about Tom and . . . and myself?' She looks at Rita with imploring eyes. Surely this hard little twenty-year-old will relent, give her some indication of understanding, compassion, sisterly feeling? But Rita hovers like a hawk watching its prey, her eyes sharp, all her instincts on the kill.

'I don't ever take any heed of gossip,' she says, 'I couldn't live in a village if I did.'

'I'm glad' says Caroline, knowing Rita doesn't mean it. 'What I meant – was trying to say – was I am very fond of Tom because I know Patrick is – I mean he has worked for Patrick for years, hasn't he? But it's rather horrible when people read more into it than is actually the case . . .' She breaks off, realising she is lying herself, doing exactly what she had come down here intending not to do. She forces herself into greater honesty, 'I do find Tom very appealing – I mean as a person – and I can understand what you must feel for him, but I wouldn't ever let anything of that sort . . .' she is getting more and more tongue-tied and involved, 'happen between us – Tom and me. Nor would he.' She breaks off. What is she talking about? Is she incapable of honesty? Then suddenly her misguided honesty breaks forth, 'I think I may have . . . encouraged Tom, when Patrick was away and I was very lonely. But now that is all behind us, and nothing as I said ever happened anyway, so I have come to ask you to excuse me for when I may have acted thoughtlessly, and to assure you I won't ever again.' There – now it is out. She looks up at Rita in a last receding hope of understanding and friendship.

Rita drinks from a glass beside her. Caroline looks at the

flowers she has brought that, like herself, wilt at the foot of Rita's bed. Rita licks her lips and says, 'I'm sure I don't know what you are worrying about, Caroline' – the Christian name jars in the context. 'I don't ask Tom what he's about, he gets on with his life and I get on with mine. I don't think anyone else fancying him is going to make much difference one way or the other. There've been plenty of them before and I reckon there'll be plenty of them in the future, knowing Tom' – and she laughs to show her complete confidence in being above Tom's dilly-dallyings.

Caroline feels reduced to something infinitely small and distasteful. A louse perhaps. Rita has successfully made it clear she is no more to Tom, and never has been, than a string of other local girls he confers his favours on when in the mood, while he and Rita continue in a partnership undisturbed by such frequent and inconsequential happenings. She sees herself suddenly as a dupe and Tom the projection of her own unsatisfied romantic longings. Her deep sense of humiliation brings colour to her cheeks, she says with touching honesty, 'Probably I have cared for Tom very much more than he has ever cared for me.'

'Tom's not one to care for any one over long,' says Rita with satisfaction, 'leastways only his own.'

'Well that's how it should be,' Caroline forces herself to say. Somehow she must get out of here, escape this ruthless wasp that stings and stings, not like a bee that can only thrust out its one load of poison. She looks almost with reverence at Rita's perfect little face and shoulders – how can anything so exquisitely endowed be so remorseless? But she must have suffered, oh yes, she must have, so should not she, Caroline, be more understanding? She makes one last effort, 'It must hurt you, doesn't it – well just a little sometimes – if Tom takes up with . . . other people?'

Rita's lip positively curls. 'I never said he did – I said they fancied him. That's all I said. I dare say plenty of the girls round about fancied Mr Ashurst when he was younger.'

'Yes – I'm sure they did. And still do.' Caroline reaches down and picks up her bag. She stands. 'It's been wonderful to see you looking a thousand times better than I 'expected' – why does she have to gush? – 'and don't forget, if I can help over the children let me know.'

Rita smiles with her mouth but not her eyes. Caroline starts to move away. 'I'll drop in again if you're not home soon.'

'Thank you ever so much for the flowers,' says Rita as Caroline goes round the curtain and leaves under the scrutiny of the two other patients.

On the way home in the car she nearly has an accident herself, so lost in thought is she over the total failure of her attempt to contact Rita. But has it been such a failure after all for Rita has made clear to her the situation that she has refused to face before – that she means far less to Tom than she would have liked to suppose, is in fact one of many. Caroline winces. All her sensibilities revolt against such a thought, she cannot believe it true. But the doubt continues to gnaw not just in the car as she drives home, but in the weeks to come. Should she then have been glad that what might have happened, didn't? She should but, on the contrary, is not, because she feels that such a happening would have lifted the feeling between herself and Tom on to a plane unknown to him before. Such is the capacity of her nature to project its own dream.

Rita, left on her own, turns her face into her pillow and weeps hot tears. Oh how she hates that woman who has taken Tom from her, if not in fact certainly in feeling, for Rita is perfectly able to gauge Tom's responses. Neither, for all the Ashurst woman's professed assurances, does she feel in the least safe. She is too shrewd to underestimate the power of sexual need.

The clocks have gone back; the evenings are light till after seven; Patrick is recovered and out ploughing, turning up the ochre bitten land into satisfying dark chocolate-coloured curves; the catkins dangle from the trees with their tiny scarlet buds. By contrast the moor is still brown, the landscape barren with white lumps of discoloured snow mounting against the banks and at odd positions in fields to mark where the deepest drifts formed. But perhaps the greatest difference is in the frequent bleating of lambs who amble weakly or jump gaily, according to age, to find their ewes devouring the few emerald blades of grass.

Caroline is in the kitchen reviving a lamb. That it is reviving is indicated by its raised head; warmth, and with it life, have seeped into the apparently dead body brought in from the fields an hour earlier. She shakes the bottle on the hotplate, tests it on her wrist. Not warm enough. She waits for a few minutes longer, then inserts the teat into the lamb's unwilling mouth, patiently coaxes, encourages. Ten minutes later she gives up in exasperation – there is nothing more frustrating than a lamb that won't suck, unless it's a ewe that won't take her own lamb. She will leave it for now, try again later. She glances out of the window, sees the light fading rapidly. She gets up, pushes a saucepan of soup across to heat, adds milk. She switches on the transistor, a women's voice reads a repeat of a programme she has heard months earlier. She turns it up:

I want this to reach you
who told me once that poetry is nothing sacred
   – no more sacred that is
than any other things in your life –
   to answer yes, if life is uncorrupted
no better poetry is wanted.

She stands transfixed, listening. The saucepan boils over with a violent hissing, drowning the voice. She rushes to it, pulls it off. The reading voice continues but now barely audibly – it has drifted off the station. She goes back to the transistor, tries to find it but can't. Sighs, gives up, and sets about wiping soup from the hot plate. Patrick comes in while she is doing so.

'What's happened?'

'The soup boiled over. It's ready.'

'Do you want this?' he indicates with a nod the sound of the reading voice under the burr of interruption.

'I did, but it doesn't matter. I can't get it clearly.'

Patrick fiddles with the set, trying to find it for her. He fails and switches off. She pours out the soup and they sit to eat.

'The lamb won't suck, but it seems quite strong.' They

both observe the offending head poking out from the gentle warmth of the stove's lower oven.

'I'll get some milk from the ewe later,' Patrick dips his spoon into the thick surface of leek and potato. 'There's a letter for you on the chest.'

Caroline gets up immediately, fetches it. Patrick reads his *Farmers Weekly* laid open beside him while she reads her letter. He is perfectly aware it is from Helen. Curiosity eventually gets the better of him. 'Well – how is she? Your soup's getting cold.'

'She sounds as though she's getting on alright.' Caroline lays the letter down, starts her soup. In a carefully non-committal voice she says, 'They want to publish one of my poems.' Her eyes are shining, and in spite of her attempt not to show any emotion her whole face radiates happiness.

Patrick who has gone back to his magazine, looks up briefly, 'Good.' He holds out his bowl for more expectantly, sees the expression on her face and helps himself. Caroline watches his head bend back to an article which seems to absorb him.

'Patrick – did you hear me?'

He pushes his magazine on one side. 'Yes – I said. That's very good news.' He finds the soup too hot so helps himself to bread. 'They've got a new breed of ram apparently, brought over from Holland – they're getting excellent results by crossing with a closewool.'

'Aren't you pleased – for me?'

'Of course. I said so – but does a poem in an unknown magazine mean much?'

'To me it does.'

They drink their soup in silence. Caroline nurses her offence but it doesn't really mitigate her happiness.

'I think it might be worth getting one.'

She pauses in the act of putting a spoonful in her mouth. Has she heard right? Does Patrick mean to start a magazine, or just to buy a single issue with her poem in it? 'What?'

He looks at her patiently, laments the need to explain. 'A Dutch ram.' He sees by Caroline's face something is wrong, assumes it to be his lack of interest in Helen. 'I'm glad Helen's doing alright for herself,' he says, watching Caroline to see if this satisfies her.

Her continuing silence makes him uncomfortable.

'You don't wish you were doing the same – you don't regret coming out here?'

'I chose it. No – I don't regret it, why should I?' Caroline asks fiercely.

'I just thought you might.'

She doesn't answer. Patrick watches her lowered eyes with a troubled expression; she hasn't managed to convince him. But with a certain wonderful Saxon insensitivity, an ability to shut himself off to all but his own concern, he turns the pages and examines in detail a modern crop-spraying attachment.

'I mean to say, she knew what she was doing.' Christine looks seriously across the counter at Rita.

'That's what I said to Tom.'

'No, I think you're right every time. I can't see it's going to do anyone good him going back up there. I should tell him if he goes back he won't find you sitting home of an evening.'

'I'm going to,' says Rita. She's only come across for a can of Carnation Milk and comfort. Ernest's weaned good and proper, that was one good thing about her being in hospital.

So that evening when Tom gets back from the Mills she bides her time till she sees fit, then lays down her ultimatum. 'Have you fixed up to go down the Forestry then, Tom?' Tom, who's had a hard day, looks across at Rita who sits timeless and unchanged before him, the tiniest scar fast fading over her left eye.

'No,' he says, puzzled.

'I thought you said you was going to – I thought you said you'd had enough of working out the Ashursts.'

'Seems a bit hard on him,' says Tom carefully.

'Why's that?'

'I always been out there, haven't I?'

'Yes – but he's got his wife to help him now, hasn't he? You should hear what they say about her down the shop. They say she's a regular one.'

'Who's they?' Tom asks resentfully. For Tom retains a deep tenderness for Caroline, if not in his heart then very near it.

'They? Why all of them. Christine was saying Martin Weller's been out there when you haven't had the time and she's been giving him the glad eye, only he's not having any of it. She's not his sort, he says.'

This is altogether too much for Tom who sits up, and starts to put on his boots. Rita looks at him in alarm, 'You didn't say you were going out.'

'Didn't know, did I?'

'Where are you going?'

'Round to tell Martin Weller to shut his mouth about the Ashursts or I'll give him what for.'

Rita goes red with anger. 'You mean you'd go picking a fight about *that* woman. Since when have you ever fought anyone for me? Oh no, they're always bigger than you are when the time comes.'

Tom ignores her, takes his jacket off the peg. She grabs hold of his arm, tears of outrage in her eyes. 'Tom, you never.'

'What?' he tries to shake his arm free.

'You never going to fight him over *her*?'

'I'm going to tell him to keep his mouth shut. It isn't the truth he's telling – he's shooting off his big mouth talking a lot of lies.'

'How do you know it's lies?'

'Because I do. She ain't that type at all – not the type to give so much as a look at Martin Weller.'

Rita lets go of him, backs away, a shrewd light in her eyes. 'You *do* know a lot about it, Tom.'

The door bangs behind him. Rita races after him, Jenny cowers behind the sofa.

'Tom,' she calls. Two people passing in the road turn their heads. 'Tom you'd better do as I ask about going down to the Forestry or else I'll be gone when you get back.'

Tom hesitates as though to answer back, sees the curious stares he's getting, and lets himself out the gate.

Rita withdraws into the house, slamming the door, takes Jenny on her knee on the sofa and bursts into tears into the child's soft hair. It all seems *so* unfair, so terribly unfair. She absolutely hates Tom. Jenny kisses her mother tenderly, it seems clear to her that her father must be wicked to make her mother cry.

Tom finds Martin Weller in his shed knocking out a dented wing of his car. He waits, leaning amongst oil drums and stacked-up tyres until Martin uprights himself. They talk of the dent, the price of spares, engines and such like for a good five minutes before Tom says, casually, 'I heard you been putting in a bit of time up at Ashursts?'

'Yep,' says Martin.

'I heard you been making out a few stories about his missus.'

'Bit of alright, isn't she?'

Tom glares at him, menace in his stance and tone. 'You ain't got no business to go shootin' off your mouth about nothing.'

'It ain't nothing – I'd say I was encouraged.'

Tom's fist shoots out, hits Martin's jaw fair and square. Martin crashes over backwards taking a drum with him. He gets on his feet while Tom waits.

'Lay off, will you – what's this all about? You're sweet on her are you?'

'I ain't sweet on no one but I don't like to hear a lot o' untrue rubbish told about Patrick Ashurst's missus, so you keep your mouth shut or you got it coming to you again.'

Martin's afraid of Tom, he stands well back, keeps a drum in front of himself.

'For fuck's sake man, if she ain't nothing to do with you what's the fuss for?'

'Patrick Ashurst's a friend of mine,' says Tom stoutly and righteously, quite forgetting other things, convincing himself if not Martin this is the reason for his aggressive behaviour.

'I ain't gonna take your job, if that's what's worrying you,' says Martin foolishly.

'You can have it,' says Tom, turning his back and sauntering away. ' I shan't be out there no more. I'm going down the Forestry on shift work when I'm not in the Mills.' He pauses, half turns back, threat coming into his voice again, 'And if I hear another word you been saying about his missus, I'll beat you up so you won't know which eye to look outer.'

Tom leaves. Martin, watching Tom's slouch disappear out of his gate, swallows and rubs his jaw, feels the tender bump on the back of his head. He won't talk any more, that's certain. Tom's family's known for coming down in a gang if someone crosses them enough and pretty well lynching whoever's done it. And as none of the local people ever go to the police unless they're 'got' for something or other, the law on the moor is a matter of strength and terrorising.

Tom driving away feels moderately relieved, moderately satisfied. He drives right on out to Greytor, calls in. Patrick answers the door, Caroline is out. Tom spends some time propped against the stove, talking, in fact the sun has set before he's finished but still Caroline hasn't come and still he hasn't got round to telling Patrick he's going to work for the Forestry.

Finally he has to leave. As he gets in his van he realises he hasn't said what he came out for – what he ostensibly came out for. Well, they'll know he's not coming when they don't see him, won't they, and meanwhile he hasn't burnt his boats and they aren't going to go offering more work to Martin Weller.

Back at their house Rita is going round silently with redrimmed eyes but she has cooked him a good supper. That night he makes love to her extra specially, tells her she's the only one for him, always has been. He doesn't give a bugger for the Ashurst woman, never has. Only right at the very end does his disappointment in not having seen Caroline at Greytor overtake him.

*

The last week in March, wrapped in warm clothes against the searing east wind, Caroline and Patrick venture forth to burn up scrub on the lower ground prior to reclaiming. Like two strange figures outside time they move from clump to clump, bending to set light to the white papery grass that sprouts from the bog ground and entwines itself with the gorse.

Patrick stands back as a clump flares up, pouring flame and clouds of smoke into the sky. Caroline, who has finished lighting along the far side of the enclosure, moves across to join him. The flames gather force and, blown by the stiff breeze, move in a long line towards the scrub and wet ground.

'Will it stop?' Caroline looks anxiously at the alarming speed with which the fire moves, then nervously at Jim Thurley's hedge. They'll just have to beat it out, that's all. But the heat already scorches her face and she knows that if it chooses it can leap over the wet ground by the tussocks.

Patrick leans on his beater placidly watching. 'If we can drain this it'll give us another two and three-quarter acres,' he says contentedly.

'Yes' – Caroline relaxes. Patrick's presence, his calm capability, reassures her. She gazes at the blazing clumps, watches in awe the flame's elemental power, feels herself shrink into impotence beside such a force. Half-mesmerised by the roar and crackle, the heat and smoke that immerse her at a whim of the wind, her mind drifts into a disembodied state where she is doubly receptive to all around her. And slowly lines of a poem begin to form, almost in spite of her – even the rhythm is there, has arrived it seems, by itself . . .

'Look after that side, will you?' Patrick's voice jolts her into activity. She takes up her beater and moves in as close as she can get without the radiation scorching her face. With her beater she thumps and wipes out the sparks that show every intention of lighting further clumps and spreading the fire too far sideways. When she is satisfied she stands, her chin resting on the old broom handle, looking at the spectacular curve of flame. Again the same two lines pass through her mind, demand that she help provide two more . . .

'Caroline?'

She looks round to where Patrick stands some way off, sees where he is pointing and makes her way to where the fire is burning dangerously near the fence. In alarm she shouts back to him but her voice is lost on the wind. Seeing he has not heard, she shields her face and treads in among the smouldering tussocks. With beads of sweat pouring off her forehead, her face streaked with black, she beats tirelessly at the offending flames until only a narrow front remains. Patrick joins her. Together they gradually reduce the fire until it is contained in a small ring burning slowly backwards.

'That was a near thing,' Patrick remarks, looking at the neighbouring hedge as though seeing it for the first time. Caroline looks at him in surprise. Could it be that he really hadn't seen the possible harm that might be done, and that she had had grounds for her anxiety? She looks down at the blackened, ash-covered ground at her feet, then away over the fields to the high hard line of Scarhill rising up to its conical summit. Above it two buzzards soar and spiral, seemingly undeterred by the cloud of smoke that blows towards them, grey against the intense indigo of the sky. And the colours, the shape of the land, stirs something in Caroline that pricks the backs of her eyes with tears, evokes in her a response she is unable to communicate.

'Patrick.'

'What?'

'The moor – it's fantastic, isn't it?'

Patrick looks. 'It's taken you a long time to see it.'

'I've always seen it but this is special.'

They both look at it.

'Is it . . . better? I mean for you now I'm here?'

'Of course – a thousand times better. You know. Why do you ask?'

'I wonder sometimes.'

'Well don't.'

'Alright – I won't.' Her eyes meet his briefly, just long enough to establish something has been said that matters.

Throughout the afternoon they continue their swaling* until the sun sinks over the dark ridge of hills behind them, slides from a red ball to a disc, a glittering lid set on earth's range. Then, each shouldering a beater, they zig-zag one behind the other, two small figures threading their way through the tussocks in a timeless landscape of scrub and bog grass.

* *Swaling:* the burning of gorse and scrub.

Susanna Moore
My Old Sweetheart

'A marvellous, intense first novel by an American, but often remarkably English in feeling. It is about the consuming relationship of Lily with her unfathomable, deranged mother and her ambiguous doctor father. The setting is 1950s' Hawaii, beautifully evoked, its postwar indeterminacy matching the shifting family relations. Susanna Moore's book is full of those vivid haunting scenes which reveal a whole emotional history. Sad, unsentimental and magical' GRAHAM SWIFT, SUNDAY TIMES

'Awash with flowers, scented breezes, exotic fish, *My Old Sweetheart* deals in the realm of the senses rather than the traumas of the external world. Its keynote is remembrance, its strategy evocation. Susanna Moore is an original and this flower-stream, jasmine scented study of childhood, love and betrayal is a remarkable debut' BOOKS & BOOKMEN

'A family world of sad, frantic charm reminiscent of the great F. Scot Fitzgerald. That perhaps no sense can be made of a troubled childhood and that in the end it may be fitting simply to let the past go by, is just one diamond sharp insight in this gem of a book' COMPANY

'I can't recall another novel like this about mothers and daughters. Lily's mysterious half-told tale delighted and touched, evoking buried childhood memories; the helpless love one feels for one's mother, the frustrating inability to protect her from pain and hurt' VILLAGE VOICE

'This is a very good novel indeed, haunting one's memory long after the details of its story have been quite forgotten' COSMOPOLITAN

Jane Beeson
Apple of an Eye

'A wonderfully powerful book' FAY WELDON

Jane Beeson's first novel is set on the Devon Moors and tells the story of Tamsin Band, an adolescent girl who lives on a remote farm with her drunken father, younger brother and her strict, churchgoing aunt. Ten years earlier her mother ran away from the claustrophobic atmosphere; now Tamsin learns she is back – not with her family – but living in a nearby farm with a boyfriend half her age. The day Tamsin crosses the moors for a secret reunion with her mother is the beginning of a time in her life which will end in tragedy and death.

  Writing about tragedy and passion in rural England, Jane Beeson's work has been compared to that of Thomas Hardy and H. E. Bates.

'Jane Beeson is an excellent writer – I read *Apple of an Eye* through in one sitting because I was engrossed in the story. She has a very sure ear and touch for terror – there is a great deal of power in her writing' ERIN PIZZEY